"This novel kept me on the edge of my seat with adventure and mystery but also touched my heart with an amazing love story! I would recommend it to anyone!"
—Erin Burbee, developmental disabilities professional

"A novel that grabs your attention instantly."
—Grant Claunch, Web designer

"A fantasy thrill ride of unexpected twists and screeching turns."
—Matt Marino, pastor

"Outstanding! As an avid reader, I loved this book, and I would recommend it to anyone."
—Sarah, elementary educator

"Unpredictable and exciting! Highly recommended for all ages."
—Myleena, accounts administrator

"A wonderful, thought-provoking journey of love and adventure that leaves you with a whiplash of an ending."
—Stephanie Allestad, radio personality

THE DARK
BEHIND THE DOOR

Janelle,
Thank you for all your support. Keep us in your prayers. May God continue to bless you and Dude,

THE DARK BEHIND THE DOOR

B. P. OBENOUR

TATE PUBLISHING & Enterprises

Published by Tate Publishing & Enterprises, LLC
127 E. Trade Center Terrace | Mustang, Oklahoma 73064 USA
1.888.361.9473 | www.tatepublishing.com

Tate Publishing is committed to excellence in the publishing industry. The company reflects the philosophy established by the founders, based on Psalm 68:11,
"The Lord gave the word and great was the company of those who published it."

Book design copyright © 2011 by Tate Publishing, LLC. All rights reserved.
Cover design by Lance Waldrop
Interior design by Lindsay B. Behrens

Published in the United States of America

ISBN: 978-1-61777-735-6
1. Fiction / Fantasy / General   2. Fiction / Religious
11.08.03

This book is dedicated to Michelle, my wife of eighteen years, who is also my long-time best friend, whom I am more in love with today than ever.

ACKNOWLEDGMENTS

The process of writing has always been a favorite pastime of mine, but a project like this would never have been possible without the support of my incredible wife, Michelle. An avid reader, Michelle scrupulously scribbled notes, circled sentences needing reworking, and laid to rest— via a thick black strip of marker or pen—many words, phrases, sentences, and entire paragraphs that simply failed to meet her standards. I can't thank her enough for the hours she's sacrificed in the constructive critique of my work. Only after passing her stringent approval did any work find the eyes of other friends or family.

It's here I must mention what a positive role our friend Myleena, another ardent reader, played throughout. Although not nearly as involved as Michelle, Myleena offered perspective that I felt was especially beneficial the several times we sat around the living room coffee table discussing the story. If not for their terrific feedback throughout the entire process and their sustaining encouragement through the difficult days, I can say rather confidently it wouldn't be where it is today.

I'd also like to take a moment to acknowledge others who have read and given feedback on this particular book. If not for the amazing eye and editing talent of Tate Publishing's own Sabrina Arndt, this book would have lacked much in form, as well as depth in many areas. She challenged me to look deeper into the lives of characters and bring to the surface more in weak areas I hadn't even considered. Andy Eaton deserves some of my warmest gratitude for his time investment into the final layout editing process. You were awesome, Andy. Also, thank you Sunnie Atkins for giving this book a chance. Your original words of encouragement prepared me for the confidence I needed to push through editing. Others who have read and given feedback include Pastor Matt Marino, Sarah Hammer, Erin Burbee, Stacey Turner, Lisa Ledezma, J. Calvin Eaton, Patty Eaton, Stephanie Allestad, for not only reading and reviewing but offering suggestions, Pastor John Pace, Jean Onstead, and my son Jaedon, who has himself become quite the book enthusiast. Those who have given feedback after a portion of reading include my parents, Bob and Pat Obenour, who encouraged me to write and express myself since seventh grade, Janelle Melton, Nick Crider, Gary T., my sons Tyler and Zach, and also Mr. Michael Pulley—you know who you are—as well as dozens of friends who simply asked, "What are you working on there?" Thank you for all of your kind words and support.

I'd like to extend an extra big thank you to my wife, Michelle, for her enthusiastic support for my writing and the journey, along with its ups and downs, that has ensued as a result. You are the one person on this planet without whom I would be lost. May your commitment to me as my best friend and life partner be equaled solely by my pursuit as your lifetime companion, husband, and last—but certainly not least—as always, forever your hero. I love you for always and then some.

Also a well-deserved thank you is due to all three of our boys, Tyler, Zach, and Jaedon, for their patience and support through all that having an author in the family is. I love you and appreciate you and am proud of each of you. Though we may never truly achieve the absolute picture we imagined for ourselves, the confidence we discover in ourselves and the scenery along the way we would have otherwise missed makes the journey so worth the while.

I fell in love with Jesus and began praying and talking to Him in second grade. I remember sitting on the playground during recess, watching other kids play and wondering if any of them ever took their questions and thoughts to the Lord. In high school my highest motivation was to let my light so shine before men that they might see His work in my life and glorify my Father in heaven. As a child I watched movies every chance I got. On Saturdays at 10:00 a.m., I'd watch *World Beyond*, a television show which aired low-budget Godzilla and other monster movies, with the occasional spooky movie thrown into the mix. As I curled up under a blanket and became sucked in to the characters' dilemmas and frightening situations, whether sci-fi or otherwise, I'd share their panic and say, "Just pray. Why don't you give your situation to God? He can help." This process of thinking stayed with me all through the slew of movies I've seen over the span of my life. I would as a child, and have as an adult, imagined God intervening in a way that shows His love, mercy, power, or His amazing ability to juggle and handle every character's situation, bringing forth beauty for the ashes of life's most difficult hardships. It is my hope that I may encourage you to let the light of Jesus shine in any and all of the areas of life.

—Bryon Obenour

FOREWORD

Is there a place for "straight talk" or "unedited commentary," void of creative writing, in the foreword of a novel? "Not if you want the book to sell" is the answer I got from all the online experts when I googled that question. Apparently, from a marketing perspective, it's my job to secretly release, in an eloquently waxing fashion, just enough of the storyline to entice you beyond the ability to put this book down. Well, first of all, you must like to read or you would not have opened this book at all, and as a reader, I doubt you are gullible enough to get sucked in that way. Secondly, if you knew the author like I do, you would know he has too much integrity to play that game. Finally, Bryon is the one with the creative gift here, not me. Through the amazing power of his truly God-given gift, he is about to catapult your heart, mind, and soul (as he did mine) into an emotionally intense, mind boggling, and spiritually challenging time travel journey you will never forget!

My life, so far, has been spent as a pastor, college professor, and counselor. So you can well imagine how dealing with the complexities of life and how its issues of the past and concerns for the future are regularly the topic of discussion with those I serve. But it is true for you and me as well. We all spend a great deal of time in our thoughts, traveling back and forth between our past and our future fighting the demons and dragons that have taunted us, ever hoping for final victory in our search for the evasive grail of our dreams.

But...what if...what if the whole context for working it all out...all of it...our dreams, our thoughts, love and relationships, our fears about the past and worries about the future—ALL OF IT—were suddenly, without warning, transported into the twelfth-century medieval world of legends unspoken and dragons and...we are the prey? What now? You are about to find out. Bryon is about to draw you into the journey with his cast, and this much I assure you: you will not return unchanged. I didn't.

—J. Calvin Eaton, MA, MS

PREFACE

The Dark behind the Door started off as a 6,000-word short story entitled *"Broga Lig Nædre,"* translated from Old English as *Terrifying Fire Dragon.* The feedback was very positive, with several readers commenting on how they would like to see more development of the story. I was asked if I'd considered expanding it into a novel. Honestly, I hadn't, but the encouragement from a few family members and a couple close friends was enough to sway me into at least taking an honest stab at it.

I started developing difficulties the characters would encounter and then brought much more character development and dialogue. It wasn't long before I felt the work was completed at 27,000 words. It had grown into a decent novella. I had two people read the story, and independently, both commented on the end of the story, saying it was lacking.

Feeling defeated, I went back to the drawing board and changed the ending, adding 5,000 words in the process. I had my wife and right-arm editor, Michelle, read the ending again. She said she didn't quite understand the twist I'd added, so again, back to the idea mill. It was then that I watched the series finale of a popular prison escape television drama, which so impacted me with its closing scene that I had a moment of writing inspiration and rewrote the ending but, this time, added a whole new character. I had to find ways to implement the newcomer throughout the story. This brought a whole new and exciting challenge and provided me the opportunity to enrich the characters even more.

Upon completion, I had nearly doubled the entire story's word count, ending up around 57,000 words. I planned to publish to Kindle as an eBook but thought first I might try my hand at submitting a manuscript to Tate Publishing. The goal was to go to Kindle in September 2010. On August 22, 2010, I received a contract in the mail from Tate asking if I was still interested in getting the book published. Through a myriad of brilliant edits spurred on by the Tate editor I was lucky enough to get assigned to, the story developed into a more gripping tale with a great addition to the ending and a word count pushing over 70,000. And that's the shortened version of how this book ended up in your hands.

1

Bracing for impact, he held his breath. The blow came slightly sooner than expected. He clenched his teeth and let out an exhausted grunt as he lost his footing and fell to his knees. He pushed himself up with a closed fist against the ground while the other hand pressed hard alongside his chest. Though most of his sweat poured from his brow, several beads pooled upon his eyelashes, and what didn't splash off washed into his eyes with burning and stinging ensuing. Wearied and spent, he turned his head to look left then right for a place to run as he dared to take a moment to catch his breath. The open field had nothing to lend. With his legs failing after several hours of evasion, he lunged forward, staggering to his right a few steps, and then once again fell. Recognizing his entire body, pounding and parched, was done, he finally relinquished the hope of escape and found himself at an unfamiliar place: the end of himself. This day would be his last. As fading optimism wilted away, the realization of the inevitable mounted, and he broke. He wept but for a moment, deeply and sorrowfully.

From the sky far above him, the great beast spread its wings and circled back around, hurling a ferocious roar from its distant height. It then pinned back its wings and dove down toward the open terrain.

Composing himself, he crawled on his stomach several feet farther, returning to a shallow trench where a friend, a young lady, lay twisted, bleeding, and unconscious. He opened his mouth to speak but only managed breathy words.

"Why? What were you thinking? I'm so angry at you. I mean, you were safe. You shouldn't have come," he said. He paused for a moment and then let out a frustrated sigh. "It was foolish. Besides, what is it you always say? 'What's going to happen is going to happen.' If that's so true, why are you here?"

He looked over her face—nearly angelic, if not for the blood and dirt smudges—then stroked her cheek. "You're one in a million, you know that? I wish we could've known each other longer than these past few months," he added. He focused on her lips and then brushed them with his fingers. "I wish things could've been different. I have to go now. Think about me, okay? Don't you ever forget me." He touched her hand then held it lightly. "I hope I make you smile when you think about me." An emerging frown betrayed the optimism in his voice. In that moment, he made a silent vow that if ever life afforded him another chance with her, he'd steal her heart. "Whoever it is you're waiting for, he's one lucky guy. All right, well, I'm not gonna say good-bye. So fare … well. And may God protect you always."

He gathered what strength he could muster and stood. To keep more harm from coming to her, he limpingly created some distance between himself and the girl. He raised his red and swollen eyes, wearily ready to accept what he never could have imagined for himself. Thoughts of regret arose as he mulled over memories of his parents and sister. He'd successfully escaped the dragon's pursuit on no less than a dozen separate encounters over the last two months. How had he managed to come to such an end? Stranded in another place, another time, and now what?

He drew in a deep breath, realizing there simply was nowhere else to run, nothing else to say, except … perhaps a prayer. Was there a God somewhere in all of this? Once again, he reviewed his good moments to the best of his ability and wondered how they stacked up against the bad.

He removed his wristwatch, a gift he'd been given for his nineteenth birthday, his latest, and held it tightly. He slid open his cell phone and then looked back over his shoulder. He figured he had less than a minute. He activated the voice recorder utility and scanned the twelfth-century landscape.

He closed his eyes, and a tear emerged from the outside corner of his right eye, followed by two from his left. Wiping the sting from both of them, he panted out what he knew would be his final words. "Mom, it's Jake. I'm sorry, Mom. I'm so sorry for everything I said the last time we spoke. I want you to know that I thought about what you said, and you were right. I never should've let a girl come between any of us. None of what happened was your fault. I didn't run away, and I'm not dead … well … " His voice trailed away. He stole a look over his shoulder and spotted the approaching shadow far off in the distance. He continued. "Please know that I love you. And Sissy, your big brother was never mad at you. You'll always be more important than any of my girlfriends. I've missed *you* more than anyone. The next time you see Dad, tell him … "—he paused for a moment, reflecting, and then added—"that he'd be proud of me. I love you." He closed the phone and prayed. "Oh God, if You are there, please help them to see that nothing was their fault. God, I don't know how to do this. Please save me." As the words left his mouth, a mighty wind arose while trees began to rock. The beast stretched out its wings to decelerate for a final approach.

Suddenly, with merely seconds remaining, out of nowhere a horse and rider materialized and then sprinted toward Jake in a fateful race against the dragon. The rider, a grease-smothered young man sporting nothing but a loin wrap and shoulder bag, leaned to one side and held out a hand. "Jake! Jake!" the rider's familiar voice called. "Grab hold. We can make it."

Jake turned, only to see his spark of hope become dashed by the beast's quicker maneuver. Its open jaws swiftly closed in upon him and the rider. Jake drew in a courageous last breath, clenched his fists, and then averted his eyes. He felt the heat of the beast's breath as a sudden light flashed about him. With a single snap, in one great sweeping motion, it was over. Jake, the rider, and the horse were gone, and nothing but a shoulder bag descending out of the sky evidenced they were ever there.

2

A large black crow cawed twice as it landed on the shoulder of the decrepit scarecrow. The eastward breeze swayed the tips of the stalks back and forth across the cornfield as it mimicked the peaceful surf of the ocean. In the distance, a Nebraska farm sat against a rapidly darkening autumn sky. Faded thunder rolls drew nearer by the moment. Lightning-charged clouds conducted a dancing ballet across the heavens.

The crow jumped and cocked its head in a startled response to an extraordinary maze of light crackling downward upon the earth. It cawed again and then leapt into flight, landing a few moments later on the weathered seat of the old John Deere. The tireless tractor sat abandoned beside the aged red barn. Parked in front of the old tractor was a much newer model, fully clad in the unmistakable green with yellow letters.

Derik and Andrea were lying comfortably on a heaping stack of hay that was situated in the loft of the barn. Derik had a piece of hay hanging out of his mouth. He fingered his unusually warm emerald amulet, which hung around his neck, as he spread out and sank in as far into the stack as his weight would allow. At his side was a bandana, with all four corners tied together, wrapped around two large peaches. Derik was seventeen, experienced with a tractor, and old enough to possess a driver's license but still not quite old enough to take Uncle Ken's truck into town for a few groceries, as told to him many times by his Uncle Ken.

"Life stinks, you know? Why can't he let me just drive into town? I've been driving his precious tractor for four years now and never even as much as scratched it or ran out of gas. I could so handle that old, beaten-down pickup." He took the hay out of his mouth and threw it onto the floor. "I wish he'd listen to Aunt Frieda. She knows I'm responsible enough."

Andrea, his down-the-street neighbor and long time best friend, was sprawled out on the opposite side.

"Must be about time to go home," she said, raising her arm to look at her watch. "Hmm, how did I know?"

"That's rich, Andi. How would you know? Your battery died two weeks ago."

Andrea was a year younger but far beyond her years in maturity. She was the eldest of five. Her siblings comprised of one younger sister and three younger brothers. She hung out with Derik simply because he was the only one around for two miles who was anywhere close to her age. Besides, his abhorrence for boredom, accompanied by his sense of adventure, culminated to keep the two of them busy when chores were finished early.

The two of them placed themselves just so on the haystack to be able to look out the loft door and watch the storm roll in.

"Oh good grief. Stop your whining, Derik. He's probably just being protective."

"What? I don't need him protecting me. I'd be fine. I guarantee it."

"I was talking about his truck, genius. Don't you remember when you set fire to the side of Old Man Cutter's barn?"

"That was over three years ago, dang it. I'm seventeen now. Besides, that was his grandkids' fault."

"He didn't light any matches to my recollection. In fact, all I remember is him daring you."

"No. He double-dog dared me, Andi."

"Oh, Lord. Here we go again." She sighed, rolling her eyes.

3

Old Man Cutter owned nearly seventy-five acres that swallowed everything directly across from Derik and all the way to the corner lot at the end of the street. Farms accounted for most of the properties for miles around, corn-yielding farms specifically. Old Man Cutter's farm was one of the largest properties in the area. He was also mighty proud of his robust peach trees. His peaches, a smaller-than-average grove, had taken on a reputation for shirt-soaking, face-wiping succulence. As delicious as they were, his peach crop generally didn't sell well at the market. This was thought to be mostly due to his open peach picking every Saturday night at sundown. For several seasons, local folks had been trying to convince him to ship a few boxes off to the state fair for the summer fruit competition. He just plain wasn't interested in the publicity or the extra work he'd be faced with in filling large orders if his peaches did well. He was more than content to watch from the front porch as his front and side yard were transformed into the weekend's social hub.

Mr. Johansen, the market owner, added to the enjoyment by bringing bottles of soda, ice packed in tubs, and selling them for a quarter each.

Every summer, about mid-July, Old Man Cutter's daughter would send her two troublesome boys out to "Granddad's" farm for a couple weeks. The plan was always two weeks. However, only twice in seven years did the visit ever last so long. And four years ago, their visit extended just three days—the shortest as yet.

Nick and Allen were one short year apart in age. Four years ago, they were nine and eight, respectively. Each year, right after the Fourth of July, Derik would inevitably get a sour stomach in anticipation of their arrival. To make things worse, Andi would make herself scarce, leaving Derik to deal with his across-the-street neighbors by himself for a great majority of the time.

This particular summer four years back, the two scalawags brought leftover fireworks from the Fourth with them. They'd deviously agreed to fire them off from the loft of Granddad's barn. From his own loft, Derik spotted the two of them sneaking a brown bag across the yard into their barn. Knowing full well what suspicious looked like, he headed over to see what they were up to.

Old Man Cutter had a small storage room behind the back wall of his loft that the boys didn't know about. Sitting directly beneath the storage room was a padlocked, walk-in tool closet with walls reaching up to the loft. The only access to the loft's storage room was via a ladder in the tool closet. Derik picked the lock on a regular basis and spent many evenings up in the old storage room with a lantern at his side. The room housed chests, furniture, and valuables that Old Man Cutter didn't care for others to know about. On different occasions, while rummaging around through some of the chests, Derik had found military artifacts from the first two world wars; old, faded pictures of people; books; paintings; heirlooms; and many other fascinating trinkets and gadgets. When he first learned of the room a few years prior, he figured if he was going to spend some time up there, he might need a quick escape route in a pinch. So he'd stacked a few chests upon one another against the wall that divided the room from the rest of the loft. The storage room's wall stretched only to the rafters, so in case he ever needed the quick escape, jumping the wall was already set up as the appointed route. Every summer, Derik also used the storage room to spy on the boys routinely. He'd then jump the wall and sneak up on them in the midst of their mischief. In their estimation, he'd simply appear out of nowhere, which also happened to be exactly what he told them he did. He also told them a phantom lived in the barn and granted him special powers. They weren't sure they were willing to completely buy that story; however, the boys were so convinced of his capability to simply show up out of thin air that they found themselves looking over their shoulders for him everywhere and every time their mischief was on the rise.

That day when Derik saw the boys head into the barn with the paper bag, he straightaway headed for the storage room. Within moments, he was observing their every word and movement as they formulated a plan through their giggles and snickering whispers. Derik quickly scanned the muddled room and found a top hat; a long, dark cape; and a gentleman's cane. He stealthily crept over the wall, with objects in hand, and then snuck into the shadows where he donned the apparel. When one of the boys took out a match and prepared to light the first firecracker, Derik stepped out of the shadows with his chin tucked into his chest. He advanced himself a few more methodical steps, and then suddenly, everything went deathly quiet. He stopped, holding his stance for a moment and then slowly looked up just enough to keep his face hidden beneath the brim of the hat.

Images of popular horror/slasher-film villains came to mind as Derik analyzed their dreaded expressions. He fought hard to keep from breaking into hysterics, believing if he gave in to even the semblance of a grin, he'd lose all composure. As Derik took one last step, Allen, the younger brother, lost it, backing away, giving into a fit of screams. He quickly gave up his brother. "Nick made me. He makes me do everything. Do him, mister. Do him."

Nick tried to say something, anything, when his hand went limp and the unlit firecracker fell to the floor. His face transformed from a blank stare into a large frown, followed by several promises that he wasn't really going to do anything. "Honest, mister, I wasn't gonna hurt your, um, barn … or … I promise, Mr. Ph-Phantom-m-m. I wasn't gonna light anything," he pleaded with big, puppy-dog eyes.

With that, Derik snickered, and the rouse was over.

Nick's puppy-dog eyes became narrow with suspicion, and then as he realized it was Derik, they turned into large angry saucers. He glared at Derik. "You're such a jerk. Man, I can't believe you."

Allen wiped his eyes as giggles of relief slipped out of a half-hidden smile. "That was funny, Derik. You scared Nick half to…" he said with a little laugh and then abruptly held his tongue when Nick swung around with a harsh look. He stole a glance at Derik again, chuckled, and then wiped his eyes once more.

"So what're you guys up to *now*?" Derik asked, snatching up the paper bag.

"We have a few extra bottle rockets and firecrackers. Nothin' major," Nick said, swiping it back.

"A few? Where'd you learn to count? There's at least three or four dozen in there, and if your Grandpa finds out, he's gonna—"

"That's why he ain't gonna find out…unless you're plannin' on rattin' us out."

"Well, maybe somebody *ought* to. Anyway, how are you gonna keep him from finding out? He's gonna hear them exploding."

"See, Al, I told you. He's turned into such a spoilsport *and* a rat. I guess he ain't what everyone made him out to be," Nick said, peeking back over at Derik.

"Wait a minute," Derik interjected. "What exactly have you heard, because I ain't no rat, and I ain't never been a spoilsport either."

Allen stood back and watched his older brother work his magic on Derik. And Derik was an older kid. Allen knew all too well how impressive Nick was when he wanted something his way. The two went back and forth until it was time to ante up.

"Okay, fine. Prove it then. Go ahead. You light the first one," Nick said, handing over the matches.

"I don't have to prove anything."

"Afraid you're gonna get caught?"

"Get caught? I get away with ninety percent of the stuff I start *because* I know how not to get caught."

Nick snapped back, "So what've you got to lose? Everyone's downtown at the market, so nobody's gonna hear anything." Then he lowered his voice into a stern whisper. "Go ahead. I dare you."

Derik rolled his eyes in exasperation, then ever-so-slightly moved his hand toward the matches but thought better of it.

In the same whispery voice, Nick added, "I double-dog dare you."

Allen gasped, then immediately placed two hands over his mouth.

Derik knew that in all his life, as far back as he could remember, he'd never passed on a double-dog dare. But did *they* know that? Would it get out that he was yellow? Should he counter back with a triple? Well, it seemed clear to Derik that everyone knew the only time you countered with a triple was if you had no intention of walking out the double dare. A hundred thoughts flashed through his mind in a matter of seconds. He placed a hand on his forehead, then dropped it down over his eyes and slightly shook his head. *Man, I can't believe I let him double-dog me*, he thought.

"Fine," he said, snatching the matches from Nick's hand. "I'm only doin' one, so hand it over, then back up."

Nick pulled out the "Deluxe Roman Candle Finale" and said, "Since you're only doin' one…"

Derik wondered how he'd allowed himself to get into such a predicament. He closed his eyes for but a moment, then drew in one of those deep, I'm-such-an-idiot breaths. "Just give it here," he said, gritting his teeth.

He pulled out a single match and struck it against the side of the box. It instantly ignited. All three sets of eyes centered in on the flickering flame as each of the boys wore the allure of imminent danger on their faces. Derik placed the match against the fuse and waited. The fuse smoked but didn't take on the flame. He sighed with relief.

"It's a dud!" Nick cried. "Dang it. That was the best one."

Derik quickly dropped it into the bag and then retrieved a much smaller one, a basic bottle rocket. He began fingering for another match when the bag suddenly lit up from the inside. The suddenness startled Derik, and he dropped the bag and then jumped away from it and yelled, "Whoa! Oh, crap!"

"Oh, no!" Allen screamed. "We're all gonna die!"

"Well…grab it!" Derik said to Nick.

"You grab it. You did it."

"It's your bag and your stuff."

The wick was burning down. A dazzling light show of sparks erupted from the bag, sending some of the sparks four or five feet into the air.

The tension mounted within Derik. He stepped toward the bag several times, trying to decide how to handle it, and with each one stepped back again.

"Do something!" Allen cried.

Time seemed to stand still as each of the boys envisioned the next few moments. Terrifying illusions spanned from half the barn blowing up, then someone going to jail, all the way to half the county blowing up with someone getting spankings.

Figuring that he only had a few seconds left, Nick turned and ran. He slammed straight into Andi, who'd just stepped off the ladder.

"Uh! Get off me, ya little weasel," Andi commanded, pushing him away and then dusting herself. With her curiosity quickly swelling into irritation, she said, "Derik, *what*"—she spotted the sparks—"in the *world…*" She stepped toward him. As she did, he cast an unnerved look at her. "Derik! Are those firecrackers?"

His eyes darted back to the bag. He shuffled his feet in a nervous prance, arms set directly in front at the ready. It seemed absurd that all common sense would desert Derik on such an occasion.

"Criminy, Derik! Get rid of the bag!" she shrieked.

"It's gonna blow us all up!" Allen yelled, backing up against a wall.

"Derik!" Andi screamed, throwing her hands up.

All at once, Derik leapt forward and kicked the bag from the loft. While it fell topside down, the Roman candle blasted into one of the sides. The bag spiraled out of control until the explosive flew out the open top, dashing straightaway into a large steel feed trough, where it exploded. The inside of the entire barn lit up and flashed like a strobe light. Smoke filled the air, along with the distinctive smell of fired flash powder and sulfur. Several embers streaked into a wall and then fell, landing into a small pile of hay. The hay caught fire almost instantly.

"You idiot!" Nick shouted.

"*Me?*" Derik asserted incredulously while running for the ladder. "You, who brought them up here to fire them off with disregard to all consequence, are calling someone an idiot?"

"Well you lit 'em."

Andi issued a horrified gasp, folded her arms in absolute shock, and then glared down at Derik, who was now on the ground running toward the burning hay.

Derik grabbed a leather poncho off an old, rusty coat hook and then leapt onto the haystack, smothering the fire. He stood up and stared at a gaping black hole in the hay lying directly beneath a large burnt char mark on the wall. He followed it up and, higher on the wall, saw the char marks left by the embers that started the fire. He slapped an exasperatingly open hand against the side of his head. Realizing he was coming down from the adrenaline rush, the weight of his anxiety suddenly took its toll, buckling his knees. He caught himself, but just barely.

That little punk almost burned down this barn, he thought. Nick's remark from a moment ago finally processed.

Derik answered, saying, "Well, if you hadn't double-dog dared me…" but stopped upon hearing yet another gasp from Andi. He glanced up to the three on the loft and noticed Andi's eyes burned straight through him. She was right, and he knew it. He looked away, spotting the bag of firecrackers. He walked over to them, picked them up with a flare of righteous indignation, and proceeded to dunk the entire bag into a medium-sized water trough.

Nick came unglued. "Those are mine! You can't do that. Oh, you're dead, buddy. You're gonna pay me for each one of those."

"But Nick, you stole 'em. They didn't cost you anything," Allen said.

"I don't care. They were mine! He ruined every one of those, and he's gonna pay me or I'm gonna—"

"You're gonna what?" Andi snarled. "Don't you know how much trouble you're in?"

Nick turned his back to her and, with a sarcastic wave of his hand, said under his breath, "He's the one in trouble."

"Am I in trouble?" Allen asked.

Andi glanced at him and then released an exasperated grunt. She threw her arms into the air, fists clenched, and then said, "Where do kids like you two come from?" She said to Derik, "If I don't leave right now, I just might kill one of them."

The next day, the two boys were sent back home. Derik was grounded for two months and had to do extra chores for Old Man Cutter until it was determined by his uncle that he'd learned a lesson.

4

Back on the haystack with Andi, Derik exhaled loudly, fingering the knot on the bandana while wondering if she was still holding the incident against him. He then laced his fingers together and raised both arms up over his head. His hands stretched to the top of the haystack. She mimicked him from the opposite side and ended up laying her hands against his. She slightly flinched, but neither one of them wanted to be the one to react and pull away, so together they sat, with her hands on top of his.

The recent news that her family had to move soon was tossing around in his mind.

Touching her hands made Derik feel like he was already missing her. "So when do you guys have to be out of your house?" he asked, trying to approach the subject tenderly.

"I heard my parents say we had a month."

"Freaking banks. Can't they give a family a break?"

"Good grief, we've had a break for six months, Derik. My mom's sickness is just not going to get better very soon, so Dad's having to carry the load by himself. His boss keeps urging him to take a position in Texas. I mean, he should. It's a promotion. His boss has even recommended him for the position to the regional manager." She looked away and sighed. "But I don't wanna move." She shook her head. "Geez, I'm so selfish."

"You? Selfish? Oh, do shut up. How long's he been the manager of the Old America Cafeteria now?"

"Eight years, I think."

"So he's pretty hot stuff over there, huh?"

"Well, he's the one that started the 'free senior lunch with a paid child lunch.' It promotes the whole grand-kid/grandparent thing, and the seniors absolutely love it. Seems like the parents eat it up too…um, no pun intended. Anyway, according to Dad, ever since he started that promotion, business has more than doubled. Now all the Old America Cafeterias are doin' it."

Derik laid his head back and grinned, listening to her relaxing voice, and then a moment later grimaced. He tried to imagine what life would be like without Andi around. One thing was certain as far as he was concerned: She would brighten lives wherever she ended up. "Well, no matter where you go, you'll land on your feet, having straight As and all."

"Let's talk about something else, okay? What's gonna happen is gonna happen," she said, trying to pick up the mood.

"Mmm, okay. Johnny J. thinks he's gonna marry you."

"Wh-what? Where did … how in the … *what*? Johnny J. is, like, two grades lower than me. And he's an itty, bitty thing. What would ever make that little french fry think he was gonna marry me?"

"I might'a told him that, uh … you thought he was cute."

"Derik!" she yelled, flipping around onto her tummy. She reached over the stack and gave his head a shove, then said, "You'd better be joking. You so better be joking. Oh, man. Is that why he's been following me around at lunch? Oh my gosh, and I've been smiling at him, thinking he was like, I dunno, lost or something."

Derik snickered. "Maybe you and the fry could multiply, and you guys could become like a value meal together or somethin'."

"Geez, Derik, I could *kill* you right now," she grumbled, trying to reach him again.

Derik ducked and leaned away, wearing a large gratified smile on his face.

She flipped back around and threw herself into the haystack in a huff. Derik then threw himself into the haystack the same way, mocking her with a chuckle, then felt around at his side for the bandana of peaches until he found them.

Andi glared off into the distance with a minor shake of her head, then considered the humor of it all and began to feel a half-grin break across her lips.

In the distance, thunder rolled, and the two turned their heads in unison to watch. The large black crow on the tractor cawed and leapt again into flight, landing this time on a bell housing fastened above the loft's doorway. The large door was held open, locked against the outer barn wall. The crow spotted the two resting in the hay.

Derik opened the bandana, grabbed a peach, and proceeded to sink his teeth into the softest part. It was a regular practice for Andi to bring him two fat peaches from Old Man Cutter's peach trees any time she was heading to meet him in the loft.

The storm was yet in the distance but was fast approaching.

"I love big storms. They help me relax," Andi uttered in a delightful, almost inspired tone.

Derik took another bite of the peach and agreed with a preoccupied, "Uh-huh," while wiping the juice from the side of his mouth with the back of his hand. They watched the display of lightning across the sky for several minutes. Andi closed her eyes in order to better take in the sounds that the storm would offer.

"That deep rumbling makes me feel like we're beneath a giant bowling alley in the clouds," he said with a full mouth of peach.

"Shhh, just listen. Isn't it beautiful?"

A few minutes of silence passed between them. They both listened to the storm's composition as it drew nearer. A breeze entered the loft and brushed against their faces. Each of them responded with a turn of their heads into the oncoming draft.

"Oh, that feels great. Couldn't you just fall asleep right here, Andi?" It continued for several minutes, occasionally gusting. He then closed his eyes while Andi pulled the arms of her sweater down over her hands. The two sat motionless for several minutes.

A sudden, powerful boom shook the barn and made both of them jump. Andi opened her eyes in a gasp. The lightning wasn't far off and would quickly be on top of them. Something was different about it, though. A reddish-orange haze was falling from the low-hanging clouds.

"Do you see that?" she asked, pointing toward the house only a couple hundred feet away. "That spray over there?"

"Yeah. What...uh...wh-where's it coming from?" Derik answered, sitting up.

"It's almost to your house," she said, sliding around to the front of the haystack so she could see him. "What do you think it is?"

"I dunno."

The storm had drawn completely around them. The rain hadn't started yet, but the lightning and thunder was as furious as they had ever seen. The wind started picking up.

"I think I'd better head home before the rain starts," Andi said, pulling strands of blowing hair away from her face. She stood up, brushed the hay off the back of her pants, and shook her hair out. A sudden, bright, flickering light lit up the area surrounding the barn. An instant later, a deafening, resounding crack exploded around them. Their eyes were blinded by an intense white flash. Andi screamed in response and jumped away from the open loft doorway, holding both her hands over her head.

When she looked up, she spotted Derik on the other side of the loft in a corner with his head between his knees. The reddish-orange fog began to settle in and around the barn.

Derik lifted his head, asking, "Are we still alive?" as he checked himself. "Andi, are you okay? What in the flaming heck was that? I don't know when I've ever—"

"Derik, get your hiney over here now," she said blankly.

He turned around and looked up to see what only could be described as a floating window. "Wh-what in the world?" he asked in a stutter while standing to his feet. The mysterious anomaly stood about as tall as he did. As a knot began to form in his stomach, he thought of Alex and Nick and their petrified faces when they encountered him as the phantom, which may have been to them something just as unexplainable and entirely as unnerving.

Derik studied the window, particularly the gathered, distorted mass surrounding it. The window didn't exist as something simply positioned before him like a hanging bale of hay. Rather, it was more like the fabric of the actual space before him had been torn and forced outward as it opened, bunching together at its edges like mounds of snow when plowed off a field. His focus shifted toward the center, a mouth of sorts. Dark at first, and drawing swirling air into it like a vortex, the oddity as a whole suddenly, and only for a moment, transformed into a scene of serenity.

The circular opening sat suspended in midair next to Andi. It drifted about a foot off the ground in the middle of the light mist. It stood between the two of them, hovering slowly toward Derik.

"What happened?" Derik asked, unsure of what to expect next. Just then, it began swallowing air once again in the same counter-clockwise current, becoming as loud as it was just a moment before.

"I can see all the way to my house through the window, Derik," she said in a bewildered tone. "What does that mean? Derik, this is scaring me."

"I can see the high school from this side," he said.

The howling wind gusted harder and continued to blow Andi's hair in and out of her face. She almost couldn't hear Derik for the wind's furious whistling and wailing.

She kept her eyes fixed on her side of the window for another moment, which maintained the identical vortex as Derik's side, and then she shot a baffled glance to Derik. "Well, that's six miles away. How can you see that?" she yelled.

"I dunno, but I don't think I can get around this thing. It's getting wider and heading straight for me. I think I'm trapped!" he hollered back. "I think it's a wormhole of some sort, Andi! Stay away from it!"

"There's a rope hanging from the beam above you! Can you reach it?" she asked.

He looked up and then jumped several times, but it was just out of reach. "It's stuck on a hook, it looks like."

"I think I can get to it and lower it before the window reaches you!"

"What'd you say? Andi! Where're you going?"

She darted for the ladder which was fastened against the wall. She scampered up to the crossing beam in the rafters and then managed to get her balance on her hands and knees despite the spiraling wind against her. She began slowly crawling across the beam, realizing she was at least twelve feet above the floor of the loft.

"What in the heck do you think you're doing? Andi, go back! Besides, I don't think you're going to make it in time! Just turn around and go back, Andi! Go back!"

Hearing that, she steadied herself and stood up, arms out, balancing herself. "I'll be right there."

"Andi, you're going to break your neck! Go back!"

"I can make it. I'm almost there."

"Don't look down, Andi, and be careful!"

She looked down at him to give him one of her looks and then felt herself begin to lean.

"What are you *doing*? Don't … look … down!"

That hole is going to get to him if I don't hurry, she thought. She glanced down out of the corner of her eye to try to spot it, keeping her head as steady as possible. "Is it gone? I don't see it anymore!"

"What do you mean you don't see it? It's as big as life. You're directly above it!"

"I don't see it. It must be paper thin."

"Gosh dang it, Andi. Why didn't you listen to me?"

"Just one more step. Yes! I've got it." She pulled the rope loose from the hook it was caught on and lowered the end down another couple feet. He reached up and grabbed hold of it. He pulled himself up to the beam and got a hand firmly in place to be able to let go of the rope.

"It's pulling me in. I don't think I can hang on for long. Andi, just go and run for help."

The wind continued to whip through the barn, throwing hay and dust into the mix. The pounding thunder continued while the lightning was more furious than ever. A sudden deluge of rain hammering down upon the roof resonated throughout the barn.

"Derik, your legs! It's got your legs! They're gone! Derik! Derik, grab my hand!" She bent down, trying to reach his closest hand. The angle she was at made her notice once again how far up from the floor she was. A feeling like a rush of pin needles ran down to her hands as she began to lose her balance. "Jesus, help me." Her body's weight had shifted; she lost her center of gravity.

"Andi! Andi, hold on. I'm right here. Andi, no! No!"

She tried to regain her balance but overcompensated. She felt her toes rise off the beam while shifting her weight and knew she was in trouble. She turned and, in a quick glance, saw Derik's horrified expression as she passed him on the way down.

Derik waited for the hollow thud from Andi landing on the loft floor. There was nothing. He repositioned his hold on the beam to be able to see beneath him. She was nowhere to be found. She had simply vanished. Realizing she'd fallen into the drifting porthole made his stomach hurt. He hung from the beam, staring into the window that was slowly engulfing him.

I can't leave her there... wherever "there" happens to be, he thought. Before another moment could pass, he drew in a deep breath and let go of the beam. As he surrendered himself to gravity, for just a brief moment, he thought he saw his emerald emit a sudden flashing glow.

The crow observed the commotion from the bell housing then cawed loudly several times, flapping its wings. It dove off its perch, glided into the barn through the loft door, and proceeded to follow the two through the open hole. The window collapsed immediately, and then the storm's ferocity subsided.

5

Derik found himself falling, rear end first, through a large dark chasm. Pictures rushed through his mind of what lay at the end of his fall. He couldn't help the re-circulating thoughts that involved lots of large impaling posts or rigid, mountainous rocks. His breathing quickened and grew shallower. His heart raced and pounded against his chest while his thoughts settled on his demise and that of Andi. A barrage of memories flooded his mind. He centered in on one. It was last spring. Andi didn't make it over to Derik's loft because both her mother and father had left for town. Andi needed to stay home and look after her siblings. Derik, full of vigor, wasn't privy to the information, so he trudged over to her place in the pouring rain, determined not to let the weather hamper a perfectly good Saturday.

Andi had lunch ready for her brothers and sister. They all sat down at the table, and then as soon as the last chair was scooted up to it, a knock was heard at the front door.

A myriad of "I'll get its" rang throughout as wooden chairs screeched backward over the wooded kitchen floor. A small charge of children dashed through the kitchen, past the living room, and down the hall to the front door. Four sets of hands landed on the knob accompanying hollers of, "Me! No, me! I got here first! No, it's my turn!"

"Yoo-hoo," Andi called, holding up a set of keys. "It's locked for this very reason. You think we're … *stupid*? You little rascals really thought you had a chance this time, didn't ya? Okay, now *I'll* get the door, and you all get back to the table and eat. Get." She stepped up to the door, but the kids were still jockeying for a glimpse at who it was. Andi started in on tickling the gang, yelling, "Oh, *you're* gonna get it, and you too! I'm gonna get all of you! Last one back to the table is really gonna get it!" The fading pitter-pattering sound of feet, together with screams and laughs, poured out the front door as it was unlocked then opened.

Derik stood on the front porch wearing a large hooded coat that was dripping from the rain. "Oh, man. I thought you'd get to ditch the li'l monkeys today. What's up? Mom and Pop in town?"

"*Some* of us have responsibilities," she said in a huff. "Come on. Get in here. And leave your coat on the porch, would you?" She took a few more steps, then, after hearing Derik's squeaky shoes against the hall's wood floor, turned around and rolled her eyes.

"What?" Derik asked with a slightly detectable attitude.

"Take off your *shoes*, please, and would you *mind* shutting the door?" She turned back around, making a gesture with her hand to her head, suggesting mindlessness.

"Geez, Andi, you sound like my mom."

"*Oy vey!* I don't need another monkey to clean up after. *Comprende?*"

"*I* don't make messes. Just take a look at my house."

"Really? Seen your room lately?"

"Well, I know *you* haven't."

"It's not hard to spot from the loft. I've talked to your mom, and radioactive mires aren't her thing. Your room needs … disaster relief." The three older kids busted out in a screaming laugh, repeating the declaration.

"Whatever," Derik said, rubbing the oldest boy's head. "So what's on the menu? Smells like chili, as in *hot chili peppas,*" he said, dancing the mamba. The kids busted up again, this time in ear-splitting hysterics.

Andi snorted, trying to swallow an unanticipated burst of laughter, then held a hand over her eyes and said, "Don't ever do that in public, please. Oh my goodness. Lord, save him from himself. And yes, we're having chili. Would you like some?"

"Only if Katie, here, helped make it," he said, giving Andi's four-year-old sister a kiss on the top of her head. Two hands eclipsed a flabbergasted smile across Katie's face as several muffled giggles escaped between her fingers. Starry-eyed declarations of love accompanied the two older boys' sniggers and woos.

Andi placed a bowl of chili in front of an empty chair and then set a glass of cola next to it. "Have a seat, lover boy."

Derik sat down and winked at Katie. Katie gasped and then gave Andi a quick look with a smile that could turn any bad day right-side up. Andi gave Katie a wink and a big smile back and then peeked over at Derik. She held her gaze for a moment while he wasn't looking and then grinned and looked away. She served herself a bowl of chili and a glass of cola and then sat across from Derik at the end of the table.

Katie watched as Derik chugged his cola, then she looked at Andi and asked, "Are you gonna marry Derik?"

Derik coughed and then sprayed cola out his nose and mouth, spewing it onto everything directly in front of him within reach. Derik tried to recover from his coughing spell as quickly as possible but found no immediate relief. The entire event had Andi nearly falling out of her chair from her fit of laughter. She managed to reach some towels off a nearby counter and threw them at Derik.

"I'm … so … sorry," he stuttered through several coughs. He glanced at Andi then started laughing about the whole thing. He took hold of the towels and began cleaning his mess. They both looked over at Katie, who had been clapping and laughing along with the boys, unsure of what might have incited such commotion.

After lunch, Andi escaped down into the basement pantry to grab some food for dinner. Her sly behavior caught Derik's attention. He followed her to the basement door and then snuck down the stairs in a stealthy manner of his own. He peeked around a corner and saw an open door to a dark room. He backed up and scanned the basement for anywhere else she might have slipped off to. There was no sign of her anywhere. He deduced that she must have slipped into the dark room. He tiptoed to the open door and stole a glimpse into the darkness.

"Man, that's dark," he whispered to himself. He cautiously stepped into the room and then took a couple more tiptoed steps. He turned and glanced behind him back to the lighted basement. The darkness started getting to him. He began to imagine what would become of him if the door suddenly closed and locked him in. He felt the regret rise up of all the monster movies he'd watched over the past few years. The Saturday night scary movie finally scored one on Derik.

"I'm outta here," he said under his breath. Suddenly, the door slammed shut. Derik nearly jumped out of his skin. "Sheep biscuits!" he said, getting ready to punch whatever was to crawl out of the walls. It was complete blackness everywhere. He started heading back to the door, shifting his feet inch by inch with his hands stretched out in front of him. He stopped, wondering if something else in the room had moved. His eyes shot back and forth, trying to penetrate the darkness. Suddenly, a small sound broke the silence. It was heavy breathing. Derik turned his head to the right, then to the left. He started swinging his arms all about. Finally, he said, "Who's there? Andi, is that you?"

All of a sudden, a ghostly face appeared out of the darkness. A face full of shadows but brightly lit. "Aaah!"

he screamed. The room unexpectedly lit up, and there stood Andi by the door with a flashlight under her face. Andi was sure if she laughed any harder her face would switch from beat red to purple and then to blue from the mere absence of breath, but not from a lack of trying. With her eyes closed tightly, spilling tears, and her lips pressed together, she laughed so hard that she simply couldn't draw a breath.

It took Derik three or four seconds of staring at Andi before he was able to break a smile. "Oh my g … You are so dead. Do you hear me? You're dead meat."

Andi fell down into the corner, still trying to breath. After her face actually turned two shades of purple, she inhaled with enormous suction. A mammoth laugh ensued.

"Oh, I've never seen you so … so … " she managed to mutter through her laughter.

"Are you crying? You *are* crying, aren't you? Laugh it up, sister. Your day's coming."

"Oh, if only you could have seen … Aaah, ha ha … sheep 'biscuits?'"

Derik started laughing simply out of watching her laugh so hard. "You're something else, you know?" He stretched out a hand to help her up. She fell into his chest and grabbed his shoulders to keep from falling again. Her laughs had subsided to a few giggles. He put his arms around her to help her keep her balance. She wore an ecstatic smile while putting her head on his shoulder and then hugged him.

"I'm sorry, but I've really needed to laugh like that. Are you okay?" she asked as she let go of him.

Derik grinned and shook his head. "I can't believe I let you scare me … I mean, I knew it was you. But still, I got all freaked out. I'm sure I'll be fine, once my heart rate gets back under three hundred."

The remark sparked a snort from Andi. She held a finger across her smile and then sniggered again. "Sorry," she said in a giggle and then looked away. "You know, you didn't have to follow me down here."

"Well, you were being so secretive about it. I was intrigued. Why were you sneaking down here anyway?"

"Well, I didn't want anyone to know," she said, turning away.

Derik bit his lip. "Know what?"

"I didn't want anyone to know that we were struggling."

"How would I know that from down here? What, because the pantry's low on food? This is how ours is on a regular basis. Besides, I've never seen your pantry."

"Andi? Are you down here?" Katie called from the stairs.

Andi reached for the door and opened it. "Yes, sweetie. I'm in the pantry."

Katie rounded the corner and then held up, obviously taken aback. "Were you guys *kissing*?" she asked in a half-way-miffed yet thoroughly disgusted tone.

Andi immediately blushed and glanced at Derik. At once, both of them tried to hide their grins. "No, no, honey. Derik's trying to help me pick out food for dinner. Is that okay?" she asked, kneeling in front of her.

Katie slid her eyes away from Andi and onto Derik. She frowned. "I guess so." She dragged her eyes back to Andi. "He's not going to break me up, is he?" she whispered.

Andi frowned, trying to disguise her smile. "You mean, break up with you?"

Katie nodded soberly.

"I think you're okay for now, sweetie pie. But someday down the road, he might decide to kiss someone his own age."

Katie's face fell. "No, Sissy. Then he will break me up with him."

"I promise, sugar bear, you'll always be his number one."

Katie studied Andi's face. "Promise?" she asked reluctantly.

"Cross my heart."

"Even if he kisses *you*?"

"Even if."

Katie smiled and then threw her arms around Andi.

"Okay, honey. Go see if you can snitch on your brothers."

Katie's eyes lit up. "Okay." She turned and trotted away.

Andi looked over her shoulder at Derik. "Well, you've got your hands full," she said. She stood up and then walked back into the pantry with her eyes scanning the floor. She stopped in front of Derik and raised her eyes to his. "Just make sure you guys always have Christmas with our family," she said with a smirk.

"Oh, ha-ha, that's hilarious," he said dismissively.

"She's afraid you're gonna drop her for the next girl you kiss."

"What? Never," he said, raising a finger.

"Hey, I'm not the one you've gotta prove it to."

Derik put his hands on either of Andi's cheeks and kissed her on the top of the head. "There. She has nothing to worry about, and you're my witness."

Andi, a bit startled, said, "Wow, from lover boy to heartbreaker in one night. Maybe it's a good thing you've never really full-on kissed a girl before because that one was kind of lacking"

"Ugh! I've kissed a girl before," he replied with a squint, trying to hide the fact that she was absolutely correct. It was his conviction that his first romantic kiss would be the perfect kiss in the perfect situation with the perfect person.

She shot him a dismissive glare.

Hey, I just want you to know that every one of my kisses mean something."

"Even that one?"

"Even that one. So ... " he said as he turned and began taking inventory of the shelves.

Andi stared at his profile for a moment and then surrendered half a grin. "Yes, back to the pantry. I'm kind of worried because we've never been this low on food," she said, dismissing the last few comments. "Well, as far as I can remember anyway. I think Mom and Dad are in town looking for a job for her. I overheard Mom calling a few places. I'm getting scared, Derik."

"Whoa, back up. First of all, let's not jump to conclusions. They could be in town for any number of reasons. If they are in town looking for work, I'm sure they'll find it. The Hendersons just packed up and moved a couple of weeks ago," he said confidently. "There's a couple positions right there."

"Where'd *they* go? For that matter, where would *we* go, if not Texas, that is? I mean, this is all I've ever known. I don't wanna leave everything—the farm and school and ... and you."

"You guys have been through rough times before, right?"

"Well, yeah. But Mom's not doing really well. I think they're spending a lot on her medical stuff. Man, Derik, she must be feeling really guilty if all this is on account of her illness."

"Well, maybe they're just cuttin' back on food. Everyone does that around here from time to time."

"I found some mail, Derik," she said, placing one hand on her hip and the other over her eyes in a fretful gesture. "It's not good news."

Derik stood quietly.

"It was from the bank. I just quickly scanned it and saw the words *four-month extension* and *foreclose in February*. They don't know I've seen it."

Derik remained still.

"The world's falling apart on us, Derik. I don't know what to do," she said as a tear fell.

"Look, no matter what happens, you and I are forever friends. Miles may separate us, but we'll always have each other, okay? I'll write you all the time and send you Old Man Cutter's peaches. And you can always come visit for a few days, I'm sure. And you know what? I'm gonna get a car soon. I'll come to you for a few days, and it'll be just like old times. I promise."

Andi slid a finger under her eye and then enveloped Derik in her arms. "Promise nothing will change between us. You won't let anyone forget about me?"

"I promise you, Andi. No matter where you end up, I'll come find you."

6

As Derik continued to fall, he felt the speed of his decent begin to slow. He cocked his head after seeing a distant orange glow. A brief glimpse of the underground lake's surface caught his eye just before he plunged deep into its tepid water. He winced as his back splashed hard, creating a burning sensation against his entire posterior. The full effects were felt within a few short moments.

Derik emerged with a large gasp of air and then an echoing breath of reprieve. Although relief was dominating at the moment, a rising sense of despair was slowly swallowing him. The desire for answers had his eyes darting in several directions. His eyes slowly began to adjust to the darkness. "Where am I?" he asked quietly. Looking around, he studied the area for any sign of light or movement. "Andi, are you down here?" he whispered heavily. The sound of breaking waves echoed against the high, far-off, dark walls surrounding him.

Catching a whiff of something quite unfamiliar, he drew in a more analytical sniff. A musty, rancid odor blending horribly with the stench of lake water caught him off guard and might as well have slapped him senseless. With a large croaking sound, he immediately vomited, followed by a dry heave a few seconds later. "Oh my g—, what is that putrid smell?" With darkness everywhere with the exception of a dim glow far above him and a hundred or so meters to his rear, he said to himself, "This must be a cavern of some kind." Reacquainting himself with the lapping breakers, he determined where he thought the sound was originating from and then began swimming. "Maybe it's better I don't see what I'm swimming in," he said, trying his best not to breathe through his nose.

As Derik approached the rocky shore, the loudness of the breaking waves made it apparent he was very close. Despite his inability to see how close or far away he was, his toes reached down, and his feet shot forward and side to side, feeling for shallow ground. He felt a rock. "Finally," he grumbled. "Thank you, God."

He managed to plod his way from the rocks and onto what seemed like a slick, muddy shore. On a small landing, he sat down and then leaned forward, laying his head against a bent knee.

"Criminy, it stinks to high heaven in here. What in God's creation could smell so bad? Andi!" he called quietly again. "Where could she be? I was right behind her." He clinched his teeth and then let out a groan. He just knew she had to be close by. "Andi, can you hear me? Answer me, dang it." His voice bounced off a few distant walls. "Fritz-a-ritz."

He felt around for some rocks, and after picking up six loose ones, he threw them in several directions to get an idea of where to go from where he was. "Andi, can you hear me?" Four of the stones sounded as if they ricocheted off large rocks or walls. "Well, probably not that way." One of the stones landed back in the water. "No, *thanks.*" The last one hit something that produced a hollow clunking sound. "Okay, little stone, where are you leading me?"

He rolled onto all fours and started crawling. The putrid odor grew stronger as he advanced toward what he could only imagine was certain danger. After crawling a short distance, his hand set down on a small, clammy object protruding out from the ground. Somewhat sticky and cool to the touch, he wrapped his fingers across the top portion of it. It shifted like a loose molar. With a little nudge in one direction, followed by a fair pull in another, the muddy terrain surrendered it with an unresentful suction sound. He picked it up and fingered it. "Huh," he huffed, wondering what it could be.

He crawled a few more steps, and then his hand landed on something that piqued his curiosity. Brushing his hand over it, he found half of it rounded and smooth like an oversized softball on one side, with two large cavities and a third smaller hole beneath them on the other side. He picked it up, grimacing, hoping it wasn't what he thought it was. He worked his way down just a bit, probing along, visualizing what his fingers felt. "Ugh! A skull," he cried, dropping it after finding the teeth.

"Great. Human remains. That doesn't bode well for me or for … oh, no. Andi! Andi, can you hear me?"

He felt along the ground again and discovered another skull, then another, and then came upon the outside edge of a large mound of bones. He took one of the skulls and, wondering how large a mound it was, skipped it across the top of the pile. The skull continued to clunk and clatter along, bouncing off bones until it came to a rest nearly a hundred feet away. He stood up and stared off into the blackness before him, allowing the bleakness he'd been fending off to finally mount.

Suddenly, the sound of rattling bones rose out of the darkness. Then he felt it—a small tremor, followed by a larger one. He felt the pace of his heart quicken.

"God, I'm not a praying person. I'm sorry I haven't followed you. I know I don't deserve Your pity or even for You to think about me, but I'm calling out to You now." He dropped to his knees. "Please, God, I'm not expecting a miracle, just a hand. I'll do anything You want if You just help me get outta here. I'll tell everyone how wonderful You are. I'll be a missionary. I'll … I'll … oh, who am I kidding? You know I'm not gonna do any of that stuff. I'm such a loser. I don't do anything that betters me or anyone else. Geez, I'm so selfish."

He leaned onto his hip, then kicked his legs out from under him and sat there. "You know, I wish I'd done things differently with my life. I could've been nicer to my uncle. Maybe I should've told my parents that I loved them more often before I lost them. Are they up there with You? Man, I can't seem to do anything right on my own. Maybe that's why I need You. Maybe You need to get in and drive for me, if it were only that simple."

Suddenly, through the darkness, a faint melodic alarm began to sound. A dim light appeared about twenty feet away. Derik jumped and then spun around to see what it was. "What the … ? That sounds like a reminder chime …" A second or two passed while he observed, and then he said aloud, "To a cell phone." He scooted onto his belly and quickly maneuvered over the bones in a combat crawl as fast as he could. "Keep ringing. Come on. Keep ringing. Oh yeah, I got you. Come on. Come on. That's right. You're all mine. Just a couple more seconds. Come on."

He was about eight feet from closing in on it when it stopped. "No, no, no! Criminy. Dag nabbit."

He felt around the hundreds of bones immediately in front of him. "Gosh dang it. I was so close. Why would You do that, God? Ugh!"

He picked up a bone and threw it as hard as he could. It landed on some soft ground way past the other side of the mound of bones. "Oh, wow. That's gotta be the way out. Maybe *that's* why. Do I even need the cell phone, God?" At once, the alarm sounded again, and the phone dimly lit up. "Yes, thank You, God. Thank You."

The phone sat under several interlocked bones at the top of the heap now nearly two feet away. He frantically separated and dug through until he grabbed hold of it. He found himself lost on the technology, for nothing seemed to do what he expected as he continued to press and slide his finger across the on-screen menus. Bright lights flickered and flashed, cutting through the immediate darkness encompassing him. Suddenly, a hologram appeared above the phone. It was the image of a beautiful young lady about his age. The image dissipated and then was replaced by a young girl who was about eight years old. A moment later, a three-dimensional family portrait consisting of an older teenage boy, the same young girl, and a thirty-something woman and man replaced it. The hologram program closed itself, followed by a low-charge warning. "Geez, I just want to make a call," he said, pressing more buttons in a senseless craze.

A quiet, silky woman's voice poured into the still air. "I'm sorry. Your voice was not recognized. If you'd like to make a call, tell me the number you'd like to call."

"I'm trying, lady, but—"

"I'm sorry," she said, cutting him off. "Are you authorized to use this phone?"

"Lady, just call nine-one-one. Nine-one-one."

"One moment," the voice said. "I'm sorry. A signal cannot be located. Would you like me to tag this phone with an EMS broadcast signal?"

"Yes, yes, that's fine." *Well, she let me try to call out at least*, he thought to himself. "Maybe I'm authorized now," he said quietly. He cleared his throat and prepared his best authoritarian voice. "Call home," he said in a deep tone.

"I'm sorry. Your voice was not recognized," she said again.

"Crap. But wow, this is cool. I've never seen anything like this." The entire phone was made up of a solid gel substance.

He sat up, trying to figure the thing out. He managed to get to the battery page, which read, "SolarCharge Lifetime Energy." "Wow! I wonder if I ended up in the future." He raised the phone to his mouth. "Tell me today's date," he said.

"I'm sorry…"

"Yeah, I know. I know. 'Your voice was not recognized.' Geez." He fiddled with it for a few more minutes and then stumbled across the voice recorder utility. There were sixty-seven messages recorded. He selected "play." A young man's voice emanated from a small, round, marble-looking piece at the top of the phone. He listened to a couple recordings and then realized that the battery would eventually drain all the way down if he didn't get it into the sunlight sometime soon. He stuck it in his pocket and then started crawling in the direction in which he threw the bone.

He returned to his crawl, and every twenty feet or so, he tossed another couple of bones ahead to help him navigate through the darkness. He eventually ran out of bones to grab and resorted to tossing large stones once again.

His hands reached a long gap in the ground. He felt along its edge four or five feet one direction, then the other. He picked up a few stones and tossed them forward. They landed a couple of feet directly in front of him. "Hmm, at least it's narrow." He got down on his belly and reached forward as far as he could and as far down as well, partially leaning into the gap. He touched a ledge across the gap, and then his fingers swept across something solid at the bottom of it. He pulled out the phone, hoping it would give enough light to see the bottom. The light was barely visible, as the battery was nearly drained. He pocketed the phone once again. *Well, it's not that deep. I could probably step down, then reach for the other ledge*, he contemplated. He swung his legs around and slid his feet down.

"Argh! Horny toads and viper venom!" an old, throaty voice shouted.

Derik lurched into a frantic jig, nearly jumping completely out of his skin, and screamed, "Aaugh!" Then in a delayed adrenaline panic, he leapt up and out in a single spring, landing on the other side of the gap on his shoulder and side of his face.

"Who goes there? I keep a redwood staff and am able and ready to employ it. This is not a warning, thou rogue scoundrel." The sound of the staff whooshed through the air and slapped hard against the moist ground.

"Whoa, whoa. I'm not here to rob you. I can't even see you."

Whoosh, whack, whoosh, whoosh, whack came the sound of the staff through the thick darkness.

"Did you hear me, old man?"

"Old man?" the throaty voice answered with a tone of familiarity. He raised his staff and prepared to thrust it once again. "I should like to have thy name. I am expecting someone. Be forewarned that if thou art not him,

I shall run thou off for Lig Nædre fodder. What is thy name?"

Derik stood still, sorting through a bombardment of thoughts of what might happen if he said the wrong name. Time seemed to speed up as he realized the man opposite him would not tolerate prolonged hesitation. He drew a deep breath, trying to decide between his name or one made up.

The staff split the air with a *whoosh*, *whoosh* and then a piercing *whack* against the ground once more.

"Thy name!"

"Uh, D-Derik. My name's Derik, okay?" He winced and ducked, stooping toward the ground and trying to make sure he was out of the way of this crazy old man's reach.

"Dar-ok?"

"No, you senseless…" Derik snarled with clenched teeth. He resolved to let it go for fear of angering the man. "Der-ik. Derik."

"Oh yes, yes, Derik," the man said agreeably. "Of course. Derik. Illuminate!"

A speck of bluish light was immediately apparent. It appeared to float back and forth effortlessly. The light brightened a smidge, seemingly to allow the man's eyes to adjust from the stark blackness. It became clear to Derik that the light was emitting from the upside end of the staff. He watched as the figure of a long-bearded man in a draping cloak emerged from the darkness.

The man stood a head taller than Derik, and his head held slightly sunken eyes that made Derik look twice.

The man's oversized nose was hidden somewhat well within his large, or perhaps long, face. Derik couldn't decide. But his high cheekbones gave his face an overall slender look, though his face was still fairly larger than Derik was accustomed to. The man's smile revealed several crooked teeth, but all were intact.

He turned his head one direction and then another, looking up and down as the brightness began to shed light upon his whereabouts. *It* was *a cavern*, he thought. He was able to take notice of the high ceiling, the encircling walls, and the heavily grooved terrain directly surrounding them.

He spotted the shore of the lake from which he crawled only moments before and then gazed out as far as the light would allow. The water easily took up over half of the entire area of the cavern he could see. Then his peripheral vision caught a large ivory-shaded mass. What followed was an unintentional, nonchalant swiveling of his head toward a repulsive sight. Derik felt his expression drop as his stomach went sour. The mound of bones stood much higher than he expected as it stretched farther back into a corner. The sight unfairly stole his complete attention. He turned his face away, grimacing. His thoughts returned to Andi, and at least one of them was unimaginable.

"Derik, I've been expecting thee," the man said, stepping toward him with an outstretched arm. Derik's emerald amulet caught the man's eye when it emitted a soft glow.

Derik flinched and then fisted the glowing stone as if responding to a burning sensation. He then stepped back, preparing to break into a sprint. "Get away from me. I don't know you."

"My apologies, young man. Allow me to explain." He stopped his approach and placed both hands on the staff that stood before him. "I was sent here to collect thee by thine companion."

A distant caw echoed against the walls of the cavern.

They both looked up.

"Blasted, Bierwul! We must commence. We haven't much time."

"Time? Time for what? And are you talking about Andi? Where's Andi? Tell me where she is you old … goat!"

The man chuckled. "Regrettably, in all mine days, I have answered to much worse than 'old goat,'" he said, glancing at Derik. "And for good reason," he added with a smirk. "But impolite was by no means among them. You can address me as … " he said but was suddenly cut short by an unexpected tremor.

The ground vibrated again, but this time more powerfully, followed by a low, deep growl from far off.

Derik looked down and noticed ripples in the many puddles laden throughout the area surrounding them. "Earthquake. The cavern's gonna collapse."

"No," the man said sternly, turning to Derik. "I'm afraid it's not an earthquake. However, we must go. Come this instant. Follow me." The man hurried off toward a small crevice at the foot of a wall. "Come. Thou must come now. She's been waiting."

"She? What do you mean waiting? I was right behind her. Wait. Are we talking about the same person?" Believing the man was speaking of Andi, Derik closely followed.

The man turned back to Derik and said, "If separation should befall me and thee, thou will find her at a small clearing to the east just outside the mountain. The way can be found in the darkness. You need not eyes to grasp vision, lad."

Derik pressed his lips together in an unimpressed fashion, as the philosophy had been enormously lost on him.

The man leaned in toward Derik and then looked into his eyes. "Pradicus," he said curtly.

Drawing a fist, Derik quickly stepped back, seizing an untrusting expression. "What are you doing? What does that mean? Are you hexing me?"

Rolling his eyes, the man sighed, then shook his head ever so slightly. "It's something mine aunt used to grumble in frustration hundreds of times a day, it seems."

"Why?" Derik asked, now clinching his other fist.

"Because, mine boy, that is mine name," he said, turning the other direction with a gentle, reminiscing laugh.

7

Guided only by the staff's soft glow, the two entered the crevice and into a passageway, a series of lumbering paths leading to an outlet. They exited out of a small fissure in the side of the mountain. Several yards below them was a beautiful lagoon that Pradicus leapt into, then swam a few strokes to shore. Derik then watched him climb onto a boulder and stand amidst a substantial gusting of wind. The airstream whipped off the mountain and channeled through a gulch, then blasted over and around the boulder on its way to freedom, wherever that might be. Derik watched the bearded man's wet hair and garments thrash about and thought certainly they wouldn't take long to dry.

As Derik stepped to the ledge, the scenery of a lush, wooded forest greeted him in the early afternoon. His sudden loss of breath caught him off-guard as he peered out across the northern horizon. Mountains, tall and short, posted far in the distance, stood valiantly in military fashion; the farther ones robed in lighter shades of violet than the nearer. Immediately before him and to the south was a magnificent forest of ivy-covered trees. His eyes fell once again on Pradicus.

"Welcome to Hellinus," Pradicus said proudly with both arms raised.

Derik eagerly followed the other's every step and hollered out a "Wahoo!" as his clothing flapped and flailed every which way in the same current of air. Enveloped within the moment, he raised his eyes and took in his surroundings with another astounded gasp, unsure of where in the world he might be. As he turned, his eyes fell on the mountain behind them, out from which they just came. "Holy cow, it's gigantic. I mean, I thought it would be big, but…"

The mountain stood several thousand feet high with the top reaching far into the clouds. The ominous sight captivated him for several moments. His eyes slowly scanned the thriving landscape of trees and shrubs decorating the mountain side. "It's beautiful!" he shouted. "I've never seen anything like it." Nearly dry after a mere few minutes in the wind, he jogged several steps down the grade to where the older man stood waiting.

"It is Mount Ablawan Liffrea."

"Abla who?"

"It means 'Breath of our Lord.' Beautiful, it is, but full of death."

The statement ensnared Derik. He turned quickly to the man with a slight tilt of the head. "What do you mean by that? Are you referring to the earthquake?"

"Lad, if only it were that simple. Come. Walk with me. Tell me about thee." They trekked a quarter mile or so, then stopped near a thick stretch of the ivy-covered trees.

In the distance, a stunning young lady in a ragged gown that extended to just below her calves rounded the corner of a widened path. Upon a log shoulder harness, she bore the weight of two large buckets, each splashing with water. One hanging on either side, they slightly swung independently with every subtle movement. Steadily, she considered her steps, head bowed, shuffling her feet along so as to keep the water spills to a minimum. Hearing a faint voice, she stopped and lifted her eyes. Standing silently with a slightly stressed grimace on her face due to her lower back pain, she paused between two panted breaths to blow her bangs aside. She caught sight of Pradicus standing on the edge of the path just behind the outskirts of a few trees. The branches, however, obstructed her view of the other he was speaking with.

She sighed with relief then mumbled to herself, "Finally, Pradicus, you're back. You are *not* going to believe what that little vermin did this time—" she said quietly in a huff and then paused. A moment later, she began toward him again, waddling along, continuing her story. "And *then* that furry little bugger tried to—" she muttered, lifting her eyes again and then froze. The long-awaited moment had come. Her countenance quickly changed, revealing the collected dashed hopes of months past. She whispered, "Derik," partially regretting that she'd crossed over, once again, into the realm of hope. Then she heard his voice carrying in the breeze. "Derik?" she said louder. He turned his head. "Oh my gosh, Derik!" she screamed, dropping the buckets of water.

"Oh! Oh, Derik! Thank God!" she cried, running toward him.

Derik spun completely around. "Andi? My goodness. Andi, is that you? What in God's creation happened to you?"

She slammed into him in a running, weeping embrace, hurling both of them to the ground.

Hugging him with an unrelenting squeeze, she nudged the side of her face into his chest, unaware of his tapering breath.

"Um, Andi?" he wheezed.

A whimper escaped her teeth-clenching smile as she grunted with one last constricting grasp around his torso. He caught his breath with a resounding gasp as she released him. She lifted her head and faced him with eyes giddy enough to put a grin on the dead.

They were her eyes. No, it was more than that, as in her look as a whole. He gazed beyond her eyes. "Wow, what happened to you, Andi?" Wiping her tears, he stared with disbelief. After finding his way up, he helped her to her feet, studying her eyes, her face, the air about her and realized she was no longer the girl he'd always known. This was a young lady who had matured seemingly over-night. The slender athleticism of her face, a developed temperament beaming from miles beneath her expression, and eyes which disclosed the enormous difficulties she'd confronted, along with the inward battles she'd lost, all culminated into the manifestation of a woman and no longer the teenage girl who lived down the street.

She leapt back into him with another full embrace. He put his arms around her and was utterly amazed at how tightly she cleaved to him.

"Thank you, Jesus. Oh, how I've missed you. I've been waiting for you for eighteen months to the day, Derik. I can't believe you're really here." She looked up into his eyes with a magnificent smile. "On my grandmother's grave, I swear I thought I'd never see anyone from home again." She dug her head into his chest and held him. "I thought I'd never see you again."

The thought that she could have lived hopelessly for *so long* seemed impossible to Derik, yet her emotional display and newly altered appearance spoke for themselves.

"What? How long? What did you just say?" He paused, placing an open hand against his forehead in contemplation. "How is that possible? Andi, we just left the barn a little while ago."

He saw her looking at him, but it wasn't the Andi he knew. It was Andrea Schaeffer, but it wasn't. She *was* older. She was different. He stepped back and looked her over in the ragged gown she wore, holding her by the shoulders, noticing their firmness. Her hair was longer and unstyled. She was a smidge taller and a bit curvier as well.

"Andi, you've filled out," he said, becoming quietly aware of the awkward pounding in his chest. "Andi, what's going on? How did all this happen? Is all of this around us what we fell into?"

"I don't know, Derik. Did the time thing pull you in too?"

He shook his head.

"Well, then how did you end up here? I mean, it took you so long. Did you wait for another worm thingamajig?"

He gave her an offended grimace. "No, of course not."

"Well, what happened then? If it didn't pull you in ..." Her face suddenly became still. "You came *after* me?"

He nodded.

"You really came after me?" she asked in a higher pitch with an awestruck smile. "You mean you followed me into the window after I fell off the beam?"

The semblance of a gloating grin peeked from his lips. "That's what I'm telling you."

"Oh, oh," she said, waving her hand rapidly in front of her eyes. "I can't believe you did that," she added, sliding a single finger under one eye. "How long did you wait before following me?"

"I'm not sure, maybe ten or fifteen seconds."

She wasn't sure why the answer startled her. She expected as much. She looked past Derik off into the trees surrounding them.

Derik's gladdened demeanor flattened out. "Andi, are you okay?"

Deciding to dismiss the sudden eccentricity, she told herself, *Chin up, little lady. What have you got to be upset about at this glorious moment in time?* She smiled again and then calculated an answer. "*Eighteen* seconds, perhaps? Somehow that explains you landing here in the twelfth century a year and a half later in time than me. Don't ask me, though. A friend of ours explained time-traveling math to Pradicus," she said with a grimace.

Derik held a confounded gaze. "Twelfth century? Eighteen months? But how can that be? It was just such a short time ago."

"Look at me, Derik. Do I really look like I just got here a short time ago?"

He chuckled. "Well, no, actually. I mean, look at you. You're gorgeous."

She raised her arms in validation. "Yeah, *I'm* the one who's been here for eighteen..." She stopped in her tracks. "What did you say?"

His face immediately began to burn while his stomach twisted into knots as the gravity of what he'd just let slip began to sink in. He looked away far into the trees, then downward—anywhere but back toward her—and started milling through the grass with his foot while an uncomfortable pause lingered.

She stepped up to him, dipping slightly to get a look into his downcast eyes. "Derik, you think I'm gorgeous? What else have you been keeping from me?"

He stole a look at her. "I've never kept anything from you. You're just different now is all. And okay, yes, I think you're gorgeous. I just can't believe this is you a year and a half later, and I don't just mean how you look."

"I think that makes me an older woman, doesn't it? I'm not sure we can hang out anymore."

"You wish. No matter what, I've still got you by fourteen months," he said, regaining some of his confidence. "I was born before you."

"Well, no matter what, I've outlived you by four months. Look at you; you're still seventeen, just a li'l pup."

"Shut up," he said, giving her a shove with his shoulder, resigning to the fact that she was probably right somehow.

"Uh-hum," the old man interrupted.

"Oh, please forgive me, Pradicus. And it's nice to have you back a day early." She stepped up to him and hugged him, then kissed him on the cheek. Grabbing one of his hands, she squeezed it. "Thank you so much. What you did I could never repay," she said and then swung her head around to look at Derik.

"Thou hast already done so, young one. Simply with all that thou hast taught me and told me of thine home so far away," he said with a cheerful, simple grin, sliding his eyes over to Derik, then back to Andi.

Still holding his hand, she turned back to Pradicus. "Derik, this is Pradicus. He's been like a father to me. He found me in the cavern the night I fell into the lake and saved me from Lig Nædre. He took me under his wing and has cared for me since he found me here."

A new joy filled her eyes that Pradicus hadn't seen in her before. He stood back and just observed the two of them while catching a flashing glimpse of the sun's reflection off the emerald amulet. Pradicus hid boyish exhilaration behind a contented grin. But she read his eyes. She drew in a long breath with everything she was feeling and then let out an emotional *squeak*. Derik smiled, noting her enthusiasm. He stared at her for another moment simply beside himself. Perhaps it was admiration. Or maybe it was something else entirely.

Derik shook Pradicus's hand and thanked him profusely for what he had done for Andi, as well as himself. "Lig Nædre. You mentioned that name earlier. What is that?"

"That is the beast thou heard inside Broga Mountain—the sound thou thought to be a quake."

"Whoa, a *beast*? What kind of a beast could shake the floor of a mountain? And wait a second. You said the mountain was called something else a minute ago."

Andi chimed in. "Okay, let's back up. The people here call the beast Lig Nædre. In our modern English, it means 'fire snake,' or, as we would say, 'fire-breathing dragon.' Broga means 'terror.' For several generations, the people here in Hellinus have called the dragon 'Broga Lig Nædre.' By the way, Hellinus is an island somewhere between Spain and Ireland."

She leaned in toward Derik's ear and spoke softly. "As far as I know, it no longer exists in our time, but a friend of ours was pretty sure it was, or is, in the Atlantic near the UK from everything he's gathered from trade routes." Pulling away, she returned her voice back to its normal level. "Anyway the mountain has been dubbed Broga Mountain because of the dragon. Valicious, a practitioner of dark magic, is responsible for the wormhole. It's his way of feeding the beast. Many say the dragon possesses what Valicious needs to practice his magic. It is also said that it guards a great treasure. Valicious feeds the dragon, and the dragon gives him what he wants: power and riches."

"So the hole opens, people drop into the lake, then the dragon hunts them down while they try to find a way out. How does the dragon know when the hole has opened?"

"He has a messenger," Andi replied.

"A messenger? Why didn't the messenger know about Pradicus hanging out in the cave? Which reminds me. A minute ago, you said he came back a day early. Are you saying you guys have been looking for me this whole time? And how did Pradicus know when to wait for me?"

"Okay, slow down. Pradicus made a calculated guess."

Derik offered Pradicus an impressed smile.

"My young lad, thou art not the first to make it out of the lake or the cavern."

"He tried to explain the mathematics to me a couple of times, Derik. I don't get it at all. But he ended up being pretty accurate, right? Every month for two days, he's waited for you—the same time each month," Andi said.

Derik's jaw dropped. He turned his expression to Pradicus. "You really are quite amazing. Thank you again so very much. Really, when we were inside … I had no idea. I'm sorry if I came across like a—"

"Please, think nothing of it," Pradicus said, holding up his hand in a dismissive gesture.

"But I truly want you to know how much I—"

Pradicus waived a finger in front of Derik's face. "Enough."

Derik huffed. Then he looked at Andi. "So what happens now?"

"Dear boy," Pradicus interrupted, "I must try to send back what is not from here."

"Send back what's not from here?" Derik immediately thought of the large mound of bones. "It doesn't look like you've been all that successful."

"Derik," Andi said, sounding shocked.

"Well, what about all the people that make up that heaping pile of—"

Pradicus hushed him with a finger while turning to look over his shoulder. "Quick. Step over here," he whispered. He struck the bottom of his staff against the ground, and the little stone at the top immediately began to illuminate. He escorted the two into the shadows of a small clearing amidst a maze of hanging ivy as a flock of crows took flight from a nearby field. They circled twice and then flew away from them in the distance. The ivy was thick and hung from oak trees large and small, comprising several hundred acres.

"Bierwul is on the hunt for thee now as well," he said to Derik. "Forgive me, dear sir. Please continue."

"What I was saying was, what of all the bones inside the mountain? Don't they belong to people who also needed to be sent back? Andi, you should've seen them. There were thousands of them. Why didn't they get to go back?"

"It's not like he's just been allowing it to continue," Andi said. "Derik, it's taken him the last two years just to get this far. Besides, technically, they'll all live their lives just as before. I mean, in the future, the time will come for each of them to be birthed all over again. They don't cease to exist because they died here. "She looked at Pradicus. "Right?"

The thought of the bones jogged Derik's memory, and he suddenly remembered the phone he found. "Look here," he said, reaching into his pocket. "This belonged to someone—someone who didn't make it back." He held it out toward the other two.

Andi looked down at it and then gasped. The object captured her widened eyes while her thoughts swam to a familiar place. She glanced at Pradicus. "Oh my God, Pradicus, what…what happened? That shouldn't be here. Well, at least shouldn't have been with the bones." Her voice began to quiver. "I thought you said he made it back." She reached her hand out toward the phone but hesitated, then drew it back. Her eyes slowly fell while discouragement and confusion captured her expression. Looking away, she exhaled a long, defeated breath.

Derik's eyes darted to Pradicus, who was slightly shaking his head in dismay. Derik then sheepishly stole a look back at Andi.

Derik lowered the phone. "You knew him. I…I'm sorry. It never even occurred to me that—" He halted with a hard swallow. A few nervously uttered apologetic fragments fell hollowly into a thick, awkward silence. "Oh, man. I can't believe that I just…" he finally mumbled, his words trailing away while he returned the device to his pocket.

Andi sniffled and then wiped a tear from her cheek. Pradicus lent his support, wrapping a sympathetic arm around her. She lowered her slightly quivering hand over her lips, then, leaning into him, broke.

Derik tried to think of something to say. While trying to get his pants to cooperate in re-pocketing the phone, his fingers inadvertently pressed some buttons on the device. A stoic voice emanated from its backside: "Pradicus was so sure of everything... It *must've* been his evil brother. How'd he know where the hole was gonna be? Well, he's gonna pay... I'm not gonna let this happen to anyone else. I promised Andrea she'd make it back when her friend gets here. One thing I do know, the dragon can't swim very well—maybe not at all. I've gotta let Pradicus know that his brother understands how to stop him. Mom, Dad, Sis, I'm gonna be back, maybe later than I thought, but I'll be on my way in a couple of days. Okay, Valicious, I see what you're doing, and now I'm coming after... Wait, what the... so *that's* what all this has been about. Oh, man. We had it all wrong. I've got to warn them. We should've known he was after the last—" A roar erupted in the background. "Oh... no." The phone clicked, and the voice stopped.

Derik said, "Shoot. I didn't mean to do that. I don't even know what I did." He looked up at the other two, who were both eyeballing the phone tensely.

Andi lowered her hand from her mouth in a closed fist. "No, he *had* to have made it back," she said with a tinge of certainty. "Pradicus, I'm sure of it. I mean, the hole was gone when you found me in the field. That means its objective … was completed, right?"

Derik held the phone up again. "It's like futuristic or something," he humbly explained, looking the phone over. "I dunno. I didn't mean for that to happen."

"No, it's good that it happened," Andi replied. "We need to try to retrieve that whole message. He was obviously going to warn us of something before he made it back." She looked to Pradicus for confirmation. She smiled uneasily. "Right? He was gonna try to tell us something before he *went* back."

Andi watched Derik handle the phone. She thought about how she'd been missing her short-term friend the past few months. "He was about ten years ahead of us, you and I. His name was Jake—well, actually, Cleveland Pasque," she said. "From Des Moines," both she and Pradicus stated together. They turned to each other and laughed. "Cleveland Pasque … from Des Moines," they said in unison.

"He despised his name and, of course, hated it anytime we said it like that." Andi said, shaking her head and with a grin. "Actually, it was a friend of ours that always said it. But Pradicus and I chimed in for fun every time. The three of us couldn't help but laugh, knowing how it bothered him. Although," she said in a chipper tone, "he liked his middle name, Jacques. Well, he said he was fond of how it sounded like Jake with an *s* at the end. So he adopted Jake as his first name." Andi stepped away from Pradicus. "I'm sorry. I didn't mean to go all blubbery on you." She tried to fight off the reemerging tears. "He was a good friend. I didn't know him very long, but we had so much common ground, and that was really important to both of us in the middle of all this. He was my only link back to our time. Well, Garren too, I guess, but I never really saw much of him."

"Who?" Derik asked.

"Garren was Pradicus's right-hand guy—an apprentice of sorts. He's an Everal—someone who, for some reason, ends up living a long life, like in the days of Methuselah."

"Methusa-who? And what are you talking about, long life?"

"Derik, geez, didn't you ever go to Sunday school? He's the guy who lived longer than anyone else. Look, it's not important. He traveled with Pradicus quite a bit and was learning how to, you know, do what Pradicus does. He was quite a character. And he had cool stuff. He always had this gold coin he'd flip into the air just before leaving on one of his outings, as if it were a good-luck charm. He also had this incredible-looking leather shoulder satchel he took everywhere. He kept everything he could possibly need to get out of every situation you could think of." She chuckled. "Not that he needed it all the time, though. He fought off a lot of animals empty-handed, some of them ferociously wicked. A pack of wolves wandered toward us once. Without a word, he simply took on the biggest one and killed it—no warning, no plan. They stuck their noses where Garren felt they shouldn't have been, and that night, we had wolf steaks."

An uncomfortable silence lingered for a minute. Her voice quieted to a whisper. "All this time, we were confident Jake made it. It's been at least six months." She gasped at a second thought, raising a hand to her mouth in a troubled expression. "Pradicus, if Jake didn't, well, then Garren probably didn't make it either." She took a small step toward him. "Pradicus, that just can't be," she said in a breaking, despairing voice.

Pradicus kept a stoic demeanor and said nothing.

She held her gaze on him as another odd silence fell. Her expression descended slowly at first and then all at once plummeted. She poured her face into both her hands and began to silently mourn for now not only two friends but the diminishing hope she'd held to so diligently for her return to her family. Derik began to approach her, but she gestured against it with the raising of a hand.

Pradicus slid his eyes over to Derik. "I tried to talk her into going with Jake, but she insisted on staying here to wait for thee. Perhaps now we can understand it was a very prudent decision." He sighed and contemplated for a moment. "It was I who closed the hole, Andrea, to keep the beast from making use of it. Jake did not use it. He didn't have the chance. My deepest apologies for keeping it from thee."

"What?" she asked in a hushed, startled voice. Her eyes dashed from one place to another, processing. Placing one hand on her hip and the other against her forehead, she continued in a quiet but betrayal-laced tone. "That can't be true." She closed her eyes. "Because it would have to mean that for the last several months"—she paused, beginning to tear up, and then continued—"you haven't been truthful with me. That can't be the case, Pradicus. We trust each other."

Pradicus remained sober.

She glared at him. "We trust each other!" she shouted with an air of incensement. A silent moment followed. "Or at least we did," she whispered. Then she walked off alone.

Pradicus didn't respond. Derik, afraid to say anything, took to humming to himself.

After a brief venting and with a creased brow, she returned and asked, "So what *exactly* are you saying?"

"Merely that the boy did what he was here to do."

Andi decided not to respond.

"The boy was a fresh breath, full of life, always ready for an adventure, exceedingly knowledgeable, and very deliberate."

"So what happened to him, Pradicus?" Derik asked. "It sounds like you're afraid to tell us the truth." He nodded at Andi. "Just tell us what happened to him."

Andi gave Pradicus a stern glare that asked, "Well?"

Pradicus sighed and ran his fingers through his hair. "Lig Nædre happened," he said grimly.

Andi closed her eyes tight, shaking her head.

"Andrea, come now," Pradicus said endearingly.

"No, no, you're lying, Pradicus. I see it."

"What you see is shame. I shouldn't have kept it from you."

With her legs feeling suddenly weak, Andi lowered herself to the ground. She scowled at Pradicus.

"You … deceived me," she snapped in shortened breaths. After a few moments passed, she composed herself. "You told me Jake made it. After I tried to stop him and was nearly killed by that flipping wicked dragon—which, by the way, was waiting for him—you all but swore to me that he made it back." She raised her voice again. "I trusted you. Heck, *he* trusted you. Do you have any idea, Pradicus, how much I want to hate you right now?"

Derik had never truly seen his long-time friend from the farm quite like this. He drew in a breath, sighed, and then turned to Pradicus. "Do you mind me asking—" he said, only to be cut off by Andi.

"Shut up, Derik. How do we know he's not in it with Valicious?" She tucked her chin into her chest. "For all we know, he could be Valicious."

8

Andi stood up and then began walking toward the other two, intending to pass between them. As she did, Derik reached out and gently took hold of her arm. Thoughts centered on the girl in the barn, whom he'd seen only hours before.

"Hey, I just want you to know I think you're amazing." She tugged her arm loose without so much as acknowledging his statement. He watched her storm off and then rolled his eyes at Pradicus. "You ever feel like you're being helpful and then someone turns around and makes you feel like a total…" He stopped, electing not to finish the statement. "Never mind," he said in a quiet huff, swatting at a patch of ivy.

Andi stopped next to a tree several yards off and rested a shoulder against it. Derik turned to Pradicus. "I guess I'm confused. I don't understand why it's assumed neither of them made it."

Pradicus stepped up to Derik, placing his illuminated staff between the two of them. "Things are not always as they seem. This was necessary and needed to surface."

"Necessary? Which one? The lie or the truth?" Derik asked.

Pradicus offered a meaningful wink and then started toward Andi.

Derik grimaced. *Oh, man this is gonna get ugly*, he thought to himself. From his short distance away, though, he marveled at Pradicus's chivalrous approach toward Andi, a refined undertaking to be sure in his opinion. After making her aware of his proximity, and while facing the opposite direction, Pradicus quietly stood beside her, just as he must have many times before. Standing rigidly, arms crossed, she scarcely turned her face in order to offer a scowl from the corners of her eyes and then slowly resumed her position.

After a moment, he leaned in toward her, made a nonchalant comment, and then glanced off in the other direction. She didn't respond. The two stood silently, the younger seeming barely tolerant of the presence of the older. With one hand, she smoothly ran her fingers through her hair, acting oblivious toward her recently professing collaborator. He stepped around to her opposite side and again conveyed a relatively concise sentiment. She turned her head away and then gazed upward through the ivy and trees and into the graying sky. Pradicus turned his head toward her and once more said something quite brief. Her eyes darted back and forth while she cupped her chin, then, after contemplating his words for a minute, adjusted her posture toward him. She answered him using expressive hand movements and, on one occasion, pointed to the mountain. The two went back and forth for several minutes until it was only Pradicus motioning his hands and arms, with Andi keeping a determined stance, arms crossed once again.

A moment later, she wiped a tear from her cheek and reengaged into the conversation with a softer bearing. The two continued for another minute, and then Pradicus turned and started back toward Derik. Derik heard Andi say, "Wait," then watched her approach Pradicus with a firm embrace. "How did he do that?" Derik asked himself. The two returned to Derik.

"Derik, I'm sorry you saw me like that," Andi said, walking toward him, stopping short. She held out her arms in a gesture for a hug.

"Please don't apologize. I can't imagine what you're dealing with," Derik answered, wrapping his arms around her. She rested her head on his shoulder and said nothing for a good minute.

"You must hate who I've become. I'm so sorry," she finally whispered.

"Are you kidding?" He caressed her back. "I meant what I said a few minutes back. You really are amazing."

She stepped away from him and immersed herself into his eyes. A small grin cracked at either edge of her mouth. "Derik, I'm so glad you're here." With Derik still palming the phone, she broke away from his eyes to glimpse down at it. "Why do I feel guilty for missing him so much?" she asked in a tender tone.

Derik took her by the chin and raised her eyes to meet his once again. "If I were him, I'd feel pretty honored right about now," he whispered.

Her lips steadily split into a brightly lit smile for but a moment, then she turned back to Pradicus. "Again, I'm sorry."

Pradicus shrugged it off. "As am I."

"So how much time did Jake spend here? I mean, in this century?" Derik asked.

Andi peeked at the phone again. "I really don't know," she answered in a hushed voice. "He stayed here with us for about four months, I'd say. I guess he showed up about six months before me and then took off on his own for a while. I was here when he came back."

Pradicus nodded.

"He was a science geek," Andi continued. "He actually taught Pradicus quite a few things."

"Wait a second," Derik interjected. "Isn't that kind of bad? I mean, don't we now have to worry about the changing of the future and all that?"

"Um, well, maybe," she answered a bit more upbeat. "I *suppose* the future, as well as the past that you and I knew, could be somewhat different once we return."

"I mean, is it possible that we'll turn in our history books to the chapters on the Enlightened Ages rather than the Dark Ages all because of how Pradicus, here, changed the world?"

An amused grin broke at one side of Pradicus's mouth, which allowed Andi to find her cheer again. Suddenly, they all broke into a brief stint of laughter. The familiar sound of Derik's laugh and the presence of his humor so thrilled Andi that her countenance took on a glow that an instant later radiated throughout her entire being.

"Derik, I have no idea," she continued. "But really, how much has Valicious changed the future by abducting people from all time eras? It seems all screwed up to me. You know what? Don't make me think about that, okay?"

"But—" Derik answered, only to be cut short by a firm finger in his face.

"Hush. No, I said."

Pradicus chuckled, turning slightly away.

"Anyway," she said, lowering her finger, "Jake told Pradicus about NASA, satellites, space shuttles, and man walking on the moon. That was a hard sell, let me tell you. He also taught him about the solar system, the earth being round, dinosaurs, and all sorts of other things."

"Wow, wish I had him for a tutor in school. Um, how old was he?"

Andi put on a small grin and looked away.

"You know what? It's not important," Derik said, kicking himself.

"No, no, it's all right. I uh, just … well, he intrigued me."

"Intrigued you?" Derik asked, speculating on how deep, or shallow, a statement that was. "What does *that* mean?"

"Derik, the future is so amazing. I know it's not too far from where we're from, but the changes in politics, technology, school—just everything. He described a world so different from what you and I know. It doesn't seem possible that so much could change ten years from where we were, but my goodness, Derik, all coins are collector's items where he was from because money's all digitally controlled. Wallets don't exist anymore because all information is stored under the skin. He showed me. The chip and scar were no larger than a freckle."

She was about to continue when she realized her enthusiasm wasn't reciprocated. She shrugged her shoulders. "He intrigued me." Then she remembered his question. "Oh, and, by the way, he was nineteen and already three years out of college. He said that with the exception of either lower income or ultra-rich districts, most all kids took classes online with automated instruction that adjusted to each individual. Because of this, students have the opportunity to combine two years into one starting in sixth grade."

He frowned with a raise of the eyebrows, wondering what part she was so amused with.

"Geez, Derik. You might try showing some *respect*, or how about a little compassion? Or maybe you should try on some concern, because if he didn't make it outta here with a brain his size, you may very well end up just like him or worse." She stepped up to him and snatched away the phone and then immediately swung her head around so as to flip her hair in his face.

Derik wasn't sure if the look on Pradicus's face was more from amusement or surprise. Her turning and walking away was something he'd experienced hundreds of times over the past couple of years. But watching her walk away this time was different. Her sway, her gate, how the breeze and the sunlight caught her hair, the way she carried herself, everything about her walking away was...older. The realization that she truly had been there for eighteen months began to set in. He stopped and tried to imagine what life must've been like through her eyes—every day looking into the horizon with a longing for his arrival, wondering if the beast would ever catch up to her, losing the luxuries of modern living overnight, dealing with the possibility of never seeing her family again, and on and on he went, drawing up challenges she surely must have endured. Suddenly, this Jake character fit into the picture, and it all made sense. What else could she have latched on to? How did the hope she held continue to carry on for so long?

"I'm sure he made it back, Andi. If he's everything you say he is, he had to have made it. I mean, it's guys like me that end up getting the ax. This Jake guy's starting to sound like someone I wish I was."

She sat down, legs crossed. "Of course he made it," she replied. "He's awesome. But that recording..." she said, looking off toward the ground. Then, as if trying to work things out in her mind, she rationalized somewhat audibly, "He must've made that recording the same day he left us. He said he was going to go back through the wormhole, and I told him I wasn't gonna go with him. Remember, Pradicus?"

Pradicus drew his thoughts upon the memory and, with the smallest glimmer in his eye, nodded.

9

It was five months before Derik would arrive through the wormhole and one day before Jake would undertake the risk of a journey back home. It had been thirteen months since Andi landed in the cavern, where Pradicus happened upon her. Jake awoke particularly early to find Garren and Pradicus already sitting around the morning fire, conversing quietly. The discussion took on the tone of a debate rather than a casual chat. "Top o' the morning, gentlemen," Jake said.

The other two tabled their dialogue immediately and turned to greet Jake.

"Oh, sorry, guys. Didn't mean to interrupt."

"What? No," Garren replied with a dismissive gesture of his hand. "What's got you up so early this morning? Nervous jitters about *mañana?*

"Nah, just wrapping up a few last things. What about you?"

Garren chuckled and patted Pradicus on the back. "Well, neither of us has had a minute of shut-eye. We've been up all night talking."

"Oh … talking or discussing?"

The other two exchanged uneasy looks.

After an awkward moment of silence, Jake chimed in. "Well, I guess that's settled. So, Andrea still sleeping?"

"We haven't seen her yet, so I guess so."

Jake pressed his lips and slightly nodded. "Okay, well, I guess I'll water the horses."

Pradicus leaned back to see around Garren. "Thou art traveling this early?"

Jake responded with a wink. "It's all good."

"My friend, this is not beneficial. This is the poorest time to be alone, the very poorest. Thou hast an engagement on the morrow to return home. Valicious would like nothing more than to impede the event."

Jake rolled his eyes. "Stop already. You know what? I'm ready to kick his little … well, you know what." He looked at Garren. "Aren't you sick of hearing about this villainous idiot? I've still yet to see the rabble-rouser. The jerk's probably dead and we don't even know it."

"Jake, just because you haven't seen something doesn't mean it doesn't exist, right?" Garren responded solemnly. "When was the last time you saw your normal flora?"

"Is that the best you got? What kind of a question is that?" Jake answered, doing his best to belittle Garren's position.

"Just proving my point."

Pradicus interrupted. "Normal flora?"

"Yeah, I think he means these itty-bitty spiders that live all over your body, feasting on your dead skin," Jake answered, beaming. "Billions of them, right now, eating you while you live and breathe."

Pradicus glanced at Garren with an alarmed scowl and then decided to bow out of the exchange.

Garren stood up. "I've seen him with my own eyes. It took a couple years of waiting and searching for that to even happen. Let me tell you, it was blind luck that I lived to tell about it. He just doesn't get around. And why should he when he's got that beast doing his bidding?"

"Whatever," Jake said, beginning to walk toward the fire. "You haven't seen him, not if you've only been here a couple years."

"I've been here longer than a couple years, and yes, I have seen him."

"Well, how long have you been here then? And how old are you anyway? Twenty-four, twenty-five?"

Garren broke away from the discussion, glanced at Pradicus, and then chuckled as he observed him nervously studying his hands and arms. "It doesn't matter how old I am. What difference does it make?"

"Then tell me when you saw Valicious. You can't because you never really did."

"Would you guys shut up?" Andi said, shuffling her feet into their midst. She presented herself in an ankle-length gown, deer-hide slippers, had one eye still mostly closed, and sported bed-head that would've vied for the cover of Vogue in the eighties. "The sun's not even up yet. What are you guys going on about?"

Jake spun around. "Sorry, angel. Go back to bed. The sun won't be up for another hour, hour and a half."

With her slippers taking turns peeking out from under her gown in little sliding steps, she made her way toward Jake, sleepily rested her head against his shoulder, and then noticed Pradicus closely inspecting his hands. "What's his problem?" she quietly asked.

"Um … yeah—" Jake proudly replied but was cut off.

"Nothing," Garren said. "Jake was just … never mind. He's just having some fun."

"What kind of fun?" she asked with a giggle.

"You don't wanna know," Garren said sternly.

She threw Jake a harsh raised eyebrow.

He confirmed her observation with a grin. "Don't ask."

"All right," she conceded, rubbing her eyes. "What is it with boys?" She yawned and then smacked her lips.

Pradicus slapped one of his own arms rather passionately and then examined the spot in detail.

Andi chuckled, shaking her head. "Good grace, you guys. I don't even want to know. Okay, I'm going back to bed, but would you keep it down?" She disappeared into the shadows, shuffle-stepping the same way she came.

"Come with me," Jake whispered to Garren. "I've got something you should see."

"Uh, no," he replied in a tone laden with sarcasm.

"Come on."

"No, I've got a lot to do, like get some sleep, among other things."

"Nothing bigger than this. I promise you."

Garren smirked, wondering what he could possibly be getting himself into. He glanced at Pradicus, chuckled, and then slid his eyes toward Jake. Tempted, he wrestled with the relishing thought of one last opportunity to put Jake in his place. A patronizing tone brazenly announced itself. "So you've got it all figured out, huh, Mister Cleveland Pasque from Des Moines?" He held his gaze on Jake, a confident, daring stare. "What about him?" He motioned with his head toward Pradicus.

Jake responded with a halfway combative glare of his own. "I think he'll probably be busy for a while. We're good. I intend for us to be back before breakfast."

"We better be," Garren retorted. Then he kicked himself for expressing compliance so readily. "Criminy, why do I always get a bad feeling about your *intentions*?" he huffed.

The two of them prepared the horses and then rode off together, Garren trailing closely behind Jake toward Broga Mountain. The huge shape, seen from miles and miles away, stood massive and tall near the eastern border of the Penumbra Forest, named for its stark shadows due to the vast overrun of ivy throughout the oak woodlands. Dawn broke an hour later as they arrived at a particularly thick patch of ivy, Garren with his apprentice's satchel looped around his shoulder and Jake with a flattened coin bag tucked under his belt.

"What in the devil's mine fields are we doing here?" Garren asked pointedly.

"You'll see in a minute. I've done this a hundred times. Just follow me."

They dismounted their horses, then ushered them the last couple hundred yards on foot. They tied the horses to a young oak and then crept closer through the ivy toward the base of the mountain.

"Okay, just listen for a minute," Jake said. "We both came out of the cavern in that mountain, right?"

"What's that got to do with anything? Now tell me why we're here before we get ourselves killed."

"I'm trying to tell you, so would you relax, please? Pradicus was there when you fell into the lake, wasn't he?"

"Jake, I swear, this is the stupidest idea you've ever come up with. In just a few minutes, we're gonna be in trouble—big trouble."

"Look, Garren, this is the only time and the only place I can show you this, so again, relax. Just follow my line of thought here. Pradicus was inside the mountain when I got here, right?"

Garren heaved a glare at Jake so pronounced that Jake felt as if holes were boring straight through him. After a lingering silence, Garren finally offered a stone cold, "What about it?"

"Don't you think it's strange that he knew?"

"Not at all. According to Pradicus, he was on a mission to save anyone he could from the dragon. I'm not sure where you're going with this."

"Okay, only two of us have come since you started working with Pradicus, right? How long have you been working with him? It's been seven or eight years, right?"

Garren nodded.

Jake extended his hand and held up a thumb, followed by an index finger. "Why only two in that long span of time? And why both of us so close together? There's something deeper going on here, like fate. I don't think she's ready to admit it, but we were meant to be together. If her friend were going to come, he'd have been here already."

"Is that what this is all about? How you and Andrea have been thrown together by fate?"

"No, I'm sorry. I got side-tracked."

Garren impatiently raised his eyebrows in a gesture to get to the point.

"The two of us were separated by six months, but in the grand scheme of things, it's only six months."

"Get to it. What are you saying?"

"I'm saying Pradicus knew. Don't you see? Pradicus is Valicious."

"Heavenly angels, stop me from killing him," Garren said, shaking his head. "You brought me out here for this, Cleveland?"

Jake held his index finger up toward Garren. "Hold on," he said in a quiet but sarcastic tone. "Before you go off on a little tirade, just listen. Pradicus said Valicious can only be spotted at dusk and dawn. Well, here we are. I've been here lots of times, just waiting, and every time, no Valicious."

"Jake, think about it. That's because Valicious knew each time that you were coming."

"Bull pucky. There's no way he could've known I was here. I hide better than a gecko."

Jake gave him a smirk. "I'm saying he knew you were coming," he retorted. "After he knows *that*, it doesn't matter how good you are at hiding."

"How on earth could he know?"

"Well, let me ask you something. How is it that you're here in the twelfth century instead of back wherever it is you come from?"

"The wormhole. You know that."

"And how can the wormhole even exist?"

"Dragon fire … magic. Oh, I see what you mean now. You're saying that's how he knows I'm coming. What if I found a way to trick him, get around his magic?"

Garren nodded while tapping his finger against his temple. "Now you're thinking. The brainiac out-wizards the wizard. You're just destined to have your head mounted on his trophy wall, aren't you?"

"Well, regardless of what you believe, I think maybe we just outsmarted him."

"I'm lost. What do you mean?"

"Pradicus was distracted this morning. If my theory is correct, what Pradicus doesn't know, Valicious doesn't know. Pradicus doesn't know we came here."

"How in the world could you come up with such"—he paused, clenching his fists and teeth, then continued— "a lame-brain idea? How do you even justify such a thought?"

Jake held out his hand. "Because of this." In his palm lay a small golden coin.

Garren gave Jake a cynical look. "What's that?"

"Oh, don't play coy with me. You know exactly what this is."

Garren offered a naïve expression.

"Don't even try, okay? It's all over your face. Fine. You wanna see if I know what this really is? This little gem lights up when trouble's brewing. That's all I need to say. And guess what? It's not lit up."

"So how long have you known about the coins?"

"Long enough to realize that Pradicus didn't act suspicious about my travels to Broga Mountain after I started carrying it on me," Jake answered with a half grin. "It's like it keeps him from knowing."

Garren slapped an open hand against his forehead. "Or perhaps it lets him know exactly what you're doing, thus removing the need for suspicion."

Jake bit his lip and scowled. "Hmm, I didn't think about that." He pondered the thought for a moment. "Do you think that's what's been happening?"

"Well, I know if you're carrying that coin, then you're a beacon in the world of Valicious and his cronies."

"Dang it. Why didn't I consider that?"

"The biggest reason I know is because I have one of my own," Garren said, fishing one out of his satchel.

"Well, I think this came from inside the mountain, and I believe there's more in there—a lot more. I plan on taking some of it back with me tomorrow."

"So is that what we're doing here?"

"Yeah. We're gonna sneak in because Pradicus is Valicious, meaning he isn't here. Valicious is a figment of his imagination. He just plays the part."

"Jake, I already told you. I saw Valicious myself."

"Under what circumstances, though? Isn't it possible that Pradicus set you up?"

"Jake, he was with me. Pradicus was right beside me," Garren said, shaking his head in frustration. "Besides, with you carrying that coin, you've basically announced yourself."

"Okay, fine. Tomorrow I'll come back without it. But Pradicus *is* Valicious."

"Look, feel free to stay here, but I'm heading back. I can't believe I came all the way out here for this. And let me tell you something else. Valicious isn't someone you want to mess with. He's wicked to the core, like the devil himself."

A terrible roar suddenly erupted from up high on the mountain. Lig Nædre perched itself on a cliff. Beside the dragon stood the barely discernable figure of a man dressed in an oversized cloak. The beast leapt off with a spring and sailed high into the sky.

"Criminy," Garren said and then let out an irritated grunt. "Now you've done it. Jake, don't move a muscle. We're both dead right now if you so much as twitch."

Keeping still as possible, Jake raised his eyes. To his amazement, there stood the evil villain himself. "What the Hellenistic? There's a man up there. He's … he's real?" He looked down at his gold piece and noticed it still wasn't lighting up.

"I snuffed it," Garren whispered. "If I hadn't, we'd have been made already."

Jake started crawling away slowly.

Garren seized his foot. "Stop moving," he growled. "You're not gonna like what comes looking for us on horseback if we're spotted." He turned his ear to the breeze and listened for a moment. "That reminds me. It goes without saying to stay as far away from the dragon as possible. You get some dragon drool on you, you're cursed for good. It'll change ya, and I don't mean give you a bad attitude."

Jake gave him a dismissive sideways look. "You're talking about the legend, the crazy belief about the half dead, aren't you?"

Garren responded with a shocked grimace for Jake knowing anything about them. "I don't care what you choose to believe. If that dragon does get a hold of you, it might just be better if it kills you then and there. You don't want to play any part in that half-dead garbage."

A squad of crows blasted out of a nearby cave.

"For the love of … can't we cut a break? So help me, Jake, if we get out of this—"

"Lay off the tough guy role, okay?" Jake interrupted. "It doesn't suit you. I'm gonna be just fine, no matter what happens."

"Dang it, Jake, you think you're impervious to risk. If you gamble enough times, it's gonna catch up to you. It's a mathematical fact. Now just sit tight and wait. We should have a window of escape here in an hour or so."

"Wimp," Jake said, taking a step out from behind the shrubs. "How are you gonna get anywhere in life if you don't take risks?" He slowly began moving back toward the horses.

"Jake, stop. You're gonna get us killed," Garren said through clenched teeth. Watching Jake slowly recede his position, he shook his head slightly. "Where the heck is Des Moines anyway?"

Jake maneuvered through the ivy all the way back to the horses, nearly one hundred and fifty yards from where he left Garren.

"Great, I'm toast," Garren said, placing a hand over his face. "Unless," he countered, pulling two small vials of powder from his apprentice's satchel. "Man, I hope this works." He mixed the two into one vial, shook it hard, and then started a dead sprint toward the horses. He threw the vial as far ahead in front of him as he could. The vial hit the ground, followed by a somewhat indistinct flash that opened a small wormhole. He hit the opening at full speed and then instantly exited another hole three hundred yards in front of him, out from under the cover of foliage. Realizing he'd overshot the horses, he murmured a few creative expletives in a fit of frustration. His feet slid along the gravel in a quick attempt to change direction. The commotion caught the attention of all eyes.

"Fart frickers," he said, wondering if he had indeed been spotted. When he caught his footing, he started immediately toward the horses. "Go, go, Jake! Get out of here!" he yelled. Realizing they had indeed been made, Jake took off on his horse in a mad dash in the opposite direction.

Lig Nædre, from hundreds of feet in the air, spun around and locked in on a target.

The crows cawed crazily, and within a minute, a distant, thunderous rumbling was heard emitting from within the mountain.

"Aw, no … no, no," Garren grunted. "The only chance I have is to get into the mountain before *they* make it out." He got to his horse and then, in a scurried frenzy, raced toward the mountain. "Come on. Faster, boy, faster. Let's go. He-aw!"

Lig Nædre swooped down with incredible speed and aligned itself with the horse and rider. Using its front claws, it reached down and seized the horse and rider off the ground, then sped into a climbing ascent.

Turning back and looking over his shoulder, Garren cried, "Jake, no!" as Jake and his horse were whisked away in the clutches of the great beast. Glancing back one last time, the breaking slices of daylight between the trees afforded him a glimpse of Lig Nædre landing high on his mountain perch. What he didn't see was Jake's self-propelled free fall into a thick patch of ivy-strewn shrubbery prior to the dragon's soaring incline. Garren made it into one of the mountain's larger entrances, then, after reaching the first pitch-black crook in the corridor, he cloaked himself and his horse together with the use of another vial. The crows blindly followed in after him, blazing past him and his horse, forwarding themselves by the mere memory of the passageway. He dismounted his horse, making sure to keep constant contact with it, lest the cloaking fail one of them. He pulled a bandana out of his bag, secured a wrist to his horse's front leg, and then, within moments, drifted into an exhausted sleep. Over the next few hours, the sporadic echoing caw of a single crow monitoring the passages occasionally registered in the shallow stirrings of his slumber. Among one such thin moment of sleep, the sound of Jake's whispered beckoning fell trivially to rest on the banks of Garren's wearied ears.

10

Derik, feeling awkward, offered a hand to Andi to help her up off the ground, which she dismissed. *Come on, you goof. Say something ... anything*, he thought to himself. "Andi, I'm sorry. I couldn't imagine going through everything you've seen these past eighteen months. Thank God for people like Jake."

"It's okay. I didn't mean to overreact. I'm sorry."

"No, don't you even. You have every right. And if you and he were sort of a couple while you were together—" he said but was silenced by Pradicus's gesture to quiet immediately.

"What is it?" Derik asked.

"Hush," Pradicus ushered. "Horses. Very *big* horses."

Derik didn't hear anything. He looked at Andi and was startled by the panic in her eyes.

Standing to her feet, she said, "It's ... the horsemen, isn't it? Pradicus, isn't it? But Pradicus ... you said ... I mean, I thought we were safe ... "

"Bierwul. He must've spotted our exit while in the cavern. There are only six known exits, so it's only a matter of time and deductive reasoning..."

"The crows. They knew where to be looking," Andi said.

A faint grumble-like thunder arose in the southern distance. Within moments, the horsemen were upon them. There were six.

Pradicus, Andi, and Derik knelt down in the narrow clearing and held still amidst the sheets of hanging ivy. The horsemen slowed to a trot, then stopped only a stone's throw away. One of the horsemen dismounted his great steed. Derik gasped as he captured a glimpse of the man—a man only half alive. Then he caught an elbow in the ribs from Andi as he dared to steal a peek at the rest of them.

"This one must be the point man," Pradicus said, bobbing his head up, down, and side to side for a better look.

None of the horsemen had hair anywhere on their heads. Nor had they any eyelids, ears, or noses. Their pasty faces seemed as though skin were simply stretched over a skull. Red capillaries intermingled with gray veins were strewn across their faces. Each one of them bore thick fur skins that draped off their broad shoulders all the way down to their ankles. A wide, worn, leather belt, housing a dozen knives of varying lengths and sizes, was fitted across each of their torsos. Each also had a silver-tipped bull whip attached to one hip and a similar metallic-looking one hanging from their saddles.

A large dark bamboo cage was slammed to the ground and its door pulled opened. A long, two-hundred-pound, ample, four-legged, reptilian-like creature with stubby, hairy antennae in place of eyes crawled out, hissing in a tirade.

Up high on the near mountain, the great Lig Nædre sprung off a cliff as a beastly roar echoed through the forest.

"Mary, mother of...was that the thing we heard in the mountain?" Derik whispered toward Pradicus.

He glanced up, then nodded.

Andi, with her eyes bugged out and feeling the need to flee frantically, began to inch away through a swathe of ivy when her foot slid down a slope. She gasped and nearly let out a muffled scream, to which Derik responded with a horrified gaze. The missed step gave way to a small landslide of gravel and leaves. Derik threw both hands over his face in apprehension. Andi turned and saw that it led to a short depression in the ground approximately three feet deep and several feet wide. Thinking the area might help them better hide from view, she alerted the other two to what she'd found. In turn, they quietly slid backward on their bellies into the shallow, rectangular-shaped cavity, each eventually taking refuge against one of its sides.

The dragon soared over the tops of the oaks, leaving a forceful wind to rush against the ground. Ivy everywhere sprung to the sky. For just a moment, Derik got a clean, unobstructed view of the point horseman. His heart leapt in a panicked frenzy, as he felt like they'd been exposed.

As the wind subsided, the ivy fell, and the clearing was again obscured. Derik found some semblance of relief and turned his attention back to the hissing beast.

Derik glanced at Andi when he heard her heavy breathing. He laid a hand on her shoulder, only to discover she had fallen into a full tremble. Her quivering fingers touched against her lips.

"Sweet Jesus … Pradicus, it's the … it's the Jangus," she whispered. "Pradicus, what do we do? We're not going to make it out of here alive. Jesus, dear Jesus …" She closed her eyes and started to hyperventilate.

Pradicus reached over and held her hand. "Shhh, we must not speak. And whatever thou doest, don't sweat."

Derik jolted his head around. "Why? What are you talking about? Because I'm already sweating … and bad."

Pradicus glanced at Derik out of the corner of his eye. "It'll smell you," he gruffly whispered.

The words reverberated within Derik. He suddenly became aware of how hard his heart had been pounding. He turned his head back around. His eyes dashed to and fro between beast and the saddled cadaverous devils looking for them.

Andi's breathing slowed, and her quivering diminished as she began to pray. Neither Pradicus nor Derik could make out her mumbling, with the exception of every fourth or fifth word. Her whispers continued while the other two observed the horsemen and their beast. They both took notice when her tone transformed from the uncertainty of, "Oh please, please, Father …" to a more controlled, "Thank you, Lord, for the shelter of

Your wing as I submit to Your will, whatever that may be."

The Jangus threw its body around violently until it was unleashed by the point horseman. It immediately turned toward the three in hiding and was off. It crawled slowly but with hungry determination while its antennae honed in and held in their direction. The walls of ivy danced back and forth as the creature nosed its way toward the rut in which they were hiding.

Derik took the hem of his shirt and wiped his face. The snaps and crackles of twigs and leaves grew relentlessly louder with every few steps of the Jangus. Derik looked away over to Pradicus, wondering why he wasn't doing anything.

"They're coming," Andi muttered with her eyes closed.

He mouthed the words "What do we do?" to Pradicus.

Pradicus laid his face into one of his hands and then slightly shook his head. He looked back over to Derik with a defeated gaze. "Nothing," he said, shrugging his shoulders.

"What do you mean?" Derik replied under his breath. "You must've gotten away from these guys before."

Pradicus shook his head.

Derik sat stunned. "How can that be?" he whispered. "You mean to tell me you've never run into these half-living creatures before?"

Pradicus shook his head again with another shrug. "Until this very day, I thought them to be a myth," he whispered back.

Derik was astounded as the unexpected answer snatched his breath. He rested his head back, then three feet from his left shoulder, the Jangus's head burst through the wall of ivy and released a wild hiss. Derik's terrified reaction landed him directly on his tailbone four feet away on the other side of Andi. His emerald burst into a brilliant illumination, as if about to rupture into flame. Derik seized it within a closed fist and then clenched his teeth under agony of its blaze.

The point horseman drew his whip and a thick, jagged knife and then leapt to the beast's side. His eyes met Derik's. Derik prepared to get up and run, but Andi placed a firm hand on his leg. She slightly shook her head. The pale figure sounded for the others. Each of the other horsemen dismounted their enormous horses, unsheathed large blades, and then approached, disappearing into the woods.

A disgruntled bat, disturbed by the stirring of the ivy, dropped from its oak branch and flapped away in an array of zigs and zags. One of the other horsemen, who bore a horned Viking helmet strapped to his back, drew his whip in lightning quickness and struck down the bat, splitting it in two, in mid-zig before it could gain any distance. The others held their positions until the Viking slayer dismissed the bat as a false alarm.

Andi opened her eyes briefly and had a clear view of the happening and then gasped. She returned to her prayer. The point horseman, reacting to the sound of her gasp, drew back his whip and cracked it twice just over Andi's head. Derik sat up and leaned into her, stretching his arm across her front. The horseman then drew the whip back again and cracked it once more, landing it upon Derik's shoulder. Derik winced in pain but held himself quietly still. The Jangus hissed wildly once again, its antennae pointing the three of them out. The horseman's large bare eyes, gripped with purpose, lay centered on Derik. The appalling figure stood void of emotion or pity, preparing to engage, breathing heavily. Suddenly, his eyes broke from Derik and then slowly scanned over Andi and Pradicus. He then turned his head and glanced over the rest of the area. He made a shrieking call to the others, and they returned to their horses. He sheathed his knife, then grabbed the Jangus by its harness and pulled it away. The Jangus screeched in protest and then lunged toward Pradicus. Pradicus grabbed his staff and struck the beast in the chest. The end of the staff lit up briefly. The horseman, busy with the Jangus, yanked it back forcefully.

Wearing an indignant scowl, Pradicus returned the staff to his side. "Hideous, filthy monster."

The creature hissed vehemently and charged toward the three in one last desperate attempt. Finally, the horseman grabbed the harness with a single hand and, in a sole mighty act, lifted the reeling Jangus off the ground and tossed it onto his shoulder. He marched back to his horse, turned the cage on its end, dropped the Jangus in through the door, and then closed it. The horsemen were quickly on their way and out of ear's reach within seconds.

Derik let out a large breath of relief, then fell onto his side and cursed, grabbing at his wound with one hand while releasing his waning emerald with the other.

Andi turned to him and put a hand on his shoulder. "Derik, are you okay?"

He winced again and then gave a reluctant nod, along with a sigh. He checked his hand and found blood on his fingers. His shirt was ripped where the whip landed.

"Derik! You're not okay. Oh my goodness, look at you." Andi positioned herself to get a better look. "Here, take off your shirt."

Derik gave Pradicus a self-conscious glance.

"Oh, shut up," she said as she began to pull his shirt off.

Derik gritted his teeth in pain as he raised his arms. Andi pulled off the shirt and cringed when she got a look at the wound. Her fingers softly slid across his back as she maneuvered around for the best angle to see the extent of the injury. "Pradicus, are you sure you've never tangled with one of those things before?" She grazed over the wound lightly. "The scar on the back of your neck looks just like …"

"Augh!" Derik cried as he flinched. "Don't touch it," he said in an enthusiastic plea.

At first, Andi cringed, and then her expression quickly flattened. "Geez, Derik, you gonna man up or what?" she muttered.

He suddenly found himself settling down quite nicely to her touch. He turned his head over his shoulder to say something, and she pushed it back. He rolled his eyes and then caught a glimpse of Pradicus sporting quite a youthful grin.

Derik grasped his emerald amulet again. "So you wanna tell me what just happened back there? And what in the name of heaven were those things on those giant horses? And I'm about to throw this thing away. It keeps burning me, and I'm getting really sick of it."

Pradicus shook his head and smiled at Andi. "Once again, thy God has saved thee."

"A sudden burst of confidence came over me, and I felt led to pray," she said.

"Hmm," Derik huffed. "What, you pray, and all of a sudden those hideous things go blind or what?"

"Blind?" Pradicus asserted. "I believe the bat has an opinion about that. No, son. Not them becoming blinded…but us becoming cloaked. Veiled, covered, hidden away, protected—take thy pick. The power of her God has overcome."

"I'm not sure it was just about us being hidden," Andi said. "Someone else was here. I saw someone. He stood in front of the Jangus. It was just a glimmer, but it was fantastic."

Pradicus pulled off a few nearby leaves and tore them in half. Then he crumpled them in his hand and squeezed them together. A few drops of a milky substance spilled out from between his fingers. He held it over Derik's wound and let the milk drip into the gash. A moment later, he placed the entire contents of his hands over the afflicted area and held it there.

Derik gritted his teeth again. "You never did answer me about the riders."

Pradicus answered in a solemn tone. "They are but a dark whisper, a forbidden fable in most circles. Rumors abound of new terrors with the shifting of the wind. But most believe those whose tongues lay sway to such darkness invite that very darkness upon themselves." He paused for a moment. "Their tongues should be cut out! Yet a sliver of truth defines the very axis around which every rumor turns, does it not? Hence, the legend and the myths unspeakable, which themselves are innumerable.

"The horsemen are said to ride as speedily as the wind, as thou hast seen, and are also said to be mistaken, quite often, for a distant rolling of thunder. It is believed that they are incessantly aware of their surroundings and are undeniably commanded to do away with all witnesses, no exceptions. Rumors have them racing into the heart of the woods and gathering at the southern end of the mountain. From there, they disappear into one of the passageways leading to the cavern, most likely. Some say Lig Nædre calls them back to the mountain, but mine eyes have spotted Valicious, more than once, overlooking the southern valley standing at Broga's Edge halfway up Mount Liffrea, or Broga Mountain. He would hold his arms apart, staff in hand, with the lengthy sleeves of his gray robes draping from his arms. Behind him, the sixth entrance to the cavern, the one used by Lig Nædre, and directly beneath him at the base of the mountain is where the riders are said to disappear.

"In the winter of the quiet year, I braved the great entrance. It is a magnificent rift in the side of the mountain heading directly to the top of the cavern through a few twists and turns, ending with one lengthy tunnel leading straight down. Wall-mounted torches lit the corridor for the first two hundred feet into the mountain. I have explored the mountain long enough to realize that a labyrinth of other paths and caves are strewn throughout the mountain's bowels, but only six carefully followed passageways lead from the valley outside directly to the great cavern.

"Given these past twenty years, mine ears have heard a myriad of stories surface about loved ones getting lost, unable to navigate their way back out of the mountain after entering it. And their reasons for entering, who but God alone knows? Perhaps they didst their villages a favor. Many attributed their loss to a run-in with Lig Nædre, which very well might have been the case. Others hold to the belief that the ghosts of their loved ones continue to haunt the mountain until they find their way out and only then are they able to give rest to their souls. Still, others believe in a magic within the mountain that keeps their loved ones alive until they find their way out. The latter belief stems from brief glimpses of vaguely familiar loved ones spotted in the mountain years after their disappearances. 'Tis these reported sightings in particular that keep the religious and superstitious folk fueling stories of mad, ghostly horsemen who ride monster stallions in submission to the great dragon's bidding."

"Well, how is it that we survived after seeing them?"

"We had help," Andi answered.

"You mean from God," Derik replied facetiously.

She tossed Derik a dismissive glare. "Well, God or not, it was someone greater than any of us sitting here, right?"

"Since when did *you* take up God?" Derik asked, turning his head over his shoulder again.

"Since I was about eleven, you goof," she answered, pushing his head back again.

"Get outta here. You never went to church."

"Well, no. But I read a few books and listened to some old CDs I found in the attic."

"Whatever. Like God's got time for you."

"Well, it's more like since I've been here, I found time for Him."

Derik frowned and bit his lip. *Can't argue that*, he thought. "Anyway, what about those god-awful monsters?"

"As I said, until now, I thought them to be a myth, a legend," Pradicus said.

"You live here, they live here, and you've never tangled with these things before?"

Pradicus shook his head.

Derik peeked at Andi. She shook her head. "What the heck? What would posses them to show up now?" he asked.

Andi stood up. "Maybe it's just the right time," she said. She turned to Pradicus.

Derik leaned over to pick up a stick and chuckled. "Yeah, speaking of time, did you get a look at that slick watch? Hey, maybe yours would work here. Did you bring it?"

Andi caught her breath then turned around. "What did you just say?"

"Your watch. Did you bring it?"

"No, before that."

"Oh, um, that slick watch that ugly had ... It was a very cool-looking watch."

Pradicus held his gaze on Andi.

"I was saying that if I had one, maybe my timing—"

"Whatever, Derik. That's really neat. Do you remember what it looked like?" Andi asked.

"Oh, it was, like, really cool. But it was slim, sort of like a girl's watch ... only not. It was definitely dude-ish."

"Could you see the face?"

"Not really. Just a bluish, silvery light."

Andi puckered her brow, shooting a look at Pradicus.

Pradicus shook his head. "Andi, please," he said softly.

"What's all this about? And is someone gonna finish my shoulder?"

"Andi, he is gone. It was not him," Pradicus reaffirmed.

"Derik, what did you tell me once about your friend Greg's computer?"

"Um, you can't get Internet here, doll."

Andi rolled her eyes. "You're kidding!" she said, smacking him in the back of the head.

"Well, what then?"

"That biotech stuff you mentioned a couple summer's back."

"That was three months ago, Andi."

She smacked him again.

"Oh, oh, right, you've been here for a ... right, the bio-tech stuff. Only Greg can unlock his computer because he's the owner. Only his bio information is stored so no one else can unlock it. There was this one time when he said—"

"Shut up, Derik." She gave Pradicus a grimace. "Only Jake could have powered that watch, Pradicus."

"He is gone, Andrea," Pradicus, with sulking eyes, said firmly in a soft tone. "Jake is gone."

Andi stood silently with a scowl, and Pradicus remained resolute with a stern countenance.

"Well, what about my *shoulder*?" Derik cried.

Andi turned and patted it gruffly. "You're gonna be okay, big boy," she whispered.

Derik grunted and grimaced. Pradicus let out a short chortle, then again met Andi's determined eyes.

"Andi, I understand. Jake presented the watch to me and explained all that thou speaks of. Thy friend is the sole owner and the only one that can power it, yes. What I'm saying to thee is that *he* is gone. The horsemen are also known as 'Gray Riders.' This pertains to no longer living. Andi, thou also hast heard the stories. Thou knowest these things. As long as Lig Nædre lives, the horsemen serve it. 'Tis too late to save him."

"Then we need to kill Lig Nædre," she snarled.

"Whoa, whoa, whoa, wh-what? Did I miss something?" Derik asked, glaring at the other two. He saw the firm look in Andi's eyes and then flinched, purposing to keep from getting hit again. Andi looked away. Behind her back, Derik crossed his eyes and circled his finger alongside his head, gesturing a *crazy* person. He immediately felt her slap once again on the back of his head.

"Dang it, would you stop?" he said, straightening himself.

She scowled back at him. "Don't be a weenie."

Derik flinched again and then looked to Pradicus in protest.

"Yes, don't be a weenie," Pradicus said, shrugging his shoulders.

Andi sniggered under her breath while holding a few fingers over her mouth. She regained her composure and then returned her glare at Derik once again.

Pradicus leaned back against a tree. "Valicious will never allow us close enough to Lig Nædre," he said. "His power is the greatest the region has ever known because of the dragon's fire. Valicious knows he is much less powerful without the beast. Besides, Lig Nædre is virtually indestructible. Hundreds have fallen in an attempt to slay the creature. The only other way to beat Valicious is for us to fulfill the prophecy before he has a chance to."

"You never mentioned a prophecy before … did you?" Andi stated quizzically.

"I believe I have once or twice. The Atlas?"

"Oh, that's a prophecy? The only time that ever came up was when you'd leave to seek out Derik each month. What does Derik have to do with the prophecy?"

A somber expression washed over Derik's face as he thought about the cavern and the secret it kept. His contemplation focused on the large mound of bones once again. With the sudden talk of prophecy and whether or not he played a part in it, he couldn't help but wonder where he might end up when all was said and done. Averting his eyes, he tuned his ear to Pradicus for an answer.

"Children, time is of the essence. If I am to send thee back, it must be soon."

Andi cocked her head. "Pradicus, what aren't you telling me? Why are you being elusive? And why the sudden rush? For months now, all I've heard is how to be patient. Then bang, Derik arrives, and it's rush, rush, rush."

Derik finally engaged. He shot a direct glance at Pradicus. "Yes, why?"

"The Atlas, the prophecy, these are things not intended for innocent minds to ponder. Let us be on our way."

"No," Andi retorted with a glare. "We're all here right now. There's something big behind those eyes, and it's scaring me. You owe me this, Pradicus. What are the prophecy and the Atlas?"

Pradicus sighed, rested his head against the tree, and then drew in a long, steady breath. He gazed back at the other two. "Valicious must not complete the Atlas," he said in a yielding tone. "According to legend, he who brings the Atlas to life will command the greatest control over it."

"So what?" Derik asked. "What if he gets the chance to *bring the Atlas to life*? What does that mean?"

Andi, holding determined eyes on Pradicus, raised an intrigued eyebrow.

Realizing this line of questioning had the potential to generate one thought-provoking question after another, Pradicus decided to back up and start at the beginning. "Mine brother was born with longer hair than was expected for a child. In mine family history, a female child had always been the firstborn. The name had already been decided. However, when I was birthed, I surprised everyone, being the first ever male firstborn. Mine grandfather's name was Pradicus, so in celebration, I was given his name. Moments later, mine brother was birthed. Having never had a male firstborn or twins, alarm fell over the family. They decided to give the selected female name Valla, meaning the chosen one, to mine brother for his lengthy hair and also for fear of superstition. Changing a baby's selected name is frowned upon still to this day. They overlooked it in mine case, seeing a firstborn male birth as a sign of goodness and prosperity.

"Growing up we were told that a clan of priests had taken our mother in and cared for her before, during, and after our births. We were also told the black sickness took her while we were yet young. Just beyond the years of our boyhood, we were confronted with the lie we were taught. The idea which Valla and I shared in creating a tunnel through time was a valiant one. We discovered that our mother had indeed suffered a terrible death, but not from a sickness. I simply wanted to undo her"—he paused—"suffering and allow her the chance to live a long life with her two boys.

"In the beginning of our work, mine brother and I together witnessed her death through a window we created in the river using a circle of gem stones I referred to as the Atlas. We didst not know it then, but small beads of dragon fire carried downstream by the current allowed us to produce the window in the water.

"It, of course, was a clan of priests who took our mother in—but priests who served an evil purpose and who identified themselves with a dragon tattoo across their backs. They served Lig Nædre. While I sought for a way to go back and save our mother using a time tunnel, Valla made his own plans to go back and spill the blood of her slayers. He took up sword and blade study. He then mastered the whip and then began teaching me. It was subtle, but I noticed him becoming quieter, more withdrawn to the point of losing interest in teaching any further. I began to see him less and less.

"It wasn't long after that he came across a tribe of merchants. At twenty years old, he befriended them, sharpened his weaponry skills among them, and even traveled with them for a short time. But somehow, on a night of drunken festivity, he spoke of his ill-will. Among the several trader families, there were two men who heard his story and stepped forward within days of each other. The two of them changed the course of his life and, as a result, mine also.

"The first was a seer, a prophet. He produced a number of scrolls and shared with Valla a prophecy of old concerning twins who might possibly discover how to fold time and, in effect, live it twice. The prophet kept company with the merchants but was not family among them. They accepted him as one of their own in exchange for the assistance of his crossbow, a weapon which greatly intrigued Valla.

"The second to step forward was a middle-aged priest—a priest with a tattoo across his back who wielded a lengthy blade himself and was accustomed to using it. One of the two men came with an extended hand of friendship, while the other approached with deceit, purposing to trick Valla and then slay him before the elders of the camp.

"During one evening gathering, the priest placed himself within striking range and, while on the sly, drew his blade. Even in his drunken state, Valla caught sight of the familiar tattoo as the man made his move. Without a contest, Valla turned, pulled his whip, and cracked it upon the wrist of the priest, disarming him of his blade. Continuing in the single swiftest maneuver any of them had ever witnessed, Valla took the head of the priest with one swipe of his sword. Realizing the disloyalty before him, he then turned his wrath onto the two dozen elders who supported the plot. In a ravishing tirade, with whip thrashing and blades flashing, he executed each of the elders within seconds of each other, leaving the crazed, fleeing women unmarked. A swelling dominance he had not known before awoke within him, and in the interest of thrusting the sensation to its fullest, he extended his massacre to every remaining man. From defenders of the camp to simple young merchants in surrender, his blades and whip spared not a single unarmed fiancé, brave husband, or pleading father."

Andi glanced at Derik and noticed his awe-stricken expression. Derik felt her eyes bearing down on him and returned the glance. "This Valla guy is amazing."

"The only problem with that, Derik, is … oh yeah, he wants to kill you."

Derik's expression flattened out as he returned his attention to Pradicus.

"Leaving the wailing women and children in his wake, he moved on, swapping knowledge of weaponry for prophecy, gaining all he could. Then together he and the prophet tracked down all the families of the priestly sect involved with the torturous death of his mother.

"His slaughtering spree covered hundreds of miles, and when the powerful men stepped in to stop him, he struck down those who interfered as well. In the end, he allowed only a single priest to live—the eldest, most experienced of them all. His vengeance became legend. Word of his butchery spread, and he was quickly branded "Valla the Malicious." It wasn't long before he began reveling in his new identity and decided to adopt the new name. He adorned himself with the title 'Lord' for his mastery of weapons and seeming invincibility. He then combined Valla and malicious to become Valicious.

"After a few years, he returned to mine home, accompanied by the prophet and the frail, nearly dead priest and demanded that I join him to fulfill some prophecy I had never heard of. All three of them were heavily clothed in furs which draped from their shoulders to their ankles. Valla and the prophet both carried a sheath of blades across their chests. Valla then told me something I refused to believe. He said he had learned how to serve Lig Nædre and that it was time to begin controlling the dragon itself for unlimited use of its dragon fire. He then told me how our window in the water played a part in the folding of time and that, with the help of the prophet and the priest, he had found a way to bring our window out of the water and into midair. He said with control of the dragon fire, he would be able not only to complete the Atlas but control it. With such control, he would bring the world as we knew it under his complete command. He spoke of abolishing all religions, priests, and sects and that it would be he alone that the people of the world looked to for lordship.

"The brother I knew no longer existed. I told him as much and then demanded he leave and never return. He swore I would join him someday or he would take mine life just the way he took countless others' lives who betrayed him. I knew mine brother was gone forever when he failed to mention our mother again.

"In a moment of hatred, without thinking, I reached for my sword. Before my hand stretched across my midsection to grasp it, I had been struck on the back of the neck in a lightning-fast lashing from the prophet's whip. With no leaf milk to soothe the burning gash, I quickly fell to my knees, then onto my back in fiery pain, screaming. I do not remember anything else after that. All I know is that I awoke at about midday the following day and Valicious was gone and mine home a pile of smoking ash.

"I tracked him to Broga Mountain and, for the most part, lived within its vastness for the next year or so, studying all I could about it. One fortunate day, I happened upon the gemstones. I laid them out just as I had years before in the river, then something amazing happened. The window I created suddenly sprung to life. Valicious spotted me from across the cavern and called upon the dragon at once. But by the time Lig Nædre made its presence known, I had already caused the Atlas to collapse inwardly upon itself, sending the stones one by one throughout all of time and then ran for my escape. Since then, Valicious has made several attempts at my life and much more so anyone I show interest in."

Derik turned his head toward Andi, revealing a concerned expression beneath a furrowed brow. Andi's demeanor remained steady, stern, and, in Derik's opinion, somewhat grave. He looked back at Pradicus and, with a lighter overall bearing, broke a grin. "That was awesome. Pradicus, he's your brother? Can you do all that stuff?"

Andi swatted him again and then slid her eyes over to Pradicus apologetically. "I don't get boys. I tell you what. You tell them there's a monster under their bed and all they want to know is how big and ugly he is and where he wipes after picking his nose. Come on, Derik. This is his brother, his mother, his family. This is real for him. He's"—she paused—"all alone now," she said, her tone quieting. "Don't you see that?" she squeaked, her voice failing her as she wiped a finger beneath either eye. She sniffled. "Oh, that's right. I forgot. You don't know what it's like to be all alone and away from your family for months or years on end."

"Now, now," Pradicus said. "That was a very long time ago."

"But you know what, Pradicus?" she stated, pointing to her sternum. "In here, it was only a moment ago."

For only a moment, a tearful heaviness arose within Pradicus's eyes as he dared to gaze upon the demons of his past which he knew full well still continued to taunt him.

Derik dragged his eyes across the ground to Pradicus and then slowly heaved them back to Andi. He paused for a moment in reflection. "You're right," he agreed, raising a palm into the air. "I'm such an idiot, always putting my foot in my mouth. Guys, I'm sorry."

Andi placed a tender hand on his shoulder. "Thank you. It's not something you'd normally think about. I know you didn't really … know."

Pradicus shook himself free of the melancholy. Feeling the necessity to get back on track, he cleared his throat while sporting a rather satisfied grin. The other two simultaneously turned to look. It was exactly what Andi needed. Her eyes lit up as her dormant lips stretched into an enthralled smile. She threw Derik an elbow, followed by a head nudge toward Pradicus.

Pradicus stepped away from the tree, then reached into his pocket and withdrew a closed fist. He held his gaze at the other two with a glimmer in his eye and, a moment later, opened his hand. In his palm sat three berries which appeared to look like medium to large blueberries. "These belong, or belonged," he said with a chuckle, "to Valicious. He has put a time restraint on the wormhole. Your opportunity to return through the same hole will expire when these berries wither." He slid them onto Andi's palm.

Derik stepped up for a closer look. "They don't seem old at all to me," he said in a chipper tone. "Ouch. Oh, hot," he whispered, grabbing his amulet.

"What's with you, Derik?" Andi asked. "What? Your emerald doesn't like berries?"

"I don't know. It's crazy. Whoever heard of an emerald—or any stone, for that matter—that just turns fiery hot on its own out of the blue?" He moved away from the berries, and the amulet dimmed. The sight caught Andi's attention.

"Derik, come back over here," she said.

As he approached, the emerald fired up once again. "Owie, hot, hot. What do you need?"

"Take a step back again, and watch your amulet."

He did, and the stone cooled instantly. She walked toward him and held the berries up in a closed fist. A spark in the amulet's core twinkled a few times, then slowly began to blossom like a tulip. As she unfolded her fingers, the amulet emitted an illuminating heat once again.

"Ouch, Andi," he snapped.

She looked at Pradicus. "What does it mean?"

"It means knock it off," Derik retorted.

"Ah," she said, raising a finger. "Pradicus, how long have you had those berries?"

"Several days now, I believe. I pilfered them from Valicious's wild garden just recently."

"Well, if these belonged to Valicious, then that's it, isn't it? It must have something to do with the dark magic he uses. Derik, didn't you say the emerald never heated up before Pradicus met you in the cavern?"

He nodded.

"Let's have a look at those berries again," Pradicus said. He reached down and scooped up a small handful of dirt. He spread it over the berries. The berries instantly changed from colorful and succulent to dull and wrinkled.

"What just happened?" Derik uttered in a panic.

"It's one of Valicious's tricks. The dirt reveals the true state of things. If he can keep thee believing that the berries are always fresh, even though they have long perished, who art thou to question him when he offers what appears to be beautiful? These berries don't have much time, which means we haven't much time. When I prepare to send thee back through this wormhole, would thou consider, Derik, relinquishing the amulet? I believe it may play a part in the prophecy."

"You get us both back, and you can have anything you want," he answered excitedly.

"Okay then. There may be a way," Pradicus said, cupping his chin. "The Jangus. It's larger than I thought it to be. It must be six or seven cubits in length, nose to tail! But the skin was smooth." He looked at the other two. "It's a water beast."

Derik held a blank stare, and Andi frowned in confusion.

"Derik, did you see those three rows of short spines on its back?"

Derik thought about it and then nodded.

"The spines are dry, closed up, giving its venom no real hole to inject from—in essence, blocking it. But I believe those spines will soften and open up in the water." He grinned.

Derik and Andi shook their heads, still wondering where he was going.

"It is said that its spines store enough venom to kill a whale." He grinned again.

Andi finally nodded. "Ah, or a dragon. So how do we get one?"

Pradicus looked back at Derik. "There's only *one*, Jangus."

"Um, well, what does that *mean*?" Derik asked.

"It means instead of being the hunted, we become the hunters."

"We're gonna steal it?" Derik cried incredulously. "Did you miss the owners of that thing? I'm not sure they're the kind of guys that'll give up their lunch money to a couple of bullies—three bullies, in fact. Frankly, I'd rather not even think about making any of them ornery, much less steal the family pet."

Pradicus stared down at the berries. "It is said that many have lost their lives in the hunt for the horsemen's lair. Some have also said that merely taking in their breath will condemn thee to the mountain as a wandering soul. Friends, we need a plan."

Derik took a step back and glanced at Andi. Andi returned his glance and then looked back at Pradicus with a determined scowl. "How much lunch money do you suppose they have between them?"

11

"If all goes well, on the morrow, we will enter the mountain. But I shall need a few things from my own collected works. Come. Let us sup," Pradicus said, starting to trek through the hanging vines.

A plan began to develop as they reached the banks of the river. Pradicus reached into a pocket and drew out a small egg-shaped object hosting a reddish-orange hue in its midst. Using his staff, he drew a sphere in the dirt, enclosing the three of them and then cast the object to the ground. A flash of fire burst out, then dissipated upon the object's rupturing.

Derik jumped. "Whoa, what's going on?"

Andi threw a hand over her mouth and giggled. "Oh, sorry. I should've taken a second to explain beforehand. This is how Pradicus moves between his home and Broga Mountain. He uses the river."

Immediately, the encircled ground broke away from the river bank and drifted straightaway into the river and then began carrying them downstream at half the current's speed.

Derik's excited eyes reminded Andi of her introduction to Pradicus's world of dragon-fire enchantment. "This is amazing." Derik laughed.

After a series of whoops and hollers of sheer exhilaration, he stopped upon encountering the engrossed grins the other two wore. He immediately began composing himself while the thrill continued to inflate within him. Andi threw Pradicus an amused glance and then returned her eyes to Derik's swelling expression.

"Come on. Get it all out already," she said.

Derik jumped into her with an engulfing embrace. "I don't know what's gotten into me. It's like I can't help it. It's so … wow. I feel like a kid." He released her and then dropped to his knees, dipping his hand into the water as the parcel of land moved effortlessly through it.

Andi turned to Pradicus. "I wish it stayed like that."

Pradicus nodded. "We certainly do forget … all too easily. It seems the simplicities we long for are naught but a heart attitude away."

"Okay, back to the plan," Andi said.

"Yes, so we shall enter the great cavern discreetly, then I shall send the two of thee back. Afterward, I will close the wormhole and put a stop to the use of them once and for all."

"Well, how do you plan on doing that with a fire-breathing dragon in there keeping it active?" Derik asked.

"That's where the Jangus comes in, and of course, Bierwul," Pradicus said with a calculated grin.

"Bierwul? Who's Bierwul?"

"The messenger," Andi answered. "Bierwul is the crow, Valicious's dark-magic pet."

"Wait a minute, a crow? Wasn't there a crow outside the barn before the storm hit?"

Andi nodded. "The crow serves as Valicious's eyes. Bierwul scouts out the areas where the wormhole is sent."

"So Bierwul steers the wormhole?"

"I don't know. Maybe something like that," Andi answered. "Actually, I think Valicious steers it through the eyes of Bierwul."

"Valicious hides his wormhole in a storm," Pradicus said. "Bierwul predetermines the path of the storm by searching for someone to, well, kidnap."

"So this is his entire fault?" Derik asked. "Ugh, the feathery little maggot. So what was the orange-reddish haze we saw falling from the storm?"

"That was Nædre fire bleeding through the wormhole. Dragon fire gives magic its strength," Pradicus explained. "It is the key to all powerful formulas. Valicious has found ways to harness it for his own use, should Lig Nædre become eliminated."

"Like the little egg-like object you used a few minutes ago?" Derik asked.

Andi peeked at Pradicus and grinned.

"Mmm, yes, *vis aduro*. It is dragon fire, very powerful," Pradicus said.

"I imagine you pilfered a few of those while you were … berry picking?" Derik added.

Pradicus returned Andi's grin with an affirming one of his own and then relented. "Perhaps a few."

"A few, my eye," Andi exuberated. "You've got a trunk full of them."

Pradicus laughed and then conceded. "I *was* referring to the most recent occurrence." The three shared a brief chuckle.

"Pradicus, how will I ever manage without you?" Andi asked. "You're always there to make me laugh and show me how to enjoy life. When all I see is how we digress, you make light of it and point out the scenery as we get back on track. I so love that about you." She began tearing up and started to speak but held back a moment. She looped her arm around his. "I'm really going to miss you," she murmured.

He patted her arm. "Veritas, 'tis true," he answered. "And thou hast been a straight edge for mine wanderings." He turned to Derik. "A blessed man assuredly awaits this one." He concluded the statement with a wink.

Believing she heard whispering, Andi lifted her face toward the other two. "Yes, back to our plan," Pradicus stammered. "Derik, I believe thou were saying something."

"Yes, of course," Derik quickly answered. "Um, yeah..." He shot his eyes from one place to another in an effort to recall his line of thinking.

Pradicus attempted to discreetly help him out by clearing his throat. "Hmm-mm. Dragon...fire, wasn't it?"

138

Andi gave them both a momentary cynical glare. "What are you guys up to?"

Derik leapt in. "Yes, yes, the reddish-orange haze … So Valicer-guy was doing his magic through the crow's eyes, then saw us and basically thought we would make good dragon kibble. Is that it?"

A small smile cracked at the edges of Andi's lips. She thought of addressing their obscurity and then relented with a quiet chuckle. "Yes, Derik, that seems to sum it up."

Derik tossed Pradicus a vague grin and then reasserted his sincerity for their plan. "Well, it seems simple to me. We can't stop at killing the dragon. We need to get rid of Velocir … raptor as well."

"Not velociraptor, you dim wit. Valicious," Andi chortled.

"That's what I meant. Valic … ious," he countered with a discontented frown.

"He knows Pradicus helped me escape and has made several attempts to catch me again," Andi said.

"So now he's ticked at Pradicus for helping you," Derik commented.

"My boy, Valicious has long been ticked, as thou hath said, at me for many years. Remember, he is mine brother, who has disowned me."

"I should say that at one time he was my brother," Pradicus said determinedly. "He's dead to me now. Whatever he has become, he is not mine brother." He paused for a moment, drawing in a lengthy breath. "Mine brother was murdered a very long time ago." He sighed as he scanned the horizon.

"Well, are you going to try to kill him if you get the chance?" Andi asked.

Pradicus's eyes fell away from the conversation and landed halfway up Broga Mountain. "Let me just say he has become the core of evil itself," he said with solemn resolve. "If ever I am afforded the opportunity to remove such evil from my midst, I will certainly do so."

Andi leaned over to Derik. "I wonder if those berries are getting to him," she whispered.

Derik answered her with a questioning smirk.

"Well, he's not been himself since you've gotten here, which is about a day after he took the berries. I think I'm going to suggest putting them in a jar so they're not so close to his body. Derik, I'm telling you, I've never seen him act so serious."

"Well, he's probably getting antsy. I mean, if the whole prophecy thing is within reach and he's been waiting this long to deal with his brother, look how close he is."

"Well, maybe. You're probably right."

The two glanced back at Pradicus, whose eyes were still on the mountain. Andi thought she saw tears drawing within his eyes. *I wonder what's really going on*, she thought to herself.

Derik caught a glimpse of her studying Pradicus before she turned her attention to the mountain to share Pradicus's view. "So ... you nervous about facing your old friend, Jake?" Derik asked her.

Andi swiveled her head around and answered him with a hurtful look.

"Oh, geez, I'm sorry. Did that sound bad? I promise I didn't mean anything by it. Really. I've just had this nagging thought that if he didn't recognize you and was bent on driving a blade into your heart"—he paused, then stood up straight and continued—"I'd have to take him out, Andi. I know he was a friend of yours, but given the chance, I think I'd … I'd … ," he said, pausing once again for a moment to consider what he was truly meaning to say. "Andi, I wouldn't ever be able to let him hurt you. With God as my witness, if that jackwagon so much as breathes your direction ever again, so help me, I'll put him down."

Andi's furrowed brow and frowning lips leveled out into a deep-rooted contemplation. It was an expression Derik had *never* seen before. Derik felt as though he'd snuck a peek into her soul in an unprotected moment. He couldn't make it out. Was it hope, heroism, incredulity? Perhaps he'd discovered something unknown to him deep down in the waiting-to-be-discovered universe that was Andi. She studied his face as the breeze picked up and flirted ever so gently with her hair.

"Andi…" Derik said, beginning to regret the statement.

She stepped up to him and put her arms around him, laying her head against his shoulder. Her gown rippled against him in the breeze, occasionally wrapping itself around his legs. She held him quietly for a few minutes while the long-disregarded agony of her waiting for him the past eighteen months caught up to her, and she broke. Clutching his shirt within her fists, she heaved several silent wails. Not sure what to say or how to respond, Derik simply held her.

"I've missed you so much, Derik," she sobbed through her tears as she began to tremble. "About a year ago, I gave up on you and the life I once had. I just couldn't continue to hope anymore. I'm so sorry for that. Can you please forgive me? Please forgive me, Derik," she whispered into his shoulder, grabbing him tighter.

"Come on now. You couldn't have known how far behind you I was going to be. I'm so sorry you had to go through that. It really must've been horrible. Andi"—he picked her chin up—"I'm sorry you had to go through that. You have *nothing* that needs to be forgiven. I'll say it if you need to hear it, but it won't be coming from anywhere within me. Andi, you've always been the soft, steady place for me to land. There wasn't a chance I wasn't coming after you. I'm really sorry for everything." He squeezed her. "All I could think about after you fell through the hole was that I should've kissed you that night in the pantry," he said quietly.

Her sobbing began to quiet. She raised her eyes to meet his.

Derik studied her face, absorbing her every crease and freckle. The words came out before he could catch them. "I really cannot believe how gorgeous you are."

He sucked his lips in, in a sudden panic, wondering if he'd gone too far. She smiled softly and then mimicked his move by drawing her lips in with a playful receptive grin. The thought of her lips eluding him once again was more than he could take.

"Oh, don't you dare," he said, placing both hands behind her head. He hesitated for just a moment, preparing to capture a memory well worth preserving, then closed his eyes and kissed her. She let out a quiet whimper as their lips pressed together. With his thumb, he wiped the single tear descending upon her cheek.

Derik savored the novel tenderness of her lips. An exhilarating thrill ran through his body like electricity, leaving his knees weak. He felt his pulse double all the while pounding like a titan within his chest. The knotting in his stomach he'd felt earlier returned twofold, then threefold, and, without notice, stole his breath. Suddenly, he realized those few seconds in time were perfect. It was the purest moment he'd ever known.

Opening his eyes, he slowly drew his head back, separating his lips from hers with a whisper-soft break. He caught her for just a second in complete defenselessness, eyes yet closed as if in a dream a million miles away. He gazed upon the face of an angel, of this he was certain.

She opened her eyes, and as she did, a tense, hesitant expression arose. "Derik—" she said but was cut off.

"I'm right here. I'm not going anywhere. I'm not ever going to leave you. I'm right here, Andi, for always." He wrapped both his arms around her and then rested his cheek against the top of her head.

12

Derik held Andi's hand over the course of the next hour as the three of them reiterated their plan on their way back to Pradicus's home. The area of land upon which they stood began to slow and then incredibly assimilated itself into the shoreline as it drifted alongside it.

The three of them stepped onto the shore just before the river waters washed into a series of rapids. They trekked a bit farther over a couple small hills, where they stopped upon cresting the second hill. The view overlooked a considerably wide neck of the Eastland River and provided them a glorious scene comprising Pradicus's home and the woodland surroundings reminiscent of lush, enchanted forests described only in fairly tales. Pradicus built his house on an ait—a sixty-acre island measuring twice as long as it was wide. The ait had formed in the center of the river as a result of an enormous ledge protruding out from the river bottom, forcing the current to separate and travel around it.

A fairly moderate downgrade led them to the river's bank, where they stood looking onward toward the house. It featured a wrap-around wooden porch and stood two stories tall and was swathed in ivy.

"How are we going to cross?" Derik asked, turning to Andi.

"Pradicus?" Andi asked, deferring the question.

Pradicus tapped his staff three times, then once, then once again against a large flat rock extending into the river. A large swell appeared from downstream and hurriedly approached. It disappeared between the island and the rock. The water then began to separate as a leathery walkway rose from under the surface. Pradicus stepped off the rock and onto the new risen walkway, continuing forward toward the house.

Derik's slow glance out of the corner of his eyes told Andi she had some explaining to do.

"It's a kraken. Pradicus rescued it from Lig Nædre's clutches when it was a baby. He said he brought it back and nursed it to health, and it apparently decided to stay. Now one of its great arms acts as a bridge for him."

"How did he get across before?"

"He said a line of enormous stones used to act as a bridge of sorts. They must have been hugely tall to be able to sit on the bottom of the river and still stick out above the surface. Lig Nædre destroyed the bridge long before I got here in an attempt to kill Pradicus. But I suppose he could just float on another land piece."

"Why not just stay on the same land piece all the way down the river?" Derik asked. Andi opened her mouth to answer, but he butted back in with, "Oh, yeah, the rapids."

"Well, we did that once. And surprisingly, the rapids had almost no effect on the little piece of land we stood on. It was a beautiful trip, but a long, long trip. The river winds all the way down there around those hills before coming back up," she said, pointing into the hazy distance. "I did see a pretty interesting-looking cave way out there that I wouldn't mind getting a better look at someday."

"Wow. Well, that thing's arm is gigantic. What's the rest of it look like?"

"I don't know. It stays hidden. It plays downstream a lot and gets all the fish it needs because of the river's neck. They come right to him." She carefully stepped off the rock and onto the massive arm, and he followed. Her eyes studied the hide for sure footing. "It talks to Pradicus, you know, the kraken," she said. "I've seen it. It's like it knows what Pradicus is thinking about."

Derik, following in her exact footsteps, looked up at the back of her head briefly and tossed her a dismissive smirk.

"You're smirking at me, aren't you?"

"I uh, oh, um … " he stammered, caught off his guard.

"I knew it," she said perkily.

A few hours passed. Andi and Derik shared a moment on the front porch, lounging on a swing handmade by Pradicus's father.

"We go to work after breakfast," Pradicus said, poking his head out. "Be prepared."

Andi smiled at Pradicus as he returned into the house. "'A penny for your thoughts' is what he always said to me. 'You can't afford it,' I'd reply, and then, of course, we'd talk. Honestly," she said, beginning to think about it, "it's been a few weeks since he's asked me that." She pressed her lips together in a frown.

"What is it?" Derik asked, putting his arm around her.

"Oh, it's probably nothing. I can't put my finger on it. Something's off."

"Hey, you said earlier that you gave up on me, like, a year ago?"

Andi looked back at him sheepishly and bit her lip.

"You know what? Don't even go there. How could you have known? Really, I'm just curious. How did you remain so hopeful for my...uh"—he moved his hand about in a gesture searching for the right word—"arrival, I guess."

She drew her thoughts in for a moment or two. "Pradicus."

The answer surprised Derik. He looked over his shoulder and then slowly returned his gaze back to Andi.

"He kept assuring me that you couldn't be far behind. But I could see through his optimism. Yet every month, he said he was off to find you, especially the last few months. He seemed surer, I mean, almost certain about your coming. That's when all the talk of the Atlas began to surface. In fact," she said, sitting up, "that's when things really started changing around here. Seriously, it's like we haven't seen much of Lig Nædre or Bierwul. Last month, for the first time since I got here, I saw people from the village. I even overheard a couple travelers joking they heard that the Gray Riders must have finally turned on Lig Nædre. They said they were finally going to get a look at the great mystical cavern. Speaking of the horsemen, they were thought to be a myth. Then all of the sudden, out of the blue, they show up. I mean, *that's* like waking up and seeing the Boogie Man standing in the corner of your bedroom. Things have certainly begun stirring lately. Wow, Derik. Do you think there could be anything to this prophecy?"

As contemplation slowly swept over her face, she drew in a deep, controlled breath and slowly scanned the outline of the hills against a tall pink-and-orange sky. Having nothing to add, Derik simply held his gaze on Andi. A few moments later, he shared her view of the sunset, and the two sat quietly.

The river's flow rushed toward them and then split at the ait's tip in raging sprays like the *Titanic* carving through the ocean. Birds sang their evening praises and melodies into the unfailing breeze, which Derik noticed was brushing against Andi's face and through her hair.

"I can't believe how peaceful it is here. You've lived here for eighteen months?" he asked.

"It hasn't been all bad," she said, drawing her knees up into her chest. "I kind of made this my spot."

Derik saw a young woman. He was mesmerized by what she'd become. The now not-so-awkward pounding in his heart returned as he studied her face from the seat beside her. His eyes traced the entirety of her profile, landing on an inscription carved into the wooded armrest beside her. It listed the names of her four siblings in lowercase and below them, in a somewhat fashioned heart, read: "Derik." She followed his eyes as they arrived at the etching.

Sporting an enlightened look, he glanced back up to her face. Their eyes met, and for a moment, nothing else in the world mattered. He slipped his hand beneath hers. The beginning of an enamored grin peeked from his lips.

"You're really here, right?" Andi asked softly.

Derik nodded.

"I rehearsed this conversation, it seems, a thousand times from this very spot, before I—" She paused and frowned, then covered her lips with her free hand. "Before I decided I would never see you again." She closed her eyes while several tears edged her lashes and fell. She took a moment to gather herself and then continued. "If there's one thing I've learned about myself through all this, it's that I—" She paused again, then opened and landed her wet eyes upon his gentle expression. "Derik, I—" she said but was interrupted by Derik's single finger over her lips.

"Shhh," he whispered. He pulled her toward him and wrapped an arm around her. She nestled herself into his shoulder, then released a long overdue breath of reprieve. He thought of the earlier incident on the haystack in

the barn when her hands fell upon his and the somewhat awkward stirring he experienced. He found himself baffled on the dissimilarity, yet a blissful grin quickly
emerged as he openly welcomed the occasion at hand.
A mere minute or two had passed since she'd emptied
herself with that alleviating sigh when a peaceful slumber
fell over her evidenced by a single, ever-so-hushed snor-
ing breath. He reached for a pink flowery quilt hanging
from a polished oak quilt rack set up beside him, then
proceeded to drape it around her. He watched as her face
erased any remaining air of tension. Only a word more
expressive than *perfect* could have summed up that single
moment in time. If only he knew what shadow loomed
down the corridor of his morrow.

Derik left Andi on the porch for the alluring aroma of
homemade roasted duck. "Mmm, Pradicus, that has got
to be the best thing I've ever smelled in my entire life. So
how do you guys cook duck these days?"

Pradicus smiled, folded up a small cooking cloth, and
neatly set it down. "Roasted duck, lad, roasted. It does
smell wonderful, does it not? He patted Derik on the
shoulder and then proceeded out the screen door, joining
Andi on the porch.

Derik watched the screen door close. *Did they even
have screen doors in the twelfth century?* he asked himself as
the image of Jake sharing future technology with Pradicus
emerged. Shrugging it off, his eyes scanned the cottage
interior. Its warm décor made him feel considerably wel-

comed with various wildflowers positioned on and along the walls and strategically placed cooking utensils hanging throughout. The wood possessed an exquisite lacquered sheen, which fascinated Derik to no end.

"This place is incredible," he said, taking the liberty to explore more of the beautiful home. He opened and closed several doors and cupboards, noting the lack of creaking and smoothness of the hinges, and then he made his way to the second floor. He heard Andi's sluggish voice trickling in on the gentle breeze through one of the upstairs windows. Two rooms and a small den comprised the upper level. Though the doors of the two study rooms were open fully, it was the darkness looming around the edges of the nearly closed den's door that caught his attention. While the overall impression was that the door should have been closed, it undoubtedly was not, as it rested ajar slightly.

Captivated by curiosity, he gave it a gentle nudge, then a second later, a slightly more robust jolt. The door objected with a groan as it drudged across the swollen wood floor.

Derik peeked in. Pale rays from the sun's western setting crept along the floor as he proceeded to open the door farther. A sudden cool gust, laced with a trace scent of something he couldn't quite put his finger on, brushed against his face and through his hair, as if escaping past him.

The door continued to creak as it unhurriedly opened to its fullest extent. He stepped in. The light entering in from behind him was barely adequate for his eyes to adjust to the stark darkness. A window positioned on the side wall to his left was blanketed with what seemed like a black tar substance. Books upon books and papers unsteadily stacked characterized the tiny room.

It took his eyes another moment to adjust, but he soon discovered it was a journaling room. Derik treaded softly as the floor popped and grumbled with every step. On the wall opposite the window, he was able to make out an almost-hidden small door without a latch.

Furthering himself into the room one small step at a time, he came upon a desk. One book lay open on it. He bent down for a closer look and, with a single breath, cleared a thick layer of dust from its pages. His amulet, hanging down freely, took on a dim glow. He turned the journal slightly toward him, trying his best to follow what might as well have been a completely foreign language. A familiar word jumped out, then another.

"Oh, okay, I got this. It's Old English. Wow," he said, then stopped dead when he recognized the word *Jake*, followed farther down the page by another, which sent a twisting knot through his stomach. The word was his own name. *Derik*.

Forty or so minutes later, Andi found him upstairs in one of the study rooms overlooking the landscape from a window. "Hey, where'd you go?"

Derik didn't answer.

She quietly stood behind him and then rested her chin against his back. Her touch snapped him out of his daze.

"Andi. I'm sorry. I didn't hear you. Did you say something?"

"Hey, what's going on?"

He had an answer but tucked it away. "I'm so enjoying how beautiful it is here. Couldn't you just imagine living here for the rest of our lives? My goodness, I mean, as long as you like fish, you'd never have to go anywhere. It's perfect here. Where are all these heavenly getaways back in our time?"

Andi smiled and then wrapped both her hands around his arm. "I have to admit, it really hasn't been bad. So spill. What is it? You gonna tell me you're thinking about staying now?"

He turned and looked at her. They enveloped one another, each in the other's eyes, for a lengthy moment. "What... is it?" she asked.

"How many times have you been up here? The upstairs, I mean."

"Why?"

He shrugged his shoulders.

"Hundreds of times, well, between the two study rooms."

"What about that room?" he said, nudging his head in the den's direction.

"Oh, no. That door's been locked shut for—I don't know—months, years probably."

"Really?" he said and then paused. "Haven't you ever wondered what was in there?"

"I suppose. But it's always been locked. I mean, I don't even think Pradicus has the key. It's not been opened since I've been here."

He set his eyes over the landscape once again. "Are you saying you've tried to open it?"

"Well, Pradicus has. He's tried everything short of breaking it down."

"Is that what he told you?"

"Uh-huh. Plus, I've seen him try. So what's the sudden *mystery* about that room?"

"I was just in it."

Shock exploded in her expression. "What? You're so lying to me."

"I'm telling you I was just in there. It's a journaling room."

"That's not possible. I've tried getting into that room several times myself when he wasn't around. It's sealed shut from the inside."

"I'm telling you, Andrea Halle Schaffer, that I was just in that room. I read something I don't think I was privy to."

She stood back away from him. "Okay, show me. Open it."

"I'm not sure Pradicus would be happy if he found you in there."

She shifted her weight and then shot him a glare. "What are you basing that on?"

"Call it a hunch."

She turned away in a giggling snort. "You almost had me. I gotta tell you, that was hands down the best yet.

Come on. Dinner's almost ready. Doesn't it just grab you, the roasted duck? He douses it with spices I've never even heard of. Can you smell them?" She drew in its fragrance in a slow extended breath. "Oh, it's the best."

Pradicus called to the two of them from downstairs. "Sup's on."

She smiled. "You so almost had me." She grabbed one of his hands. "Come on," she added in a gleeful tone. "Wait until you taste this. This is the best cooked duck in the world."

"Roasted duck," Derik replied.

She laughed. "Oh … yes. Of course. *Roasted* duck."

13

After supper, Derik and Andi headed back out onto the porch. Andi snuggled up under the large pink quilt. She sat sideways, with her shoulder against the back support of the swing, facing Derik and wearing a contented smile. "I could so do this forever. Now that you're here, I mean."

Derik grinned, trying to hide his blushing. "Yeah, it's amazing. But you haven't forgotten what it's like back on the loft, have you?"

A yearning expression washed over her face. She cracked a trace of a smile. "No, home will always be the best," she said with a tinge of sadness.

Derik noticed her sliding her fingernail in and out of one particular grooved design on the arm of the bench. He'd not noticed it before, but how could he amidst the many etchings? "We'll get home, Andi. I promise. We'll get home."

She slid her eyes over to him and extended her smile in a manner that Derik perceived as particularly patronizing.

"Come on. I know that look. What is it?"

She inhaled slowly, turned her face entirely toward him, and then dismissed the impulse, returning her eyes to the etching.

"Hey, what was that?"

She didn't respond.

"All of a sudden I'm not privy to your thoughts, your ponderings? Since when?"

"Since a year and a half ago, Derik."

"Andi, that's not fair. *You* haven't been away from *me* for more than a few hours since the loft."

She nodded slightly, appearing to remind herself of the fact.

He touched her arm. "Whatever it is, it seems big," he said in a solemn tone. "Come on. We never kept secrets from each other." He sat up straight. "So spill already. After all, who would you share it with if not me?" he said magnanimously with one of his famous smiles.

She blew away the little shavings her finger had made and then took another long, contemplative look at the etched pi insignia Jake had left for her several months ago. She dragged her tearing eyes away from the etching and then slowly raised them to meet Derik's. "Jake," she said, "I would've told Jake."

Her bottom lip started quivering and, a short moment later, curled into a pathetic frown. Derik placed an open palm against her cheek, caressing her lips with his thumb. "You really need to get something off your chest. Tell me what happened," he said.

One particularly large tear streamed her cheek. "It's all my fault," she sniveled. She pressed her cheek into Derik's hand. "I told him not to go. But he said he had one last thing to do. I messed it all up by trying to stop him."

"You mentioned this a little earlier. How is it your fault?"

She raised her face to the sky and took in the incredible starry sight with a large inhale, letting out the air slowly. "He and Garren went out one morning. It had something to do with proving that Pradicus and Valicious were the same person. I don't know. I never got the whole story on their outing. Jake came back that night without Garren. He said he found Garren sleeping in the darkness of one of the pathways inside the mountain. I don't know about that either." She chuckled. "Actually, he said Garren hacked off a good ten years of his life there in that darkness." She chuckled again and then sniffled.

Derik cut in. "Oh, with how badly Garren caught Jake off guard?"

"Mm-hm. It reminded me of your 'sheep biscuits' that night in my basement," she said with a reminiscent smile.

Derik grinned with a dismissive rolling of his eyes.

"Anyway, they found each other just inside the mountain. Garren told Jake to come back here for a few things while he was going to go farther into the mountain since the horsemen were gone out looking for the two of them. Jake said he had something to take care of before he went back to the mountain to find Garren. Long story short, we had a fight, and I told him I didn't care if I never saw him again. Then I said I thought he was stupid for risk-ing everything and that I hoped he—" She paused.

Derik waited.

She finished her sentence somberly. "I said I hoped he met up with Lig Nædre. But I didn't mean it."

A momentary silence fell between them.

"I couldn't leave things like that, so I tried to find him that afternoon. I knew where he was going but didn't know when he would be there. He had this gold coin that he gave to me before he left. He said it would let me know when trouble was near. So I took it with me. I told Pradicus I was running an errand. I took the only horse he had and left. It was amazing how quickly that huge beast tracked me once I got near the mountain. I swear it's like it knew I was coming. I got off the horse and ran into the ivy. I think I must have run two miles without stopping once. But everywhere I went, there was Lig Nædre, just a few seconds away.

"The sun was starting to go down, so I thought I'd have a chance to run for it in the darkness after the sun had set. The coin kept a steady glow, so I knew trouble was still near. After waiting for a couple hours and not hearing a thing from the dragon, I took off in a dead sprint. I knew there was a wormhole across the plains. That's where Jake was headed. I got about halfway there when I twisted my ankle. I fell hard and smacked my forehead. I didn't know how badly I was bleeding, but I knew I had to keep going. I found out later it wasn't all that bad.

"I got to a place where I couldn't put any more weight on my ankle, so I stopped to rest. I was terrified being out in the open with Lig Nædre on the hunt. I realized the coin could probably be spotted in the darkness, so I threw it as far away from me as I could in the other direction. I hopped and crawled for a little while until I started feeling sick. The giant bump near my temple was throbbing so badly. Every time I moved even a little bit in one direction or another, it screamed at me. I know I threw up a few times because of the pain. So I stopped hopping and then only crawled for what seemed like miles until I found this safe little ravine. I fell asleep for who knows how long. But what awoke me was a heated burst of air. When I opened my eyes, I didn't know where I was, and the sky was still dark. It all came back to me so quickly, though.

"I rolled over onto my stomach, and when I did, I saw something; I wasn't sure what, but something told me it was the Jangus. In a sudden terror, I completely seized up. I didn't know if it was the Jangus, but something was definitely in the ravine with me, not far in front of me. I tried to move an arm, a foot, anything, but Derik, I was petrified.

"It moved toward me using the shadows. Since hot breath had awakened me, I thought whatever it was had paused to inspect me as it traveled the ravine and then headed away from me. But that couldn't be right because this creature seemed to be coming toward me while making a strange sound every few seconds. I couldn't tell what woke me. There was no wind, no breeze. Fearing it was the Jangus, I was sure I was seconds from death. I actually remember whispering to myself, 'Don't breathe. Dear God in heaven, help me not to breathe.' I caught glimpses of it but only when parts of it passed through the moonlight. I didn't know if maybe it was a small bear or perhaps a mountain lion.

"Then the trembles started in. I couldn't move any part of me at will, yet my entire body shook like crazy. The thing crawled closer—a few steps then a pause, then a few more steps and another pause. I imagined it tearing into me, thrashing me against the walls, and I wouldn't be able to do a thing to stop it. I wanted to scream, you know, to scare it off, but even if I wanted to, I couldn't. I was frozen. And then what if it didn't know I was there? If I did scream, would it attack me and kill me? Would it eat me? Or did it already know I was there, quivering like a cornered mouse with no defense to fight it off? Had it already determined I was its next meal?

"I heard the stirring of the soil just a foot or so in front of me. The thing had become quiet. It stopped. It made that strange sound once more. Suddenly, I heard thunder, and it was really thunder from the storm that had been brewing, not the Horsemen. It was about to rain, and all I could think at that moment was how this couldn't get any worse. I saw a crack of lightning shoot across the sky out of the corner of my eye. Then another one flashed somewhere between where I was and Broga Mountain. It lit up everything around me. I saw the thing in front of me. It was"—she stopped to swallow hard and then contorted her face while shaking her hands and arms—

"an ugly, furry, giant spider," she added in a high-pitched grotesque voice. Good krevins, Derik, it had like half a dozen or more black eyes, each the size of the tip of my thumb, all attached to a big, round head and body. Its fangs hung down like a sabertooth tiger's.

"I saw it and remember thinking it couldn't be real; it was way too big. I don't know where my voice came from, but I outright screamed like I never knew I could. I was suddenly free to move. I reached for anything and everything and grabbed a rock, then threw it at its face. The hit made this icky, soft-sounding thud, kind of like the sound you might get if you threw a baseball into a bale of hay. It was sickening. Then it spun this wet web around my leg and started dragging me. I clutched everything I could that was sticking out of the ground. I was screaming my fool head off. I got a hold of this little root and hung on. It seemed like my leg was about to be torn off, as hard as that spider was pulling. The lightning flashed again, and I saw the tunnel web in the side of the ravine it was pulling me toward. It finally stopped pulling and then began to crawl on top of me. I swear I punched it in one of its eyes, and it broke open like an egg. But it was much thicker and gooier than a yolk.

"It backed off for a second. I took the opportunity to reel my legs up underneath me and then started yanking on the root as hard as possible. I pulled it loose. On the end of it was a big clod of dirt. I started swinging it at the spider's face, but with every swing, it darted away and then lunged back at me.

"Finally, I threw the root at its face and the dirt clod exploded. I guess it blinded it. It backed off for a second, then made that noise again and rushed me. I put my arms across my face and screamed, waiting for its attack. It didn't. When I looked up, it was gone. Suddenly, its carcass fell from the sky and landed a few feet from me, making a sound like ten pounds of wet beef hitting the ground. Just a single splat, no bounce," she said, shuddering at the memory. "Right after that, out of the darkness came this very deep growl, then a rush of heated air. All at once, the entire area lit up with a burst of fire from behind me, followed by a roar that deafened my ears. The roar sounded like a lion's roar but being blasted out from a cruise ship foghorn.

"I got to my feet and limped away from the dragon as fast as I could. It found me, Derik. After eighteen months, it caught up to me. I remember wondering if it never really wanted to catch me but was just playing with me, feeling like if it had wanted to, it would have and with certain ease. I fell down before I could get very far.

"It was too dark to really see the dragon well. But it just stood there as if following some preconceived plan. It was so enormous, like a strangely-shaped cathedral. It must have been three or four stories tall. It blocked half the sky as it stood over me, with its wings stretched out and all majestic looking.

"I started scooting away, then made it back on to my feet and ran again the best that I could. But Lig Nædre stuck one of its feet in front of me, and I tripped over a claw. I got up again, and then, with a swipe of its foot, it

163

knocked me across a clearing to another ravine. I felt like I'd broken every bone in my body after that landing. Oh, I hurt so bad. I was so tired, so worn out. I remember just rolling myself into that second ravine. That's it."

Derik wore an incredibly intense look upon his face. Flabbergasted, he stammered out a few broken syllables and then decided to shut his mouth.

"After that, all I remember is the taste of blood in my mouth and how hungry I was. I don't even remember falling asleep or being sleepy. Derik, it was the most scared I've ever been in my life. But I do remember praying that Jake would find me. I guess not every prayer can be answered how we want.

"The next day I was awakened by Pradicus, who was holding Garren's satchel. He said he didn't know why it was left in the middle of the field but that he wanted to keep it for him in case he'd lost it. I don't know what happened to Jake. But I think if I could've found him that day, I at least could have told him I was sorry for what I said. I thought Jake and Garren both made it back home until you pulled out his phone earlier. Come to think of it, I'm not even sure where Garren's from. He's been here so long, and being an Everal, who knows where he calls home. Hmph. I never gave it any thought before now. But I knew where Jake was from and how badly he wanted to get home. Oh, wow. I can't even go there. And then you saw his watch." She placed a hand over her face. "This is going to drive me crazy." She looked over at Derik, who was still in shock over the spider story.

"You're serious. You were really attacked by a giant spider?"

She laid her head back and scanned the starry sky. After a moment, she turned her head toward him, and then her eyes slowly descended upon his smirk. "Does it really matter? After all, I'm alive."

"I'm sorry. I'm just … in shock."

"Can we forget about that?"

"If we get a chance, will you show me its webbed tunnel?"

"Are you really that dense? Has it occurred to you that spiders come from eggs? There's gotta be more of them out there. No, I'm not showing you were the web tunnel is. I would say you had better be kidding, but I know you better than that."

Derik grinned, then said, "Okay back to, uh, Jake. What was it again?"

"Geez, Derik, what is up with you? A girl might feel a little less transparent around you if you actually took the time to listen to her."

Derik rolled his eyes. "Whatever … yeah, a giant spider," he said skeptically under his breath.

She turned her head so she was looking perfectly straightforward. And there she sat with a saddened expression.

"Hey, I didn't mean to hurt your feelings," he said, briefly resting his hand on her knee. "I'm sorry. I can be such an idiot sometimes."

She slid her eyes toward him. "And a jerk," she said, shaking her head. "Still such the boy, for goodness sakes. I can tell you're an only child, believe me."

"Well, maybe if I'd been the one here by myself for a year and a half, I'd have little patience for me too. I'm sorry. I'm still the same me from yesterday—the same juvenile little teenage brat."

"All right, I guess I'm not being fair. But can you at least try to act just a little bit…older?" she asked with a diminutive wince.

He smiled and then sighed, gazing across the starry heavens and then landing his eyes back onto hers. "Look, there's a rugged older guy deep down in here somewhere; perhaps a masked super hero and debonair billionaire-type waiting to be discovered and chiseled out by the right…girl," he placed his hand onto hers, "with the right hands."

Andi grinned and then turned away, rolling her eyes, unsure of why she felt a sudden blushing. She rotated her head back toward him, wearing a smile that shouted she'd just been slapped across the face with a generic line from a sappy romance novel. "Why do I feel like I'm fourteen all over again?" She giggled.

Derik joined her in a chuckle and then squeezed her hand. "No one makes me laugh like you do." A sudden comprehension washed over his face for her last comment. "That was a slam, wasn't it? You just slammed me," he said, continuing in his laugh.

"I, uh," she stammered, "I didn't mean it as a slam," she said light-heartedly. "I was just meaning that…"—

she paused for a moment—"well, that." She then looked him straight in the eye and conceded with a laugh. "Okay, you got slammed."

Derik smiled quietly and then shot a gaze straight into the brightness of the moon. The moment sharply turned. A serious tone settled between them.

"Okay, you can't take the blame for Jake, Andi. Promise me you'll try to let that go." He released her hand and then stroked her arm with a finger. "Promise?"

Andi nodded. "Well, it feels a lot better having told someone." She then took Derik's hand and placed it within both of hers. "Especially you."

The comment produced an air of worth in Derik's expression that Andi had never before witnessed. The two of them shared a quiet moment within each other's eyes.

"So now what?" Derik asked.

"Now we trust."

Derik decided to leave that one alone and was more than content to sit quietly with Andi for a while longer.

The moon hung low in the southern sky, beaming in a bold brilliance unmatched by any evening either had seen back home.

Andi pulled out a ruffled paper scrap from beneath the quilt. She unfolded it and then began studying it under the low light from the oil lamps at either end of the swing.

Expecting that she'd share in its significance, Derik simply waited. "What've you got there?" he finally asked after a few quiet minutes.

"Mmm, nothing," she murmured without looking up.

He shrugged it off for a few more minutes, taking in the night's sky. He turned to her again. "Really, what is that?"

"I told you. Nothing."

"Come on. Let me see."

She sighed and then held it out. "Its nothing you'd be interested in."

He snatched it away from her. "What is this? A page out of a book?"

"Okay, so you've had a look. Now can I have it back?"

"Wait, what is it? Is this a page from the Bible?"

"Just give it back, Derik. It's not like you'd know what to do with it."

He handed it back, deciding not to hassle her about it. "So where's the rest of it?" He turned, giving her a skeptical glare. "Did the dog eat it?"

"You're not funny. It's all that's left of the book of Romans."

"So … what? You just reread the same page over and over?"

She held it against her chest. "I can't get enough of it. I've memorized every word on both sides of this page."

"How did you end up with a Bible anyway? That doesn't seem like something you'd usually come across at this point in history."

"Oh, but a gel-based, solar-charged phone does?" she retorted.

"Okay, point taken," he said with a partial grin. "I guess I'm wondering why someone would bring one with them. I mean, we came so suddenly. I guess that leaves me to assume someone had to have been reading it when they were taken." He thought of the mundane silliness of it all. "Come on. Really, who sits around and reads the Bible?" he added with a scoffing tone.

She quickly threw him a dim-witted look, holding up her page.

"Besides you," he said, sniggering and shaking his head. "Geez, I don't see why or how anyone could slave over the same dreary thing day after day. Well, I hope you at least get something out of it," he said rather patronizingly.

"Whatever, Derik. Like I said, it's nothing you'd be interested in … or understand."

"But how can anyone be interested in it? It's just a bunch of 'thou shalts.' Who needs it?"

She ignored him, returning to her reading.

"Okay, what do you get out of it?"

"Don't worry about it."

"No, really, what keeps you reading the same old thing over and over?"

"You don't really wanna do this, Derik. Just … never mind."

"Look, I'm *intrigued*," he said, mocking her earlier use of the word.

"Intrigued?" she said with a grin. "We're back to that, are we?"

"Look, if you don't wanna tell me, fine. I just thought you might want to share—"

"Share what?" she interrupted. "Share something precious to me that you'd just as quickly toss to the wind? No, thanks."

"Don't get all bent out of shape. I didn't mean to step on any toes."

"You still don't get it, Derik. You've only been here a few hours. You're still the same you who ate peaches in the barn yesterday. I'm not. I'll never again be that naïve person who sat in the haystack with you. I've had to search for answers, for understanding. And when those things didn't reveal themselves, I had to look deeper. I had to look down deep into myself. And what did I find? I found an emptiness that desperately needed filling. That's when I came across the book of Romans. Back then, it was just a slim, vinyl-bound book with printed notes and comments on how to read and understand Paul's writing. And nobody even gave it to me, Derik."

She looked away briefly, taking a moment to revisit the memory. "I came upon it by accident—trying to ditch the rain—and there it was, safely tucked under the cleft of a rock, as if it were waiting for me to find it."

She looked up at him, pausing as tears filled her eyes. Then she continued in a slow, solemn tone. "I found it on the very day I gave up on you. It was the only time in my entire life..." She sniggered, cracking a small transparent smile. "Yeah, my long-lived nineteen years, right? Anyway, it was the only time I actually came to the end of myself, Derik. And God was there to meet me. I poured myself into the pages and used the comments and helps to gain understanding. As I read each day, I found, not only answers, but truth. The words spoke life to me. And each time I read through it, I discovered something completely new, like I'd never read it before. I can't wait to read the rest of the Bible. I don't even know how many more books there are.

"Then out of the blue, Garren walked by and asked what I was reading. I told him. He suddenly took tremendous interest in me. He sat down and asked me to tell him about it. Well, after I did, he leaned toward me and said I was right on track. He started spouting off all this stuff about faith and difficulty, so I asked him to slow down and explain what he was saying. He said something I'll never forget: 'It's just around the corner.' I asked him what was around the corner. He said, 'What you need to sustain you.' He said God puts these promises along our way and we can tell when one is near because the road starts getting tough to walk. In fact, he said he can tell by the look of almost any person how far away or close they are to that next promise. He said he's seen it over and over again. It's always during that last bit when people start to give up and they don't realize what they need is just around the corner. He said that's what hope is, according to the book I held in my hands. Then he showed me. It was right there, Romans chapter five." She took note of Derik's unmoved expression and sighed. "I just wish you could show that you cared even a little bit. I mean, you don't have to be an Everal to understand there's more to life than just what we see here."

"You don't have to be a what?"

"Sorry, an Everal is someone who lives a very long time. It's kind of like in the days of Adam and Enoch and them. For some reason the gene reemerges after several generations. Everals' bodies age much slower than the average person."

Derik groaned rather dismissively. "That's such hogwash. What have they been feeding you all these months?"

"I don't expect you to understand any of what I'm saying."

"That sounds a little … demeaning," he snapped back. "But I'm not offended."

"You know what, Derik? I'm the one who got the raw end these past eighteen months, yet somehow, through it all, I can see how I came out on top." She paused, coming to a realization. "I've never quite thought about it like this, but when we get back, I get to pick up where I left off with so much more than I had before." The tinge of a gleeful titter sparked in her voice. "Oh, I can't wait. Derik, I'll get to see my little darlings again and Mom and Dad. Wow, it's gonna be so good to see everyone."

She summed it up with a weighty sigh, then turned her attention to the vastness of the star-swarmed sea blanketing the night above them. Her thoughts centered on the sheer goodness of her Lord. "God has been here every step of the way with me. My old life seems so empty now when I think back on it."

"What if you go back to what your life used to be without all these changes?" Derik asked. "What if you don't remember anything about any of this?"

Andi looked at him with utmost sincerity. "If I knew that going into it, I'd stay here. There's no way I want to separate myself from Jesus and all He's become to me. But that's not really a consideration. I've been over this so many times with Pradicus. He's gotta be sick to death of explaining it. Let's see. How'd he tell me to say it... 'Under the skin is my measure within.' What that means is, as I develop and mature in my own progression of time, I'll continue to advance despite how time bends around me."

"Wait. You're saying that if I were to go back by myself, then return in a week or two, I wouldn't skip over time and somehow become older or younger?"

"No, because time as you know it only advanced a week or two."

"Well, what about you? Would you be the same age?"

"Here's where it gets tricky. You'd leave my time plane, but I would continue to age as normal. But the next time I see you, I might have lived twenty years in my time plane while yours only advanced two weeks, meaning I actually lived twenty years while you were gone."

"And then if we went back together at that point?"

"I'd almost be as old as my parents, and you'd still only be two weeks older but only because I actually lived those twenty years. It's the same reason I'm eighteen months older right now."

Derik gave thought to everything she just said. "So you'd actually consider staying here?"

"You still don't understand. This is my life now. I've moved forward, and my past will always be a part of me. Don't get me wrong. I desperately want to get back to my family. But if it meant losing all that I've gained here, meaning losing what I've learned about who I am, who Jesus is, I'd choose to stay." She looked down at her ragged page. "That's what this means to me."

Derik smiled softly. "That's cool. Wow, you so are not the same person I knew this morning."

Andi exhaled a belabored sigh that waned away into a contemplating pause, followed by soft chuckle. "I can't tell you how strange it is to hear you say that. It's such a long time ago for me, like maybe that entire part of my life was just a dream. I can't imagine what things look like from where you're sitting. Well, that's not true. I guess I can. But you'll never know what it looks like from where I'm sitting."

"Honestly, I hope I never have to."

"I've learned so much about how people lived without modern conveniences. It makes me sick to think how spoiled I used to be. I feel it's much more rewarding to live this way. There's an appreciation for the small things, things we take for granted, like roasted duck. We had to hunt for that little guy. It's not like running down to the local market place and picking up dinner for six so we can make it home in time for television. Geez, I might never watch television again. I love living like this. The world moves slower, we talk, we get to know—I mean really know—one another, and God is so good. It's amazing how much I've had to lean on His provision. What an opportunity for Him to reveal Himself." She yawned. "I know we don't have air conditioning. I have actually missed that. But most of the months have been okay." She yawned again. "So you ready to call it a day?"

"I'm not tired. It's only eight o'clock. I've only been up for, like, thirteen hours." He felt a reciprocating yawn stir and begin to well up but ceased it in his throat before it could engulf him.

"Well, I've been trying to keep busy since sun up and, of course, didn't sleep a wink last night," Andi said, recalling the mixed feelings she encountered each time Pradicus ventured off to wait for Derik.

Derik replied with a somewhat patronizing nod. His indifference tore at her.

"Geez, Derik, really?" Her sudden shift in tone fell on hollow ears. "I just told you I've been trying to keep busy all day. That doesn't mean anything to you? And you have no idea, no concept, of why I wasn't able to sleep last night?"

He shook his head nonchalantly.

"Have you gotten denser over the time I've spent here, or is my memory just that bad? I guess I've forgotten what a piece of work you can be sometimes."

"Huh?" he said quite obliviously, trying his best to follow the last thought.

"Good Lord, what is the world coming to? Every month, this being the ump-teenth time, Pradicus went off for two days—"

"Oh, to find me," he interjected and probably with more cheer than would've been appropriate.

Andi rolled her eyes. "Unbelievable," she muttered. She glanced away for a second and then swung back around with a fierce look. "I gotta tell you, Derik, it wasn't easy all those times wondering if I was ever gonna see you again, dealing with the downside of hope."

"Wow."

"Wow? That's all you have to say? Do you know what I've been through this whole time? I've changed. I've grown up. And you? You're a jerk. You haven't changed a bit. You're exactly the same as you were the last time I saw you." She stopped, realizing how ridiculous a statement it was. She held him in her glare until, crease by crease, her firm visage shaped into a half-relenting grin.

He chuckled. "Yeah, I was gonna say—"

"You didn't deserve that," she said, cutting in. "Well, you kinda did, but—"

"Yeah, okay. I get it," he said, placing a hand on her arm. "You gotta know, though, it's so out of my universe to put any of this together."

She nodded with yet another yawn. "I know. It's still dizzying, even after a year and a half."

Derik's suppressed yawn finally won out, overtaking his every effort to restrain it. He grunted. "Now you've done it. There'll be no going back from that one. Well," he conceded, "it's not like I'm gonna be able to grab a soda and a slice of pizza and fall asleep watching TV."

"Oh, that sounds really good right now," she said, licking her lips. "With wings and buttermilk ranch. Oh, I'm so all over that. And not those wimpy mild wings. I'm talking hot," she said with a declarative nod.

"Nuclear," they said together. Both broke into a fit of laughter.

176

Derik realized her laugh had changed, even if only minutely. It seemed to him that it had, in a sense, matured. "Yeah, see," he said, putting aside the observation, "you really do miss the good stuff back home."

She held a quiet gaze for another few seconds. "Seriously, I can't tell you how delicious that sounds right now. I wonder how long it's been since I've actually sat and thought about pizza, not to mention wings and a soda."

"How about we make it a date?" Derik said. "Tomorrow night, after we get back, we'll get some pizza, nuclear wings, and a couple sodas, and then together watch a good chick flick."

The certainty in his tone struck her—the ease with which he discounted the unforeseen, the unfathomable, so unfamiliar, so confident. "And, of course," he continued, "I'll spring for some chocolate ice cream. And I'm talking the good stuff with hot fudge, nuts, and whipped cream. But only after you catch up with your family, that is."

She sat forward, frightfully aware of the mounting air of hope. How many times had she promised herself she'd never return to that place where notions like faith and possibility are exchanged for words like *impeded*, *thwarted*, and *despondency*? Would things be different this time? Could they be?

"Derik, I don't know if I can give into that again. If anything happens, anything at all, preventing our return..." she said, pausing, gravely concerned for her emotional soundness. She closed her eyes. "You just don't know, Derik. You really have no idea."

He took her by the hand and held it firmly. "Hey, it's not the same as it was before," he said, smiling gently. "I'm actually here with you this time. That's gotta mean something." Her eyes held to his without release. "Let me tell you something. The last thought I had hanging on to that beam had nothing to do with bringing you back. It had everything to do with being with you and making sure you weren't alone."

The apprehensive frown she wore slowly stretched into an optimistic grin.

"Look, I fully plan on making it back. It may not be tomorrow, but it'll be soon. I just know it."

She glanced away, reflecting on his thoughts back on the beam.

He released her hand for a purposeful gesture. "Besides, I have to make it back for Mindy Blake."

Her tone quickly swelled into annoyance. "I could've gone a lifetime without hearing that name ever again," she said through gritted teeth.

"Mindy asked me to clean up the audio from her video of Principal Haring—you know, the 'Teacher of the Year' interview she's submitting for Channel Six News. Well, tomorrow, they're previewing it at a school assembly—of course, in her highness's honor, don't you know. Word is she's already prepared a 'shocked' acceptance speech, even though they don't announce the winner for three more months. Like the evil witch even has a chance. Give me a break."

"Oh, my crackers, what have you done?" Andi charged with a cynical squint.

"Well, you know that audio recording from about two years ago that we've kept under wraps? Come on, you have to remember … Principal Haring … the brownies … "

A blank stare washed over Andi's face. She began to wonder what other memories her twelfth-century excursion might have stolen from her.

"I cannot believe that this, of all things, has somehow fallen out of your brain. Okay, fine. You at least have to remember how she always confiscated student's sweets, especially brownies, during oral health week and then stuffed her face with them after lunch was over."

She shook her head with a detached smirk, somewhat surprised at how her memory was failing her.

"Well, I suggested double chocolate with laxatives, but you came to school with double chocolate, double laxatives, stating how you were gonna get her good."

Andi's jaw dropped as she sat lingering in suspense.

"Jenny, her disgruntled aid, took your recorder—voice activated, mind you, or sound activated, in this case—and planted it behind the toilet … any of this ring a bell yet?"

Her face contorted, as if reaching for a faraway memory.

"Well, it wasn't but an hour or so before she was spotted heading down the hall back to her office in the 'I have to go *now*' quickstep."

Andi burst out with a short giggle and then slapped a hand over her mouth while her eyes jolted open like saucers.

"It wasn't all the cussing that had us on the floor laughing when we finally listened to the recorder, but your comment about the tommy gun."

A screaming laughter ensued but only for a moment as recall instantly dawned. Caught in the midst of a full on noiseless belly laugh, she gasped so profoundly it completely stole her breath as her frenzy continued breathlessly.

"Yeah, now you remember," Derik affirmed. "Well, I laid her tommy gun over the background music that Principal Haring handpicked specifically for one part of the video."

Her hysterics continued, now combined with foot stomping and tears.

"She's gonna drop a brick. I mean, considering the expletives on the recording, we can all pretty much imagine the theatrics that took place."

She reached out and grasped his arm. "And you want to go back?" she managed through winded breath.

"I wouldn't miss it for the world."

She gained some control. "You are so dead," she replied. "Wait a minute. Didn't we get her cussing *you* out on that recording?"

"Yeah, but she couldn't prove anything. I'm the first person she points at for everything. Don't you remember?"

"Well, she's gonna know it was you after the recording plays on the video."

He shrugged his shoulders. "She's got it coming. And the best part is, it'll be one of those life-shaping moments psychologists talk about. You know what I mean. Some mumbo jumbo about all of us having five or six defining or life-impacting moments that affect us forever and ever. This is gonna be one of those," he said, chuckling maniacally.

"You are horrible."

"But she so deserves it," he said, feeling satisfied.

"Well, I know you well enough to know you're gonna do what you want to do."

"That's right. My ways are set. I'm too far gone."

"Well, I can say life is so much more *interesting* with you around." She eyeballed the heart with his name carved into its center, then glanced back at him. A peculiar smirk, unfamiliar to Derik, crept into a contemplating grin.

"What does that look mean?" he asked.

"Mmm, never know. I'm going to bed. Thanks for the laughs, really. I very much needed that tonight." She stood up, offered a good-night smile that sent Derik's stomach into knotted fits, and then entered the cottage.

"Wow," he said, rubbing his eyes amidst a drawn-out yawn. He then stood up after a minute of reflection and followed her in.

Fighting to keep his eyes open, Derik laid a sheet out on the floor of one of the upstairs rooms and then collapsed on it. He was lost in slumber within seconds.

Later that night he visited the dark den again, except this time the room had called to him in his dreams. He found himself standing in front of the small door. The eeriness, the scent of something familiar, the unfriendly presence, all of it met him there. He looked over his shoulder, into the deeper darkness, to where the journaling desk sat. A shadow hovered over it, and as his eyes adjusted, he recognized it as the silhouette of a man. He was writing. Derik's overall impression was that this was not Pradicus.

A small bump from the other side of the small door stole his attention. His heart leapt in fear. He quickly cast his eyes toward it. Listening to the pounding of his pulse within his ears, he wondered if a part of him knew what lay in wait for him. The door narrowly moved back and forth, as if being stealthily tested by whatever loomed on its opposite side.

Derik snuck a peek back over his shoulder to find the corner empty this time. His focus returned to the undersized gateway, but gateway to what or from what? Clenching his fists in unrest, he thought of turning away from it but then knew he couldn't or, more importantly… wouldn't. Something was awry, and though he felt terror teetering at the edge of his emotions, he couldn't explain the sudden allure. He felt for his amulet, probing the tips of his fingers about where it normally lay, suddenly aware of and stumped by its absence.

He drew in what courage he could gather with a weighty inhale, swallowed hard, then took one short, shuffling step toward the small door, and then abruptly halted as the pungent stench of death filled his nostrils. Not malodorous decaying remains, but simply death, , an unexplainable smell which captures the very absence of life itself. It suddenly registered with him—the familiar scent. He'd caught a trace whiff of it in the cavern. It was the underlying, almost indiscernible odor which lurked beneath that of the musty lake water and putrid human remains.

Pressing on beyond the trepidation, he reached his hand out toward the small door when suddenly the entire wall was met with a fierce *slam* from the other side. The room shook violently. Derik jumped; then there was another *slam*. Derik jumped again. Dust and wood particles fell from the ceiling while cracks splintered the wall. A final brutal smash blew a gaping hole in the wall six feet wide, floor to ceiling, sending the door whistling across the room. The explosive surge threw Derik aside. He landed on his hip and shoulder and slid several feet across the wood floor.

Quickly sweeping the dust and debris from his face with a forearm, he gazed in horror at what entered the room from the other side. It was a Gray Rider upon his enormous, terrifying horse. Suddenly, an emerald-green light cut the darkness and burned brilliantly from the amulet which the rider wore around his neck. A deformed face glowed radiantly among the cast shadows. It appeared to him at first as Jake's face, but as his vision sharpened, he gasped in stunning horror to discover it was his own. The realization turned his stomach so pointedly that the startle jarred him right out of his sleep. He sat up, sweating, panting, wondering what could have possibly stirred him so, for his memory served no recollection. He closed his eyes after taking a minute to settle, then lay down again and fell back to sleep.

14

Waking to the smell of coffee and flapjacks, Derik smiled, recalling traces of one outlandish dream involving an older Andi. Expecting to see the old red barn out his second-story window, he opened his eyes and sat up in a panic, realizing it wasn't a dream at all. It was his first glimpse into a world that Andi spoke about the prior evening. Her words reiterated in his thoughts: *You just don't know, Derik. You really have no idea.* Mulling over the rampant barrage of "what ifs" and "what nows," he felt his pulse quicken and, for the first time in recent memory, had no bearings for what on earth to expect. The lack of solid footing in his current circumstance lent itself to a rising uneasiness. After taking a minute to reorient himself, sitting silently, he came to rest on one soft, reassuring thought. A second later, her voice carried into the still air where he sat. Listening to the sound of not just a familiar voice but her voice at the top of his morning had warm fuzzies chasing away all apprehension. A chord struck in his heart as he listened to the melody of her tone while she milled around downstairs, preparing breakfast with Pradicus. In that single moment, disquiet melted away into serenity, and he found himself challenging whether he would actually want to go back. Gazing around the room, he took in all he could of Pradicus. The thought occurred to him that if for some reason they did stay or had to stay, Pradicus would probably fall into a father-sort-of role for Andi, which followed logically to father-in-law. He smiled then shook it off, curtailing the notion.

"Hey, sleepyhead," Andi said in a welcoming tone. "Now what would put a smile like that on your face this early in the morning?"

Her sudden presence startled him and, in his estimation, was the reason for the unexpected myriad of thoughts and feelings rushing through him like a current.

Wondering if she could have possibly read his thoughts through the smile, he grimaced and looked away. He quickly recovered, though—a strength on which he played well. "I, uh, was actually thinking about you."

She stepped into the study with a grand look about her. "Really? Please do tell."

"The truth?"

"Of course," she said, emitting a soft glow of anticipation.

"I was thinking that if, um, you and I didn't go back for whatever reason, you know, that there's a pretty good chance that, well, we—you and I—would probably become more than good friends and move on to the next level." He watched her try to hide a look that—at least in Derik's estimation—piqued her interest. "Yeah, you know, like getting to be neighbors and no longer good friends but *super* good friends … forever."

"Smart aleck," she said, shaking her head with a grin. "You're what my grandfather calls a 'whippersnapper.'"

"What do you mean? You wanted the truth."

"Truth, my horse's behind. Since when have you ever stood on the truth? Come on down. Breakfast is ready," she said, turning away, chuckling.

She made it down the stairs when she heard him retort, "You have a horse?"

Finishing breakfast, Derik pushed his plate away. "Pradicus, how do you cook so well without the modern stove?" he asked.

"I must say, it is a process. And a process one must learn quickly if one wishes to enjoy the food he prepares."

"We've cooked everything, haven't we, Pradicus?" Andi stated proudly.

"Ah, yes, and the pleasure has been all mine to have thy company."

Derik looked at Pradicus squarely. "So you've been trying to get into that room upstairs, huh?"

Andi gave him a kick in the shin, along with an equally painful glare. The table became quiet.

"Why, yes, my boy," Pradicus answered.

"He didn't mean to bring it up, Pradicus. Did you, Derik?" she said with firm intention.

"Well, I only ask because—" He was interrupted by another kick in the shin.

"I happened to mention it last night, that's all," Andi said, cutting in. "I probably shouldn't have, but it kind of stands out when you're up there."

Derik directed an offended scowl toward Andi. He turned his attention to Pradicus. "I'm sorry. I don't mean to pry."

"No, no, it's fine," he answered. "The room was once a map room filled with all sorts of charts, plottings, and such." He began fiddling with his beard while a blank stare caught his gaze. "One day, long, long ago, mine brother and I had a falling out. The house belonged to me, but through a chain of events set in motion by his evil mind, he stole it out from under me. In the process, he thought to have killed me. It was none but the mother of that young kraken who saved me from Lig Nædre and the clutches of mine malevolent brother. After he realized I was still alive, he made a final attempt to finish me.

He chose this very house with which to carry out his purpose. I managed to gain the upper hand, at which time he retreated into the map room. He locked the door shut. Never had he known me to be a life taker, but he knew all too well I was prepared to take his that very day. He remained in the room for several days. I was sore afraid he would destroy my every work, so I kept from breaking down the door. Knowing he would need to exit at some point, I locked the door from this side and placed a group of crossbows just off the window to hinder his escape there. He sealed the window from the inside with a resin or tar to keep the window from shattering, as well as to keep me from seeing in, even though I haven't

187

had access to it from the outside. He became quieter as the days drudged on. I didn't know whether he eventually fell dead or simply loomed amidst the darkness. I pleaded with him to come out and make amends but was never answered. I decided I would break down the door. I needed to. After repeated attempts, I realized he had an extended lock in place—a lock of supernatural or perhaps magical operation. Finally, I thought to smoke him out. I forced enough smoke into that room to kill ten bears. I concluded he must have died despite my attempts to reconcile. But as we all know, a body without life produces quite the stench."

His eyes regained focus and alternated between the two of them. "Mine brother is alive, and he isn't in that room, and I have yet to open the door. Where he went and when he left is still a mystery. I do know that only since then has he been using Lig Nædre for wormholes to hunt people."

"Hunt people? Specific people?" Derik asked, his brow furrowed. "What would be a reason for such a thing?"

Pradicus, venting his anger for the locked room, gripped the cup before him, squeezing it, obliterating it with a brutal glare. "Tell me, Derik, what didst thou find in there?" he asked without so much as the flicker of a lash or stir of an eye.

The question came so unexpectedly that Derik completely lost his breath. His eyes, widely held in startle, held fast to Pradicus's suddenly firm expression upon him. "I…I…" he stammered, searching for a way out. The typical quick recovery eluded him.

Pradicus slammed a fist onto the table. "What didst thou find?" he demanded with authority.

"Journals. N-n-nothing else. Well, maybe a map or two."

Andi sat dumbfounded. A whisper passed her lips. "You were serious?"

"Show me!" Pradicus exclaimed.

"Well, I didn't open the door. I don't know how or why it opened."

"Show me," he repeated, standing up. "You're the key to all of this, young man." He leaned in toward Derik. "You will stop Valicious."

Derik swept his eyes across the table to meet Andi's. The general sense of her expression emanated well beyond flabbergasted and on to holy Jiminy Cricket.

Derik led the other two up the stairs to the locked door. It wasn't resting open as it had been the night before, though the eeriness remained. The door seemed to know they were coming. It was as if it dared them to approach. Derik wondered if the slit between the frame and the top of the door had suddenly begun seeping obscure shadows, somehow unable to contain the thick, billowing darkness stirring from behind the door. If Derik didn't know better, he'd have sworn he felt, for just a moment, a sudden awareness that at least one of the other two he was with was vehemently unwelcome.

Holding his breath, he grasped the knob gingerly, turning with a cringe to look over his shoulder at Andi while he did so. Anticipation swelled as their eyes met. She nodded slightly in a gesture to proceed. He glanced past her to Pradicus. The man's stern countenance gave Derik the impression that suspense had given way to concern. He turned back to the door, exhaled, and, with a firm squeeze, rotated the knob. Pressing his shoulder into the door, he nudged it. It objected. He stole a quick half look over his shoulder and then cleared his throat, beginning to picture what may lay in wait for him on the other side.

"Come on, Derik," Andi asserted.

Derik mustered his courage and gave it a heartier jarring. The door gave an inch. His amulet offered a dim glowing.

"Just give it a man-sized push," Andi declared, driving herself into Derik's back. The amulet exploded into a radiating green illumination and then was suddenly and mysteriously snuffed.

"An-di," he retorted, falling into the door along with her and then onto the ground as the defiant door was thrust open. Papers scattered abroad amidst the whirling dust.

Andi sat herself up while her eyes traveled the room. "Wow," she said. "It *is* a journaling room."

Pradicus stepped in, hesitant, cautious, scanning every detail. His attention fell on the new little door in the wall. He lunged toward it, tearing away at every obstruction between himself and the anomaly. "Blast. I should have known." Having no knob or lever, he ran his fingers along its edges and then rammed it several times with a shoulder, followed by a few determined kicks. "Blast."

"What is it?" Andi asked, taken aback by the unexpected outburst.

He turned to her. "I need something... the material Jake described months ago, the explosive..."

"Dynamite?" she suggested.

"Yes, yes, and to use dynamite as a reference, Andrea and Derik, what we've accomplished here today is the lighting of a fuse, and a short one at that, I'm afraid. Derik, I do not think Valicious counted on thy presence here. I believe we have just changed everything."

Andi and Derik exchanged looks.

"We haven't much time," Pradicus said, beginning to peruse the room.

"Pradicus, what do you mean?" Andi asked.

He stopped in front of the volume that Derik had laid eyes on the evening before. He cleared a thin layer of dust with a quick, firm blow.

Derik watched him skim over the pages. The memory of seeing his name within the very same pages began to haunt him. Feeling like a pawn at someone else's hand of play, he clenched his teeth. The words simply fell out. "How'd you know? How in the heck did you know to expect me?" The cynicism in his voice grabbed Andi's attention.

"Whoa, what's going on? Why all the excitement all of the sudden?" she asked.

"Ask him," Derik replied.

"What's with you, Derik? You're being kind of rude."

"Remember last night when you found me standing at the window in the study?" She nodded. "I saw something—more like read something. I was so floored that it, well, changed everything."

"You're not making a lot of sense right now, Derik. What's all this about?"

"Tell her, Pradicus. What's sitting right in front of you that you never told her about?"

Dismissing fearful thoughts of sedition left and right, she directed herself toward Pradicus with a loyal demeanor. "It doesn't matter, Derik," she said. "Whatever you saw or thought you saw has a reasonable explanation."

"Oh, you don't understand—" he retorted.

"Derik, you're being extremely rude. Now drop it," she asserted.

Pradicus closed the journal, then whisked away with it under his arm so quickly that the underflow gust from his gliding morning robe left the floor whirling in dust.

Andi took another mesmerizing glance around the room, landing her gaze on Derik. Without a word or acknowledgment, with the exception of a scrutinizing squint, she turned on a heel to exit.

"Wait, Andi, you have to know what's really going on here. It's not at all what you think."

She held her stance, facing away from him. "How would you have any idea what I really think or know?" she said. "Honestly, Derik, I'm not who I was. And you've only known who I am now for, what, twelve hours?" She glanced over her shoulder. "There's a lot you don't know," she muttered sourly. Then she proceeded out of the room.

While standing quietly amidst the stillness, a tingling sense lingered about him—a feeling that clutched his inner soul, screaming he was no longer alone. It accompanied the scent he'd smelled earlier, barely discernable and trailing away as quickly as it had come. An unfamiliar acuteness had him focus his attention straightaway on the small door. As he approached it, his amulet, unbeknownst to him, began to flicker dimly once again. His eyes lit up as the perilous curiosity of it all enthralled him. He stopped two feet short of the door, however, studying it, suddenly convinced that an unfriendly presence loomed on its opposite side. His stomach turned at the thought that a mere arm's length separated him from whatever it was and yet engrossed him at the same time.

The sound of a sudden cold thud from the other side of the door made him jump. He turned to take a step but inadvertently lost his footing. He didn't stumble just anywhere, however, but fell toward the small door and, in fact, into the door face first. He quickly pushed himself away, staring the door down as if it had something to do with his tumbling into it. A bit startled, he slowly backed away when suddenly a blot of condensation, like heated breath on a cold window, appeared on Derik's side of the door, followed by a second, more resounding *thud* that shook the floor.

"Stick it in your ear," he unconfidently snarled, then hastily left the map room. The door slammed shut behind him as he left. He quickened his pace and nearly leapt down the stairs, landing with eyes scanning the room for the other two. "Andi," he said, spotting her across the room, "what's, uh, the plan?"

She stood in the corner where she kept her bedding and clothing. A partial wall separated a similar area where Derik assumed Pradicus slept. "Leave me alone," she replied.

"Am I missing something? I mean, didn't you say you two have been trying to get into that room for months? I would think you'd be a little appreciative."

"Oh, is that what this is about, Derik?" she said, busying herself with minute detail touch-ups. "Well, here you go … thanks. Will that suffice?"

"No, it won't. What the heck is going on here, Andi? The door opens, and the two of you suddenly take on entirely different identities? I'm not the bad guy here."

"You were a real jerk up there. Sometimes I just can't stand you, Derik. Sometimes I wish I never knew you, and right now, I wish you hadn't come."

"What do you mean? Andi, I don't get it. If I've done something so bad, tell me what it is."

"You've ruined everything, Derik. We had a good thing going here, and then you show up and shatter it right in front of me. Why'd you have to come here?"

"What? And you think *I* wasn't making sense? What the heck do you want from me?"

"Just go back to that room where you belong."

Watching as everything in his new little world began to implode around him, he took a flabbergasted step back, his eyes dancing about the room. They fell on a familiar partial page. He snatched it and held it up in front of Andi. "This is where we were last night. Romans. Remember?"

She swept her eyes away with disinterest. He took the sheet fragment and began reading. "Do not be conformed to this world, but be ye transformed by the renewing of your mind, that ye may prove what is that good and acceptable and perfect will of God."

She glared at him with a blazing disgust, but as he continued, her eyes found solace.

He scanned the print for something, anything he could easily understand, and then continued. "Be kindly affectioned one to another with brotherly love in honor preferring one another; not slothful in business; fervent in spirit, serving the Lord, rejoicing in hope; patient in tribulation, continuing constant in prayer…" Preparing to continue, he looked up to find her in quiet tears. He slid the paper into his pocket then reached for her.

Stepping into his arms, she rested her head against his shoulder. "I'm so sorry, Derik. Please, please forgive me. I didn't mean any of what I just said. In that room, it's like something got a hold of me. I didn't even see it until you started reading. That's the power of the Word of God, Derik. It keeps you balanced. It keeps you… well, it keeps you. I had my guard down, and whatever it was knew so."

"I'm just glad you're back."

"Derik, I need to share more with you on that later. But right now, you need to tell me what you saw in that journal. I think Pradicus is in trouble, like he wasn't supposed to find it yet."

"Well, long story short, someone knew—" he said with pause, and then he continued, "that I was coming."

"That's true. I told Pradicus long ago to expect you."

"No, I mean, someone planned for me to be here."

She cocked her head. "What do you mean?"

"My name was in the journal, which means my name's been in that journal since … before any of this, before you got here to tell him about me."

A blank look washed over her face, which, after weighing a few considerations, fashioned into a concerned frown. "Are you sure? It was dark in there. Maybe you're mistaken."

"Not only my name, but Jake's also."

Silence filled the room as the declaration shook her. *"What?"* she asked, placing an open palm against her forehead. "All of this … has been part of some stinking, conniving plan?"

"Well, I thought you already knew that."

Her eyes raced across the room from one spot to another as she tried to put pieces together. "Well, I did, I guess, just not quite like this. This is different. All of a sudden, we're talking maniacal, cunning, planned out." She was quiet for several seconds. "Did you see my name?" she asked with a determined stare.

"Andi, at this point, I don't really think—" he said before she cut him off.

"Did you see my name?" she snapped, wondering if any purpose surrounded her lengthy absence from family and good ol' Nebraska normalcy.

He was reluctant to answer, seeing where she was going with it. "No."

Fury arose out of her determined countenance. "That reptile-loving bastard."

"Andi…" Derik said while fishing for something more to say.

"I'm not even supposed to be here? I've been through hell and back by accident?"

"Who's saying that? Just because your name isn't in the journal doesn't mean you're here by accident."

He watched her pick up a glass and hurl it against a wall. It exploded into pieces and hundreds of shattered slivers. She picked up another and drew her arm back.

"Whoa, whoa, time out. That isn't the way to handle this. I'm sure Pradicus has a good idea of what's really going on."

"Pradicus, yes, of course. He must know something." She called to him, but he failed to answer. She stepped out onto the porch and then called for him again.

"Look, I thought we had something to do today. Remember our plan?"

She hesitated for a second, then walked to the edge of the porch and called for Pradicus yet again.

"Andi, his brother doesn't know what we're planning. We can talk about this on the way. We've got to get going if we're gonna have any chance of getting back home."

She stopped and looked at him. "Yes, you're right. I'm sorry"

"Now here's what we need to do first—" he said just before a sudden thundering rumble distracted him, followed by a surging boom that penetrated the air from above. Water from the river immediately ignited up and out in a reddish-orange hue like an underwater atomic blast. A second ball of fire struck the river and exploded. Then seemingly out of nowhere, an enormous long-necked, winged beast swooped in and hovered sixty feet above the river's shore. A ferocious roar escaped its black orifice, followed by a lengthy mass of fire. The wind from every flap of its widespread wings gusted downward upon the treetops.

"Pradicus, it's Lig Nædre!" Andi yelled in a panic, rushing into the house. Ominously, Derik looked onward toward the mythical beast. He stepped to the edge of the porch, watching in terrified wonder. Bierwul circled above the great dragon, once again serving as the eyes for Valicious.

Andi came bursting out the front door back onto the porch. "I can't find Pradicus."

Derik turned quickly and caught her in midstride into his arms. "It's fine. I'm sure he's aware Lig Nædre's here.

They heard Pradicus's voice bellow from above them. They stepped off the porch and into the front yard, ducking the wind-driven flying debris. They found Pradicus standing atop the house with his arms raised, speaking loudly to himself, hurling curses toward the dragon in a deep, authoritative voice.

The dragon wrenched its neck and then dove toward the house, with Bierwul following close behind.

Pradicus bent down and picked up a large crossbow. He took aim and pulled the trigger. The arrow rocketed forward, piercing its target with a deadly strike into the heart. The crow instantly fell lifelessly through the air. "Blasted, defiant little cuss," he said through gritted teeth.

Lig Nædre held up from its descent for a moment, watching its companion unresponsively arrive at its final resting place. It then redirected into an ascending climb and continued until it reached the silvery mist on the underside of the clouds. Its eyes, fierce and unshakable, locked onto the shooter, its intended target. Then in a furious plunge, the dragon pinned its wings back and dove toward the earth. As it neared the hills, it spread out its mighty wings and leveled out, brushing the tallest treetops with its underbelly, intent on closing quickly. It opened its mouth wide, heaving a blanket of fire upon the grassland, preparing to snatch its mark from the rooftop.

Andi and Derik both dove for the ground.

On a speeding approach, with a single snap of its jaws, Lig Nædre took half the roof off.

Andi careened her neck around to survey the aftermath. Part of one wall, a large portion of the roof, and Pradicus were simply gone. She jumped up and chased the dragon for several steps in sheer devastation.

"Pradicus, no!" There was no sign of him. Pieces of roof fell to the ground, trailing the dragon's flight. Andi fell to her knees.

Derik ran to her in a consoling effort. He scanned the sky as he held her. "It's circling back around. It isn't finished, Andi. Do you hear me? It's coming back."

She remained in her position, disoriented.

"Andi, we've got to run. It's coming back. Lig Nædre is coming back."

She looked up at him with sopping eyes. "This wasn't supposed to happen, Derik." She then lifted her eyes to see where the beast was. Derik's optimism began to fall. She glanced back at Derik and saw the switch in his eyes as his awareness of the inevitable loomed only seconds away. Both of them knew it was too late to begin running.

In a high circling arc, Lig Nædre followed the same approach. Focused and purposeful, it found the two of them on the ground and then drew in a large breath for a final blast of fire.

"Let Your will be done, oh Lord Jesus." Andi mumbled through her sniffles. Thoughts fell on Pradicus, her friend, confidant, and father-figure. Her lips curled into a large frown as the blank expression she attempted to keep collapsed into grief-stricken mourning. She covered her eyes with a hand and wept. A myriad of wonderful Pradicus moments dashed through her memory, but the one that leapt out at her was her most recent discussion with him concerning things she and Garren had been talking about quite a bit lately. She had approached Pradicus just days before Derik's arrival.

"Explain to me again why you resist so much, Pradicus. You're the sweetest guy I've ever known. You're giving, considerate, kind, and just an overall beautiful person. What in the world could possibly keep you from reaching out to God?" It was the first time in their several brief discussions that Pradicus hadn't sidestepped the question. Perhaps something deep within him knew things were about to change.

"Andrea, I suppose the reason thou sees me as a good person is because I have tried to turn from mine past. I have committed unforgivable deeds, as well as witnessed the same, namely the assault and butchering of mine mother. I cannot forgive them for what they did; therefore, I cannot ask forgiveness for what I have done. She called out to God in her terror. He didst nothing. I see what God has done in thy life for thee, and I am happy for thee. However, thy God is not a God for me. I am sorry, Andrea, but I shall take that to mine grave."

"Well, I'm going to pray that He opens your eyes, Pradicus," Andi said. "I'll ask Him to make sense to you someday, and then you'll forgive yourself for what you've done. When God changes your heart, you'll find it within yourself to forgive them for what they did to your mother. It's the kindness of a loving God which leads to repentance, Pradicus. Maybe someday you'll see such kindness in me."

"Andrea," he said firmly but gently, "I wish not to forgive them. But you do that child." He grinned, then turned and walked away.

"Pradicus," she called with a tinge of concern, "forgiveness is freedom."

He wasn't sure why, but that particular remark struck him quite oddly. He paused for a moment and allowed the word to settle upon his lips as if never having considered it before. "Freedom ... ?" He then continued on his way.

Derik kneeled behind her, laid himself across her back, and then closed his eyes while his mind spun through a collection of their fondest memories together. He chuckled. "Remember, Andi, the first time we went down to Crapola's Italian Place?"

In her determination to be strong for what few seconds remained, the words took a moment to settle amidst a countless number of surging thoughts. "Carpolla's?" she asked, trying to focus. "Oh, yes, yes," she answered in a sniffling laugh. "I remember you getting stuck in the bathroom when they lost power," she added, giggling.

"Yeah, I never told anyone, but I had to sneak in to the girls' bathroom in complete darkness for a roll of toilet paper. I crawled the entire way. I'm not really sure why."

"Oh my gosh," she said, hesitating, trying hard to stay distracted, "are you serious?"

"My hand bumped into that young, really sweet orphanage lady, Sister Kathryn, when I crawled under one of the stalls." He started cracking up. "She screamed somethin' horrible when my hand touched her ankle, let me tell you. You talk about losing your religion."

"Derik…I—" was all she could manage before he grabbed her arms and squeezed.

"It's gonna be over quickly. Don't look," he said as the down wind surged upon them. A pillar of fire unleashed upon the two of them, consuming everything it reached, leaving a two hundred yard band of destruction. The beast pulled up and, with a fling of its tail, demolished an entire side of the burning house. Two charred strips laid smoking across the meadow, stretching from where the two took cover all the way past the remains of Pradicus's house. Lig Nædre circled once, then soared westward in an ascending climb until out of sight.

The dragon landed on its crest high up on the side of Broga Mountain. The horsemen on their steeds were assembled together there already. Lig Nædre made a few sounding gestures to the riders, then they unhurriedly turned and dispersed into the mountain. The dragon rested its jaw on the ground and made several regurgitating thrusts. A stone-like cocoon covered in saliva slid out from its mouth and onto the ground. It breathed on the object, which then began to soften. A body began to take shape as the shell around it melted away. The dragon nudged it a few times, then cupped it in its mouth and crawled off, entering the mountain through the large crevice.

Only a matter of minutes later, Lig Nædre was in a descending drift in the midst of the cavern. It landed on a ridge and released a long fiery breath and triumphant roar. Sporadic stones within the cavern's walls gleaned the heat and began to release light. As the particular stones brightened one by one, they charged others nearby, and within moments, the vast cavern was lit up in a remarkable array of illuminating white, green, blue, pink, and yellow stones. As the stones ignited into brilliance, they gave off a sweet fragrance that quickly filled the cavern.

In single-line fashion, one following the other, the horsemen arrived through one of the passageways. Their stallions plodded across the muddy terrain toward a ledge overlooking the lake, upon which Lig Nædre stood. The horsemen gathered to the side of the ridge and waited. A few moments later, a ghastly figure stepped out onto a higher overhang opposite Lig Nædre's. The fiend took a long look around then disappeared into a crevice.

15

Upon Lig Nædre's final pass when the beast rained its fire down, incinerating everything around the two of them, Andi felt a sudden supernatural peace and opened her tearful eyes and gasped in awe. Derik opened his eyes and looked over his shoulder. They were safely enveloped under a sea of fire. But the fire looked different, as though being viewed from beneath a crystal shell. When the fire passed and the shell shifted away from them, they noticed it wasn't a shell at all. It was a fantastic translucent person standing over them with arms raised to heaven. Then before they could blink, it was gone.

Derik stood up and took Andi by the hand. "Did you see that, Andi? It was *in*credible. It was amazing."

"No," she said, sliding a finger beneath her eyes, "it was angelic." She sniffled and, amidst the inner-settling peace, found the capacity to smile. "*That* is what stood in front of Pradicus in the ivy." She placed a hand over her chest and raised her face to heaven. "Thank you, Lord Jesus."

Pradicus's house smoldered, and half of what remained standing collapsed at once. An aerial view would reveal the devastation reeked upon the ait. Billows of smoke plumed into the air from the wreckage while a thinning smoky haze from the charred trails Lig Nædre left behind wafted into the quiet breeze. The rich foliage had been consumed within the two lengthy blackened streaks leading toward the house, with the exception of the tiny sphere in the center of the second streak.

Andi's thoughts turned to Pradicus, and her eyes softened as she looked back at the house. "Pradicus," she whispered in a sigh. She glanced at Derik despairingly. "How is it that we made it and not him? I don't understand, Derik. I thought we were all gonna finish this together. How are we supposed to do this without him?"

She glanced back at the unscathed sphere in the grass. She imagined the posture of the two of them in the midst of the circle. The picture triggered a memory she had while listening to one of the CDs she found in the attic. "Wait a minute, Derik," she said in a somber tone. "I'm not really sure, but I think we're supposed to pray."

Derik held out a hand straightaway after what he'd just witnessed. "Can you teach me?" he asked.

"I'm not well versed at this. I'm not exactly sure I know how to pray with someone else. But right now, I feel like that doesn't even matter. Will you pray also? I mean, maybe if we both say something..." she said with a slow shrug.

Derik kind of nodded with a slight gesture of his head. "Well, maybe I, uh..." He saw a soft smile split her lips. "Um, yeah. I will…Sure, I'll say something," he added with a more exaggerated nod.

She took his hand and closed her eyes. He watched her and then closed his. She didn't say anything right away, so he peeked at her. Her lips were just barely moving. He took the opportunity to steal a long look at what he thought to be a truly beautiful angel. He'd never really seen her with her eyes closed like that before. He smiled secretly and then closed his eyes again. She opened hers a smidge to check on him, making sure he was taking the quietness before God seriously. A thrilled half smile arose.

She drew in breath. "Um, God, I'm still kind a new at this. I just really want to say thank You. I really don't know why we made it and Pradicus didn't. I guess You have a plan, and in that plan, I really hope we can get back home. I really miss my family, God. I guess You would kind of already know that. I really don't know why I'm telling You that. And God, could You keep a couple of those cool see-through guys—angels, I guess—around us until we do get back home? I really, really thank You for saving us. God, I hope he's there with You right now—Pradicus, I mean. Tell him…"—she paused—"that…I'm really going to miss him," she added with a crackling voice. "Can You say thanks for me? And kind Father, your kindness always leads me to repentance." She squeezed Derik's hand. "Okay," she whispered.

"Oh, uh, hmm-mm," he said, clearing his throat. "Well, that was very cool back there, God. And thanks for watching over this little girl here. Help us get home, I guess…" he said, trailing off.

"Amen," Andi said, opening her eyes.

"Oh, yeah, amen," Derik added. He glanced at Andi for approval, and she mouthed the word *thanks* to him with an excited grin. He nonchalantly nodded back.

"So what'd you think?" she asked.

"Well, you said, 'Really,' like fifteen times. Did you know that?"

"Ugh!" she said, furrowing her brow. "Shut up. No, I didn't. Besides, I was asking what *you* thought about what *you* said."

"I guess it was really, really cool. I mean *really, really*," he said with a smirk. She answered back with a smirk of her own. "I'm just playin'. It was kinda weird, I guess. But I knew I was talkin' to someone on account of seeing that angel thing that stood over us. I guess I felt like someone was listening. It was cool."

"What, not really, really cool?" she said, sneering at him.

"You know what? You're really cute when I get under your skin, really. Really."

She glanced back at him with a contemptuous squint. "Really?"

His uneven smile gave way to a sharp, pompous grin. "Yeah, really."

"I thought it was awesome," she said, looking away. "The preacher on that CD said that God works through people's prayers. And you know what else? There's a bigger reason he's not here—Pradicus, I mean. I think that he's not *supposed* to be here. And I also think we have to go to Broga Mountain. We're supposed to do this with or without him. I don't know how or why. I just know what we have to do. And I'm feeling like we need to go now."

"What? How do you … how are we … hold on a second. How are we supposed to get there?"

"I'm not quite sure yet."

"Well, what makes you think we need to go now?"

She held out a closed fist. "This, for one thing," she said. The unfolding of her fingers revealed three wilted berries. Derik grabbed at his amulet in the hopes of keeping it from burning him. "Andi! It's gone. My amulet's gone."

"When's the last time you remember having it?"

Derik's mind, still yet whirling amidst the pandemonium, found focus and recall nearly impossible at that particular moment. "I can't even remember."

"You can't remember? Fantastic. Hold on a sec. It kept glowing, didn't it? And it glowed around these berries. Maybe if we walk around with these berries, it'll glow."

"Right."

The two walked toward the house. Suddenly, a large series of splashes erupted from behind them. They both turned and looked. A colossal kraken arm waived into the air, then heaved itself down to the earth.

"Whoa. What's he upset about?" Derik asked.

"I really don't know."

"Come on. Let's keep looking."

"Wait," Andi said, staring at the water beast's tentacle. The kraken flipped it up and down several times along the shore.

"It's talking to us, Derik." She laughed in amazement. "Pradicus isn't even here, and it's talking. Oh my gosh, Derik," she said, turning and grasping his arm. "It's talking to me." Andi squinted her eyes, trying to remember a conversation Pradicus and she had pertaining to the river and the kraken. "It's trying to tell us something."

Derik took a step forward, scoping the shore. "The shoreline?" he asked.

"The only thing that's over there is a getaway tunnel leading under Pradicus's house. Of course, that's it. Pradicus built it as a flood safety. It's a second home he rarely used. Pradicus used the tunnel to feed that thing when he was nursing it to health. Pradicus said that it would flap its arms like that to warn him of a coming flood. I never did see it do that before."

"So is there a flood coming?"

"Um, I don't know."

"Well, maybe there's something down there we can take with us to the cavern. We could always use torches."

"Yeah, okay. Let's go."

The two ran across the meadow to the shore. They jogged the shoreline until Andi saw the opening. "Here it is. Come on."

Derik cut in front of her, realizing the large door would have to be watertight. That being the case, it would be difficult to break the seal. He unbolted the door and then turned the cranking wheel counterclockwise several times. The seal released; then he yanked on the door and pulled it open.

"My hero," Andi said, batting her eyes.

Just inside the tunnel, a shelf held a small heap of flint stones. Andi grabbed one of the nearby rags and laid it out. She took two stones and smashed them together. The sparks dropped onto the rag and caught fire. She quickly wrapped the rag around a torch and then touched the torch to a trough. A fire ignited within the trough, then spread all the way down the tunnel, lighting it up. Derik gave her an impressed grin, grabbing another rag and a few more stones.

She winked at him. "Living here for a year and a half you learn a few things."

As the door shut behind them, Derik focused his eyes in the glistening light as they proceeded down the long corridor of the tunnel. The dense, stale air of the musty tunnel filled their lungs as they shuffled along the cold, rocky ground. As Derik led the way, Andi stole a look back down the corridor, running her eyes along the ceiling and walls, painting mesmerized strokes left to right and back again until she covered the extent of their distance, landing her sight on Derik once again. A thought occurred to her, and she suddenly found herself awestruck within a mystery. *I wonder if Pradicus meant for us to come this way*, she asked herself. *And did the Kraken know his intentions?*

The tunnel led into a midsized room with a short ceiling. Two doors stood on opposite sides of the room—one leading up to the house, and the other leading to a room full of trinkets, collectibles, and scrolls. Derik entered the latter. The trough, accompanied by an attached tin strip along its walled edge throughout, encircled the entire dwelling so the room was already equipped with reflecting light. He stopped and took in the splendor of collected history.

"Oh, wow. Old Man Cutter hasn't seen anything," he said, looking over at Andi. He picked up a couple of handmade pieces of jewelry and studied them. He then noticed the scrolls. All of the walls had shelves, which kept rolled-up scrolls sticking out every which way. Derik made out some writing along one of the shelves. "Look at this," he said, pointing out a word that had been etched into the shelf.

"Ivory," she said. "It says ivory."

"You can read that?" She looked at him and shook her head incredulously. He smiled, turned away, and then scratched his nose, feeling dim. "Oh yeah. Year and a half. Sorry. So, uh, what about this one?"

She peeled her eyes away from him and then attempted to read the word. "Um, I think that says 'jasmine.' He pulled out the scrolls and opened them on a table in the middle of the room. They looked like star charts with hundreds of lines intersecting one another.

"Whoa, what is this?" Derik asked excitedly.

Andi took a step back. "Derik," she whispered. "I know what these are." She began scanning the room. "Oh no."

"What?" Derik asked, eyes flaring.

Her scan escalated into a frantic search. She ran from wall to wall, reading the lettering on the shelves, sighing louder and louder as she went. "It's not here. Oh, Derik. What have we done?"

"What? Tell me what you're talking about."

She went back to one of the shelves. "Oh my goodness." She sighed. "Here it *is*." She pulled out the scroll and opened it on top of the others. It looked just like the others. She put her finger on one of the lines, followed it to an intersect point, and then pursued that line until it moved on to yet another. She maneuvered herself around the table, keeping track of the lines with her finger as they repeatedly took her to and fro around one side of the table and back again.

"Andi, you're about to drive me crazy. *What* are you looking for?"

"You, Derik. I'm looking for you."

A somber expression fell upon his face. He swallowed hard. "What do you mean?"

"This chart has been tracking your emerald. Ah! Look, look! It ended here. According to this, he lost track of it in 1756, Asia. That's what he's been looking for! It completes the Atlas so he can fulfill the prophecy. Look here. Each of these maps has the same depiction and Latin heading at the top. It illustrates the Atlas's progress. The emerald was the last stone."

"Well, I don't have it. We've got to find it."

Andi frowned then pressed her lips together. "No. We just need to get it back."

"What? From who?"

"Pradicus. I think he's trying to stop Valicious from fulfilling the prophecy." "But Pradicus is … dead."

"I'm starting to think that's only what he wanted us to believe. He's alive, Derik, and he's gonna try and take on Lig Nædre by himself." She looked down at the wilted berries. They were beginning to harden. "When these berries wither all the way, the window back to home closes. Come on. Let's go out through the house. There's a way out near the back porch."

They quickly ran to the other door, and just before exiting, out of the corner of his eye, Derik caught a small section of aged wooden signs. In the failing light, he made out one in particular and stepped closer to it out of interest. It measured about two feet in length and one in width. It hung down awkwardly from a single nail in its upper-right corner. In exquisite, hand-carved modern English, it read, "Welcome to Laminus." Beneath those words read, "In Christ, all things hold together."

Scanning the rest, he took a step back toward the door when something caught his eye, stealing his breath. On a newer sign, which obviously had taken a blow but wasn't completely broken, were the words "Cleveland and Andrea Pasque." He heard himself mutter the name "Andi" in an enlightened tone that surprised him. It began to dawn on Derik that she had indeed lived eighteen months without him, moreover spent the entire length of time with absolutely no guarantee she would ever see him again. He covered his face with both hands in a frustrated gesture and then sighed.

"Derik, what are you doing? What's wrong?" Andi asked, stepping back into the room.

"I thought I saw something. It was nothing."

"You look upset. Are you okay?" she asked, beginning to eyeball the room.

He placed a hand on her shoulder and then paused for a moment, taking in her eyes, her face. "Yeah, I'm okay." He slid his hand around to the back of her neck, then drew her toward him and hugged her.

Entirely lost on the incident, Andi stepped away from him with a firm look. "This isn't the time to get all sentimental or melancholy on me, Derik, or whatever else this is. We need to be thinking about how we're going to get all the way to Broga Mountain from here. It's half a day's journey, Derik. By then, it may just be too late. Are you coming?" she asked walking back out of the room.

He heard her exasperatingly going on about boys and their trinkets as he shut the door and followed behind her. A ladder leading upward to the basement of the house sat at the end of the tunnel. Upon reaching it, Derik stepped in front of Andi once again and started climbing. About halfway up, Derik stopped beside a wooded board. "Does Pradicus own a horse?"

"Not anymore. Why?"

"Because I hear a horse on the other side of this panel."

"You're hearing things, Derik. Keep going."

Derik managed to pull off the panel in the wall of the tunnel. Andi climbed up next to him, and they shared the step. They both peered into the mysterious area. Multicolored rays flickered and danced as they filtered through the small opening Derik and Andi created. Cobwebs graced the corners of the room—a sign no one had been in the room for quite some time. Out of the darkness, a horse passed by the light.

"Derik," Andi whispered, "we've got to get out of here. Don't you recognize that? It's a Gray Rider's horse."

Derik felt his pulse begin to thump hard. He looked into her eyes, "A horseman?" He paused for a moment. "So where's the rider?"

"I don't know, but obviously not here. Now get going. Move."

He stepped up the ladder a few rungs and then halted. "Hey, do you remember how fast those things are?"

"Why don't you just send death an engraved invitation? How many lives do you think you have?"

He gave her one of his adventurous looks, which, in her estimation, often stemmed from a wild idea and was accompanied by a vast lack of planning.

"No way, Derik." She leaned in toward him. "No."

Five minutes later, the two were riding bareback on the colossal stallion whizzing through the forest. Derik sat in front, sporting the most enormous grin he'd ever produced. Andi sat behind him, head tucked and arms clenched in a death grip around his waist. The animal raced with smooth, graceful, lengthy strides.

"Jiminy Christmas, Derik! Can't you slow this thing down?"

"What? I can't hear you. It's too loud up here."

The highest visible portion of the mountain grew closer and closer with every passing second. Derik realized they were approaching much too quickly and started trying to slow the animal down far before reaching the entrance he and Pradicus came out of. Rather than the two of them flying off the horse in a sudden stop, he began to think about coming to a stopping point slowly. He pulled back on its mane, at first lightly, gradually increasing his draw. It responded. The great steed took a few hundred yards to slow all the way to a complete stop.

"Woo-hoo-hoo! How about that ride?" Derik exclaimed while helping Andi down. "I bet we covered ten miles in the last few minutes."

"You know what? I think you could've ridden that thing a lot slower. I think you just decided to see how fast you could push it. No matter that my *rear end* was in the air most of the way. Criminy, Derik!"

"Yeah, about that. You were kind of clawing your nails into my stomach," Derik said, wincing while lifting his shirt. "Could you take it a little easier on me next time?"

"Oh! If I could walk right now," she said, rubbing her lower back.

"Hey, there's plenty to go around. Tell you what. Whatever's left after we take out the horsemen, release the Jangus without it killing us, kill Lig Nædre, and stop Valicious from fulfilling the prophecy, you can have. Promise."

"I think I'm gonna … oh." She grunted. "Huuurrrl."

Derik stood still for a moment, arms crossed, tapping his toe.

"Derik! Remind me never to listen to one of your bright ideas ever again. Oh my goodness."

217

Derik softened his eyes, realizing she was probably right about pushing the great horse, and stepped toward her.

"Don't you dare come over here! Keep your little hiney over there."

"Geez, that seemed a little uncalled for."

"Derik."

"Okay. I'm sorry about the ride," he said, brow puckered. "But we're here, and we are in one piece, right? Hey... I'm sorry."

Andi sighed and then bit her lip with a half smile. She glanced over and chuckled at his crazy, wind-blown hair, then relented. "Okay. I guess I'm all right." Then she stopped to think what hers must look like.

Derik boasted a satisfied grin. He waited for her to take a step toward him and then walked over to her as she brushed fingers through her hair. He then swung his arm around her shoulder in a confident gesture of her dismissal of his recent misjudgment.

She gazed into his eyes. "Derik, will you tell me something?"

He offered her a rather egoistic nod.

"Ten minutes on that steed wasn't such a treat with my nose in your back. I was just wondering. You've only been here a day, so when on earth did you have the time to wallow in bear poopy? Or is that just you?" She ducked under his arm, lifted his shirt, and then slapped him in the stomach hard enough to pull prints. "And just so you know, we're not even yet," she snapped, placing an open hand against her lower back.

Clenching his teeth, he heaved a piercing shrill. "How in heaven's name do girls know just how to slap a guy? Holy cow," he begged after gathering himself. He stole a look at her, noting the elated satisfaction she wore.

He cracked a smile. He discreetly nudged his nose toward one of his armpits and drew in a couple quick sniffs. He immediately winced. "Geez, hello," he coughed out. He glanced back at Andi. "Oh, come on. It's not that bad.

She tossed an annoyed "Yeah, whatever," turned quickly, and then started marching.

"Oh, you're leaving. I'm right behind you."

A few minutes later, the two of them were stealthily heading into the shadowy abyss that was the thick of the Penumbra Forest. Derik glanced at Andi. "So how fast do ya think we were goin'?" he asked with a smirk.

She slid her eyes over at him in a bitter squint.

"Well, not that it's important or anything."

She slightly shook her head and returned her attention to her footing.

"I bet we were pushin' eighty," he mumbled, clenching a fist. His eyes scanned the trees. "Maybe a hundred," he added, marveling at the thought.

She gazed high up on the mountain and found the clouds rather interesting. They sat lower than normal, enveloping the entire top third of its height, and stirred slowly in a counterclockwise direction. Faint, quick bursts of light emanated from within the mountain's top, penetrating through the clouds like an electrical storm.

She glanced at Derik. "They've already gotten started," she whispered.

"I can't wait to ride one of those stallions again. Wasn't it fantastic?"

"Would you shut up about that, Derik? We've got a job to do."

He halfway rolled his eyes and then sighed. "Fine."

She stopped promptly and looked straight into his eyes. "What's your deal? What's up with you suddenly? Has the animal really got you so mesmerized that you can't move on?"

He said nothing, looking away.

"Look, Derik. I'm going in there with or without you. I was hoping we'd do this thing together. Now I'm not so sure I want you involved. Either snap out of it or stay here." She turned and took a few steps toward the mountain again.

"All right, I'm sorry."

She stopped and faced him again. "Derik, I've lost everything. Can't you see that? Everything that meant anything to me has been stripped away all due to that stupid beast and his villainous, evil partner in crime. I'd like to kill them both. In fact, I plan to. I hate them for what they've done to me."

"Whoa, hold on a second. It's not like you to sound so … vengeful."

"People can change in eighteen months, Derik, especially when everything they've known has been yanked out from under them in a matter of seconds, and even more so if it was all for *nothing*," she said in a tone of agitation. "Haven't you changed in the last year and a half of your life?"

"What do you mean 'by a matter of seconds'?" Derik asked.

"The *time* hole thing, Derik. Remember, back in the barn?"

He nodded slightly. "The *worm*hole."

"Yes, the wormhole. My life as I knew it was gone instantly. And I'm really mad about it, Derik."

"Well, but I thought you said you found God. This doesn't sound at all like the person I was listening to last night."

She exhaled slowly, placed her hands on her hips, and turned away from him. A silent moment passed between them. "You're right. I'm sorry. I wish I had someone who could tell me how to deal with situations like this. The CDs I used to listen to didn't explain that after turning my life over to God I'd still have to deal with becoming angry and all these emotions. I mean, I guess I thought maybe God would somehow make them go away. But He hasn't, so I guess part of my life then is about making sure I don't give in to them—at least until I can learn to better control them."

She stopped and pondered over the words she'd just spoken. "Wow, Derik, I didn't really think about it like that until just now. Maybe that's what it's about. Could it be that God wants me to work through these things? Maybe He's teaching me to use His tools to deal with and overcome these things that seem so difficult. That actually sounds more like what I've read in Romans."

She turned back toward him. "Derik, again, I'm sorry I lost control. Jesus is way bigger than any of this. I don't have the right to harbor that kind of bitterness or blame. Thank you for pointing that out. In a moment of resentment, I abandoned His strength. 'For I am persuaded, that neither death, nor life, nor angels, nor principalities, nor things present, nor things to come, nor height, nor depth, nor any other creature, shall be able to separate me from the love of God, which is in Christ Jesus our Lord.'" She smiled. "That's from Romans chapter eight."

She closed her eyes for a brief moment and prayed in a quiet, regretful tone. "Please forgive me, Lord, for putting myself and my agenda before Yours. Amen." She gathered her gown, stepped up onto a small boulder, and then continued walking toward the base of the mountain.

"Wait, wait just a second. How can you say all that? How can you mean that?" he asked, remaining motionless. "After everything you just said about killing someone, how can you simply make nice? Aren't you still ticked?"

"Of course, I still feel angry," she said from a short way off. "But it's not okay for me to get to the point in my anger of wanting to kill someone. So because I let the angry mess come in, I have to acknowledge it. But it's not about me anymore. It's about God and my surrender to Him. It's His strength I choose to lean on. So now it's His deal."

"What? That doesn't make any sense."

"It's kind of like your game of football," she called back.

"What do you mean? Are you saying *you're* one of the teams? No, I got it. You're saying you're the ball, right?" He frowned and reconsidered the last statement, wondering what he might have meant by it.

"What in heavens are you talking about?" Her reply trickled through the woods. "No, I'm the trophy."

Derik furrowed his brow. "Huh?" he asked quietly with a tilt of the head. He then leapt up onto the same small boulder she'd stepped onto and then started after her. Her last comment jogged through his memory. "I don't get it. Trophy?" He whispered to himself.

The two of them entered the mountain through a narrow gap at the base. Derik had secured the torch he'd used earlier to his waist. He unfastened it and then repeated Andi's earlier steps in lighting it. Within moments, they were on their way with Derik leading, torch in one hand and keeping hold of Andi's hand with the other.

They stepped, stooped, scaled, and slid their way through the mountain's passageway in silence. The passage floor leveled out, and the ceiling grew tall as they neared the cavern. Derik's thoughts turned to the Atlas.

"Do you think the Atlas could be the treasure Pradicus was speaking of?"

"I dunno," she answered back in a quiet tone.

"Well, who came up with this Atlas time gate thing in the first place?"

Derik, I know I've been here a year and a half, but really, it's only been a year and a half. I haven't talked to anybody other than Pradicus, Garren, and Jake the whole time. I really don't know that much about it."

The passageway started widening. "Okay, here we are, Andi," he said softly. "Hey, something's really going on in the cavern. Remember how dark it *was*?"

Andi nodded. "Like it was yesterday."

The two of them peeked into the great cave. It was magnificently enormous. The colorful blending of light emanating off the stone walls was breathtaking. Strewn stalactites hung majestically in various sizes throughout its ceiling while the lake enveloped a great majority of the floor of the cavern. The lake, primarily large in the middle, broke off and pooled into several sections, some with high cliffs either arcing over or simply hanging over the water. Derik wondered how it could possibly be the same place he'd crawled out of just a day before. Numerous ledges and handmade pathways carved into the cavern were identifiable. Off to their right was the ledge where the great beast itself was perched. They heard the clopping and rustling of the Gray Riders' horses farther off to the right but couldn't see them when, in fact, they assembled on a ridge directly above Derik and Andi. Across the cavern on another ledge, a man stood chanting ceremoniously in words foreign to both their ears.

"I think he's speaking Latin," Andi said.

"Is *that* Valicious?" Derik asked.

"I don't know. I've never actually run into him. It must be, though."

"Otherwise wouldn't Lig Nædre and the horsemen be after him?"

"Of course. Now how are we gonna sneak in there? We can't even see the Jangus," Andi said, sitting back against the wall. "We need a diversion."

Suddenly, a sharp, deep snarl escaped the dragon's snout, followed by a distinctive grunt, and instantly, the horsemen were on the move. Derik and Andi exchanged inquisitive glances. Andi leaned forward slightly, listening intently to the sound of the clickity-clacking hooves. As near as she could tell, it sounded as if the horsemen were moving away from them. She shot a look of determination toward Derik. "Ready?" she whispered.

They both leaned forward onto their hands and knees and then, in unison, jumped backward when the horses suddenly appeared in a thunderous landing upon the moist sand in front of their passageway.

The lot of them dropped off the ten-foot ledge from directly above. Derik and Andi froze. The bamboo cage holding the Jangus slammed to the ground. Footsteps approached the opening, where Derik and Andi were holding up, then stopped at the cage. The horseman knelt down to open the lock when Andi saw the watch. She gasped loudly, then covered her mouth and glanced at Derik. Her face beheld a new depth of panic. Certainly she'd given their position away.

The horseman stopped what he was doing and spun around to his left, glaring directly into the crevice. Devoid of fear or any emotion, he rose to his feet and, after a decent stoop, stepped in. At his foot, Derik hid, crouched into a shallow nook with his face against the wall.

The torch lay several feet back, indicating that someone had indeed been there. Its flickering flame shed light throughout the small chasm, casting shadows behind ridges all along the walls. Andi sat with her knees pulled up to her chest. She hid against a wall in the darkness under a narrow overhang. The horseman stepped over to the torch and picked it up. The weak light against the walls shifted. He quickly turned. The torch protested against the little gust while shadows realigned. The horseman's eyes fell on Andi's now unhidden feet. He reached for his whip. His eyes followed up her leg to her face.

Andi jerked and then lost her breath. Sickened by his appearance, and terrified at what loomed in the next few seconds, she gathered what breath she could. "Jake … please, Jake," she whispered through a quivering voice. "It's me, Andi." Her wide eyes splashed off the first of several tears while those following spilled out and streamed her cheeks. "Jake, remember me? You've got to remember me. Jake, don't do this. You and me on the swing, remember? You showed me your watch and told me about your family, Jake. They miss you. They want you back, Jake."

The horseman unsnapped his whip and then let it unravel to the ground. He drew up the handle, preparing to cast a lethal lashing down upon her.

"Jake!" she cried, raising her arms in front of her.

The horseman stopped when he caught sight of his watch out of the corner of his skinless eye. He shook off the hesitation and then proceeded with the rearing back of his whip. Suddenly, the sound of his own voice began to echo off the walls as Derik held out the cell phone. The horseman swung around and faced Derik, who stood behind him. Having pilfered a large blade from the horseman, he held it up in one hand and the cell phone in the other.

"So this is Jake," Derik said in an annoyed tone, recalling the painful writing on the sign he'd read earlier. The thought of Jake laughing, sharing tender moments, and ultimately desiring companionship with his Andi had Derik's blood boiling until it was steaming out his ears.

Through gritted teeth, and with tears suddenly welling up within his eyes, he said under his breath, "You so much as breathe in her direction again, you filthy puss bag…" then paused to steal a look at Andi. His eyes quickly shot back to the imminent threat. "Caught ya sleepin', didn't I? I'll take you down right now, man," Derik said with a raging fire in his eyes. The horseman showed no threat by Derik but was caught up in an instant internal identity crisis. The person speaking from the cell phone no longer existed, at least as far as he knew. The words "I'm sorry, Mom, for everything" challenged his memory, and then on it played.

"Jake," Andi pleaded. "It's me, Andi. Jake, you've got to remember. We're gonna make it home. All three of us, Jake. You're still in there. I see it."

Jake reached for the phone. Derik stepped forward, quickly handing it over, and then stepped back with blade still held up. Jake's eyes softened as they glanced from one wall to another and back several times.

A sudden roar from Lig Nædre snapped Jake out of his moment. The conflict arose within him once again as his eyes regained their sharpness. Torn between two worlds, he clenched his fists.

"Jake, don't listen to it. It's you and me, remember? Let it go and help us. We can win this, but we need your help. Jake, please. I have a chance to get back to my family."

Jake held still, turning his head about. Finally, he looked up with conviction, eyes certain. He turned, drew a blade, and then lunged for Andi. She screamed. Derik immediately dove after him and tackled him before he could reach her. Derik drove his blade into Jake's shoulder. Jake threw Derik off and then turned to face Andi again.

Hearing the commotion, the Jangus hissed loudly and thrust its jowls against the bars of its cage, then violently threw its body into it several times. The other Horsemen casually looked down at its activity, then back up at each other with mounting curiosity.

Derik jumped back onto Jake, this time wrapping the whip around his neck. He then pulled it tight. Jake waved his arms around in a panic, grasping at whatever he could, dropping his blade.

"Derik, stop! You'll kill him!"

"He's already dead, Andi."

"No, he isn't. I couldn't tell until just now. Stop, Derik, please."

"Andi," Jake muttered in a slow, raspy, almost stripped voice.

Derik froze. "It spoke!"

228

"Jake, I knew it. I knew you were still there."

"Let him finish me, Andi. I...I can't help you."

"No! No, Jake. I won't let him. Dang it, Derik! Let him go. Now!" she said furiously.

Derik reluctantly released his grip. Jake fell forward, then pulled the blade from his shoulder and released it. Derik quickly kicked it away. He turned, then picked up the one Jake attacked Andi with and stuck it securely behind him in his pants.

"If you won't finish me, then I'm doomed here forever. I remember now and can't go on like this. My soul is black. There's no hope for me."

Andi searched her heart. She looked at Derik, squinting and pressing her lips, and then looked back at Jake. "Then I'm going out there and giving myself up. If you're staying, so am I."

"What did you just say?" Derik snapped at Andi. "Wh-what? What are you doing?"

"Andi, to turn against the fire beast would be my torturous death. I'm not capable of turning on it."

"Then you better figure out a way to stop me," she said, walking out the crevice into the cavern.

The Jangus spotted her and lunged against its cage yet again, hissing frantically. The Horsemen dismounted in a single leap and seized her. Grasping her by the wrists, they stretched her arms out and dragged her to Lig Nædre. The great beast roared in a victorious rave.

The spectator across the water, whose face had now begun to resemble that of a Horseman, bowed out into the shadows. With her back to the dragon, Andi raised her eyes as an ominous silence commanded the moment. They arrived on the shape of a man in an oversized, gray, hooded robe who seemed to materialize out of the shadows. He withdrew his hood just so, revealing only his nose and mouth and the appalling skin that comprised them, reminiscent of shriveled reptilian scales. Andi gasped as a terror she'd never known gripped her. The sheer presence of the fabled devil stole her breath. She surprised herself with the tone of angst she used in speaking the name. It simply dropped out of her mouth in a murmur. "Valicious."

She locked her gaze upon the phantom-like figure while awareness sharpened into focus. The decision she made to reveal herself would indeed cost her her life. The sudden comprehension shook her. "Jake, help me," she cried in a regretful plea.

Dearest memories of parents and siblings raced to the forefront of her mind. Convulsing violently, she pulled, twisted, and contorted every which way in an attempt to escape, to no avail. "No ... please!" she bawled out in tears. Her thoughts returned to the field where she and Derik were rescued from Lig Nædre. "Jesus, please!" she cried out. "God, help me."

Valicious spoke out in a repulsive, rasping voice. "Be done with her. We have what we needed her for. Rid the boy as well. He's with her."

Before the words could leave his mouth, Derik stormed out of the cave with his blade drawn. "Over my dead body, you sick, ugly toad!" he yelled.

His emergence elicited renewed tenacity within Andi and had her captors loosening their grips on her wrists. With one tremendous heave, she broke free of both their holds, then tumbled to the ground several feet away. She quickly stood to her feet and then waited for someone to move toward her.

Valicious turned to Lig Nædre. "Breathe hence forth thy fire," he bellowed. "Empower me. For it is nearly finished. The Atlas is complete, and its power is finally mine! Feast now, my pet." The dragon's neck reeled around, and its jaws swept down after Andi.

"Derik, the Jangus!" Andi yelled, jumping and stumbling out of the way while Lig Nædre's jaws snapped once after her, then twice. Enjoying the game, Lig Nædre raised its head toward the cavern and heaved a bellowing length of fire that blanketed the ceiling of the cavern in its entirety. It came back around with renewed focus in its eyes. It gave off a partial roar, as if encouraging her to engage in the sport.

Everyone froze, watching the great dragon work its strategy out with the prey. Andi stood, caught her footing, ran several steps to a horseman, and drew a twelve-inch blade from a sheath on his hip. The horseman had no intentions of interfering. The dragon let out a cry announcing the contest was under way.

Andi stole a look over her shoulder, trying to ascertain how involved Valicious was with the Atlas. Realizing he'd paused his work for the entertainment, she grinned. She returned her attention to her enormous foe while the grin she wore shrunk to a scowl. Her glare was returned by its snarl. She took a quick scan of the cavern while maintaining her role as challenger, blade held up in front of her.

Her eyes landed on the mound of bones. The insignificance Valicious held for each of the lost lives tore at her. Her eyes arrived back on Lig Nædre. She felt the rising pressure of her gritted teeth as her thoughts swam to a recent place, one in which she felt insignificant. "I mean something to someone. Do you get that?" she said. "They all meant something to someone," she screamed, pointing toward the bones. Her voice then fell to a firm, enraged tone. "And who are you to decide? And for what? We're all significant." She took a step forward and lifted the blade. "Do you hear me, you illegitimate murderer?" she yelled. "We all mean something to someone. We're all significant." A single tear arose in her right eye and spilled out. "With God as my witness, I'll see you dead before this is over," she said to the dragon, then turned and ran, cutting toward the lake.

The dragon swept in swiftly. Andi took three long strides and then leapt off the ledge, turning her entire front side back toward the dragon, then threw the blade. The blade found its way into the beast's mouth and stuck itself in back of Lig Nædre's throat. Andi then glimpsed over at the crevice where Jake was. "Help me, Jake!" she cried, then plunged into the lake.

Lig Nædre let out a furious wail and then followed her underwater descent with a heated blast of fire. It then thrashed its long neck around in an attempt to dislodge the object which proceeded into a series of coughing snorts. Andi surfaced twenty feet away and then began to swim toward the other side in a sudden and powerfully fierce resolve. Refusing to allow her escape, the dragon snarled, extended its winged arms, and then leapt off the ledge in an attempt to snatch her from the water in its jaws. It soared quickly as it passed over Andi and then hurriedly circled back around. Suddenly, two marvelously looking, light-emitting arrows hit the dragon's right wing, disabling it, followed by two more on its left, sending the behemoth spiraling into the lake.

The horsemen turned their attention to the direction from which the arrows came. Two shimmering men stood on a high ledge with bows, reloading.

Andi flipped around and immediately recognized them. "Yes!" she screamed, followed immediately by, "Oh, no," when she realized Lig Nædre was about to send a wave around the lake of massive proportion. The archers turned quickly and then took aim at the horsemen.

Finally, Jake jumped out into the cavern and drew his combating blades. He delivered a powerful slash against the door of the Jangus's cage and then heaved it several yards through the air into the water. He then engaged one of the horsemen in a battle to the death. While he faced the one, the others used their blades and whips to knock the arrows from their lines of descent.

Derik snuck his way to the edge overlooking the water in search of Andi. She was still swimming but was closing in on the opposite shore. She was fifty feet directly below Valicious. Derik glanced up and saw Valicious beginning to open a wormhole in the middle of the upper expanse of the cavern. Slipping behind one of the great horses, methodically, he stopped when he bumped his head on a large crossbow.

Jake did his best to keep his combatant's back to the archers. Soon enough, the opposing horseman took an arrow, followed by two more, but kept fighting. Jake took his encounter to the lake's ledge, and when his opponent took his fifth arrow, he began to slow. Jake then maneuvered himself in such a way as to deliver a kick that sent the other fighter over the edge into the lake. One by one, Jake engaged the other horsemen, repeating his strategy, and, one by one, they fell.

Finally, there was only one horseman left, the leader, the one who wore a Viking helmet across his back. He was the biggest and by far the strongest of the riders. He'd already taken one arrow in the chest and another in either side but wasn't showing any signs of letting up. Jake knew he was out of his league. His rival wouldn't allow his back to face the archers, and he meticulously continued to knock the arrows down one after the other, all the while wearing Jake down.

From its lower position in the lake, the dragon caught sight of the skirmish between its loyalist and the betrayer and then hissed horribly. Jake entered into a state of pain he never could have perceived. He clenched his fist and pounded his white knuckles into the soft, moist ground while the pain splintered throughout his entire body, causing him to emit a shrill scream of panic. He doubled over, dropping his blades. He then tumbled to the ground in agony, pleading for a merciful death from his former cohort. The horseman stared down upon the conquered warrior and spit. Then he skipped over to his stallion, dodging the descending arrows, and unsheathed an enormous double-headed axe. He then bounded back to Jake, swinging the atrocious weapon around in an impressive maneuver so as to land a clean strike.

As the axe swept through its final descent toward Jake, a thick, unusual arrow struck the horseman in the chest just below the neck. The horseman instantly halted, and the weight of the axe carried him several feet away. He stood frozen as four more of the shimmering archer's arrows struck him in the side and back. He dropped the axe. He looked up to see Derik, just now lowering his aim, with Jake's crossbow.

Jake rolled around in pain, gnashing his teeth in a squealing whine, and then took notice of the dead horseman. While thrusting his head into the ground, he spotted the unrelenting dragon reeling in the water. Jake unsteadily stood to his feet and screamed through his agony, "You lose, you little—" but was cut off by a shrieking roar from Lig Nædre. The Jangus had finished with the horsemen, now evidenced by several floating limbs, and had loosed its fury on the dragon. Lig Nædre whirled around and then began to sink, hissing and screeching.

Valicious had nearly completed the gate. Derik watched as the rays of colored lights began to merge in a counterclockwise swirl. He quickly loaded another arrow, took aim at Valicious, and then fired. The two archers followed suit. Derik's arrow nicked Valicious in the arm. The others' arrows narrowly missed on account of his painful flinch. Valicious panicked, then leapt off the ledge into the gate and disappeared. Andi reached the ledge and just missed, grasping his cloak as he jumped.

Derik saw one of the translucent men draw his arrow on Jake. He ran a few steps toward them, raising his hands frantically. "Noo! Noo! You've got it all wrong! He's with us!"

The archer fired. The drawn string on the bow snapped, launching the arrow into a piercing flight. Derik watched as it traveled the vast distance with speed, grace, and ease. A silence fell upon Derik as he realized he was too late. There was nothing he could do. The arrow took on an ice-blue hue as it crossed the cavern. It struck Jake in the right shoulder.

Jake dropped to the ground, holding himself up on all fours.

"Jake!" Derik cried, rushing over to him.

"I'm all right. The beast released its hold on me. We're no longer tethered. Get Andi and go before the gate closes."

"Where's the arrow? We've got to get the arrow out right away."

"Arrow?" he asked. "I'm afraid I don't know what you mean."

Derik searched his back. There was no arrow, just as Jake had explained. Derik glanced back at the archers, who were both gone. He looked back at Jake. "Jake, your face. It's changing. Some of your skin is coming back. That's great!"

Jake felt his face and found lips had begun to reform. He immediately took a fleeting look toward Andi, but when she stepped to the ledge Valicious had just leapt from, looking back at the two of them, he quickly hid his face from her, glancing down and away. His eyes shot to and fro as he considered the ramifications of what was happening. For the first time in months, he generated a happy thought. "I'm released," he said to himself quietly. "My God, I'm released." A droplet of water splashed onto his arm. Another followed. He paused for a moment, recalling the feeling of—"Tears, Derik. Oh my God in heaven, He heard my prayer," he said, now sitting up with hands in his face, beginning to wail in a joy long forgotten. The film over his eyes started dissolving, leading to a burning he was no longer familiar with. Instinctively squeezing his eyes shut, he was surprised to find he had developed transparent, thin membranes returning as eyelids with which to blink. All at once, what began with a moment of enlightenment ended with a titanic resurgence of emotions. His blubbering continued as he tried to iterate his matter to Derik, who was so amused with the display that he just watched endearingly with a grin.

"Derik," Andi called. "Is everything okay with Jake?"

"He's fine," Derik answered in a laugh.

"The berries ... do you have them?"

Derik looked at Andi incredulously. "You gotta be kidding me! I don't know where they are!"

"Then we gotta go! Come on. Let's go." Andi turned around and saw a glassy sphere loaded with strategically placed jewels, all connected by white, almost indiscernible mapped lines. It was the Atlas. It sat on a rock-carved table just inside a passageway off the ledge.

She began walking toward it in awe. It was beautiful. The lines' white shimmer had Andi thinking in terms of controlled lightning, only on a much smaller scale, as in delicate thread. As the light passed through each particular gemstone, it emitted a brilliant glistening, which gave off the overall glassy effect. "The other end of this is what we must have seen in that room," she said to herself. "I bet he created a window here for that horseman to travel through in order to get to that horse." She raised a cynical eyebrow. "Too bad it won't be there." She chuckled. She took a closer look at the gorgeous glimmering stones without getting too close out of respect for the white vibrating lines. *He doesn't have absolute power if I take one of those stones*, she thought to herself. She took another step toward the Atlas, then tripped and fell. She sat up and then rotated around to see what it was she'd kicked. It was a small bag. She tipped it toward her.

Derik helped Jake to his feet. Jake studied Derik's eyes for a moment. "So you're the one."

"Come again?"

"I used to pray you'd never show up. To look back at those days from here, wow. I was such an inflated coward. And I'm betting that's how she saw me." He took one step back and was working on another. "Listen, Derik, I can't ever thank you enough for—"

"Whoa, wait a second. We're all in this together now. Let's go. You're coming too."

"I can't go back like this. I'll stay here and go after—"

"No. It'll be okay. We've got to try."

Jake shook his head, looking away.

Derik frowned. "Fine. I'm not gonna twist your arm, but we've got to go. At least escort us to the gate that will get us home."

Jake conceded, then whistled. His muscle-bound stallion sprinted to his side. "Hop on," he said after swinging onto its back in a single grasp of its mane.

"Um, yeah, okay."

Jake held out a hand and yanked Derik up, then pulled his fur hood over his head, hiding his face.

Derik glared at him. "She's already seen you, man."

Jake paused. A thought stole his breath. He turned to Derik with a hopeful air about him. "My phone, do you still—"

"Here," Derik answered, pulling it out of his pocket.

Jake tapped a few buttons, producing a holographic image of his family. He smiled gently and then safely tucked it into his garments. He leaned back toward Derik. "Hold on, friend." The two were off in a sprint. They sped through a series of tunnels, ending up in front of Andi.

"You happen to get a good look at those two archers at all?" she asked.

Derik shook his head. "One of them took a shot at Jake here, though." As soon as he spoke the words, he realized the archer had delivered a dose of something quite incredible. He glanced at Jake. "You didn't feel it, did you? The arrow, it didn't hurt you." With his face hidden within the oversized hood, Jake began looking

239

back at Derik but spotted Andi. Before the hooded opening could completely compromise him, he resumed his straightforward position, resigning himself to silence.

Pulling empty hands out of her pockets, Andi frowned. "We couldn't have done it without them."

Derik nodded, looking down at Andi, and asked the more pressing question. "Where are the berries?"

"I'm sorry. I guess I lost them in the lake." She stepped up to Jake's leg and patted his knee. "Jake, thank you so much." She covered her mouth while her eyes fell to the ground. A tender, breaking voice announced, "I thought you were dead." She returned her tearful gaze to Jake. "I can't imagine what you're going through right now. But I want you to know, Jake, that I know you're no longer that horrid thing. No matter what you look like, you'll always be my Jake." A quiet, awkward moment passed while she waited for any kind of reply.

Andi switched her gaze to Derik. The beseeching expression she wore tugged at Derik's heart, kindling a tender response. She stepped away from Jake and toward Derik. He reached down and held her cheek with an open palm. His task-oriented grimace softened into a compassionate, welcoming grin. He stole a look at her lips, and she took notice. She slid her eyes over to Jake and then quickly ran them back to Derik, tossing him a puckered kiss. Butterflies instantly ran amuck throughout his stomach.

The silent giggles were enough to motivate Jake. "Come on, Andi. Hop up," he said from under his hood. "We have to jump through the gate. This gate isn't at full strength yet. It won't get you back. There's still a fragment of the one Derik arrived through yesterday. If we jump through this one, it should lead us to that one."

Derik tapped him on the shoulder. "Why do we need to go anywhere? Wasn't it right here in this cavern? I mean, because this is where I fell through."

"Not anymore."

"Where'd it go? If it was here, why isn't it still here?" Derik asked.

"Bierwul took it with him earlier, along with Lig Nædre. He was trying to speed things up for Valicious."

"So where is it?" Andi asked.

"Wherever Bierwul was last."

"Pradicus's house," Derik said. "Bierwul was shot there by Pradicus."

"What?" Jake asked, turning to Derik. He held his gaze for a moment. Derik then looked to Andi, wondering what the matter was about. Jake rotated back around.

Derik reached down, clasped Andi's wrist, and then pulled her up.

"Hold on," Jake said. The huge horse took a couple of galloping steps and then leapt into the gate. They exited the gate just behind Pradicus's smoldering house.

Andi jumped off the horse, followed by Derik. "If this gate took *us* here, shouldn't it have taken Valicious here also?" she asked.

"Perhaps, but unlikely. He wouldn't have wanted to risk us following him, wherever he jumped to," Jake answered. "We are only permitted to jump between windows unless we're mapped, in which case we can jump anywhere."

"We've got to find our gate, guys," Derik said.

Jake turned toward Derik and Andi. "It's usually hidden in a confined area like a cave or a room or—"

"Yes, over there under the house, where we found the horse, Derik," Andi interrupted.

The comment snatched Jake's attention. "What horse? There are no extra—"

"Wait a minute," Derik said, cutting in. "Pradicus didn't even know about the riders, so how did he have one of their horses?"

Jake offered a perplexed sigh. "Perhaps a plant by Valicious. But that would only be necessary if Pradicus were expected to become like...me," he said, glancing toward Andi.

An enormous *bang* cracked the sky, followed by a massive roar of fury. Lig Nædre burst through the time gate and heaved its most substantial swell of fire ever. The Jangus fell from the sky, lifeless and limp, and slammed to the earth with several *snaps* accompanied by one large *crack*. Derik and Andi ran then dove for the ground, reliving their recent horror with the beast.

Upon his noble steed, Jake stood his ground. The wing injuries sustained by the archers' arrows were evident via its unsharpened maneuvering. Nonetheless, it was alive and very much seeking a reckoning. It swung down and tried to make an attempt at Jake. Jake unclipped his whip and unleashed a thrashing upon the beast's face, causing the dragon to flinch on its pass. The horse stood true, fearless. Jake re-secured the whip into its clip, then grabbed his crossbow and proceeded to shoot and reload in a rapid and precise effort. Many of the arrows simply bounced off the scaled armor. But the arrows that did land fell along the neck. The beast was careful not to open its wings into a full span within firing range on this occasion.

As soon as Jake emptied his quiver of arrows, he slammed his crossbow to the ground and drew his long blade. The wind created from the wing thrusts had trees swaying and clothing dancing loosely.

"Jake, no!" Andi screamed.

She arose and took a running step toward Jake but was grabbed at the ankle by Derik. "Let me go. He can't do this, Derik. We can save him." She broke free and ran. The dragon circled around wide in the distance and came in shallow. There was no escaping this time.

"Andi! Andi, don't! I can't lose you again!" Derik screamed as the hope he held for the two of them began to fade before his eyes. He stood to his feet. The memories poured in: her lips in the basement pantry, her tranquil voice while weathering storms from his loft, the glow of her skin on moonlit Saturday nights at Old Man Cutter's, her smiling face waiting for him on his stack of hay, and the flitting of her hair every time she turned away from him.

"Oh my goodness..." he said quietly, then bit his lip. "I'm in love with her. Oh God, I'm so in love with her." Time stood still for but a moment. Clarity found him. No matter where or when, he made a decision that it would be he who would stand beside her, before her, and behind her. The honor to be the standard in her pursuit for love stood solely as utmost privilege. "Andi!" he cried. "I *love* you!"

Andi held up and gazed back at him. Her expression exhilarated him and was worth the adventure's every daring second. She said nothing at first. Then her countenance fell as she exploded into a tearful tantrum. "Derik! Why? Why now?" She clenched a fist and then threw it down. "I can't. I've got to go. I have to do this! Derik!" she yelled and turned back toward Jake, beginning to run again.

"Then your fate will be mine," Derik said quietly, breaking into a sprint.

Andi reached Jake and seized his foot. "Come on, Jake. We can make it." She looked over her shoulder, and the dragon had just started its final approach. "Jake! Don't let me die with you."

Jake looked down at her. "It's too late for me. This is the end that has been chosen for me. I'll face it boldly. Go."

"Let me see your face again. Please."

Jake looked up and held off a second, then removed his hood. Then he glanced back down at her as Derik reached them. Andi saw the monster still, but who Jake was and what she knew of him were more pronounced. His voice had returned, for the most part, with the exception of a shift from time to time, most notably when raising or lowering his pitch. He'd formed new skin, which made up his lips; his eyelids had begun to return; his eyes weren't as bulgy; and the veins had begun to recede. But the overall skull emphasis remained. It wasn't so much that his face seemed thinner; rather, his skull was more prominent as if it had expanded a bit while under the dragon's control. His overall beefier size hadn't begun to shrink either, a side effect he'd hoped to hold on to for a while longer. His strength remained as well, as in the way he pulled Derik up onto the horse with considerable ease. But most importantly, the way Jake held his eyes was back.

There was something about the confident, laid-back, "I've got it all under control" kind of look within and around his eyes that had always intrigued Andi. It was certainly something she never would have guessed about herself. He didn't come across as "prince charming" or "the knight in shining armor" to Andi but rather the "James Dean" rebel sort who had an itch for trouble and had become well adept at handling it and in cool fashion. He was perhaps something along the lines of Derik but rougher around the edges and quite a bit further out there on the edge itself. A bigger risk-taker for sure, but he almost always knew what he wanted and had the knack for getting it.

"You're beautiful, Jake. And I am your friend … always. Always, Jake," she said slyly, unclipping his whip. She grasped the handle, then stepped away and turned her face to Derik's chest.

The wind picked up mightily. Jake stood in his stirrups and held his blade high. "Fear me, behemoth!" he yelled. He pulled a bottle of black powder from his saddle and flung it as far into the air ahead of him as he could.

"Hold on to me," Andi said to Derik. Then she turned around and cast the whip around Jake's waist, then pulled him. Jake only fell back slightly and then turned to Andi. "No!" he cried in surprise.

Lig Nædre swept in. The bottle landed next to its left eye and exploded. The dragon recoiled as it began to pass over Jake. Beginning to lose its bearings and with its eye disintegrated, the beast extended its neck back around and blindly snapped its jaws. Its orifice snatched a wide heap of grass, along with Jake and his horse. The beast repositioned the two within its mouth as it careened uncontrollably out across the river. The whip quickly reached its extended length and yanked Andi and Derik off the ground, ripping the handle from her grip. She could only watch as her friend was swept away, attached to the listless leather hanging down from Lig Nædre's mouth.

"Jake!" Andi cried, reaching her hand out after him. "This can't be the end. It's not supposed to go this way." She dropped her head and began to grieve for her friend. "Lord, I thought You were going to save him," she sobbed through her tears and with a defeated frown.

Suddenly, an eruption exploded. From the water beneath the dragon, the kraken reached its arms up and seized it, pulling it down in a grand splash.

The plunge knocked the wind out of the dragon, causing it to hurl what it had just filled its mouth with. Huge splashes of water soared as the titans fought. Bursts of fire lit up the horizon. The kraken continued to reposition its arms for a better hold, all the while trying to avoid the snapping jaws of its larger opponent. Finally, Lig Nædre swung its great tail around, landing a crushing blow against two of the kraken's arms, breaking itself free of the powerful grasp. It strained its wings in a powerful effort against the river's current and managed to extend them fully. With several enormous thrusts of its tail, it propelled itself up and out of the water enough to begin an ascent. Several more great flaps of its mighty wings gave it the boost it needed to break away. Against its smaller, less powerful, and certainly dispirited foe, it turned and blasted a prevailing pompous roar.

Basking in a confidence laden with vengeance, it heaved its tail one last time in a lethal swing toward its river rival. The kraken countered with a sharp swerve, then seized the dragon's tail in a mammoth grip and immediately propelled itself downward deep toward the bottom. Lig Nædre screeched in an unexpected panic as it plummeted once again into the river with a fantastic splash. The kraken wrapped its tentacles around the dragon methodically and purposefully until it had the hold it wanted and then squeezed with all its might. Several deep cracks and snaps made their way to Andi and Derik's ears. Hundreds of bubbles great and small rose to the water's surface for several moments. Suddenly, all at once, they stopped. The kraken led the limp dragon down near the bottom of the river, then, with its massive strength, systematically dismembered it, tearing limb from body. In its final act of triumph, it wrapped one of its wounded arms around the head of Lig Nædre and crushed its skull, leaving the carcass to drift to the bottom of the riverbed.

Jake stepped out from the woods unscathed, covered in dragon phlegm.

"Jake!" Andi hollered, then leapt up and ran to him. "Thank God! Oh, thank you, God." The three of them glanced over to the river and watched as the water settled.

Jake pulled his hood over his face again. "You tried to save me anyway, Andi. Thank you. It's over now."

She turned to Derik and laid her face in his chest again. "Really? It's over? It's really over?" she said, nearly unable to dare to tread there. She placed her arms around Derik's neck and then found her legs giving out.

Derik held her in his arms and then knelt with her. He placed her head on his lap and stroked her hair. "It's over, Andi." She cupped her hand over her eyes and wept.

"Hey, come on. We made it," he said, touching her face.

"Wait, the berries. Is your gate still open?" Jake said.

Derik looked up at him and shook his head. "We couldn't find them. We don't know if it's still open."

"Well, you said you saw light in a small room under the house?" Jake answered.

Derik nodded. "Behind the house, over there," he said with a flick of his head.

"There may still be time." He whistled. In a second, his stallion came galloping out of the woods in a head sprint. "Come, my friends."

Derik helped Andi up, and out from a hidden pocket under her gown fell the three berries. Andi gasped in cheerful surprise. She and Derik both fixed their eyes on the three bouncing bits of hope until they came to rest, only to find them dried up and completely withered.

"No!" Andi cried, throwing her fists.

Derik sighed. "I guess we're stuck here for now." He held Andi by the shoulders. "Look, it's okay. I'm okay if we have to stay a little longer, just until we can figure some things out. I want to learn about Romans and more about this amazing God. It'll be fine."

"Maybe you're not stuck here," Jake said. "If I remember correctly, we were after Derik's emerald. That stone was taken from your time period. It will return to the same period unless it's been allocated to another. This time period doesn't count because this is where it was forged."

"Wait a second. Are you telling me that my amulet started right here and made it all the way to me in the twenty-first century?"

Jake nodded.

"Then who forged it?" Derik asked.

"Valicious. About twenty years ago."

"What? Twenty years ago? But it's been, what, almost a thousand years missing?"

"No. Pradicus dismantled the Atlas and used time gates to spread the gems throughout time. Valicious has been after the gems ever since. If you had the emerald, you could go through any time gate and return to the time period from which it was taken."

"How did you end up here then?" Andi asked.

"You're not going to believe this. My watch. The number twelve on its face held the tip to a powerful stone, a diamond. That small diamond was cut and shaved into a hundred pieces, and each piece had to be tracked down."

Derik thought of the mound of bones in the cavern and the people they belonged to and then shook his head in disgust.

"It was a very dark time here for many years, according to the traders. Many people fled the island and refused to come back after Valicious went crazy; he went on some kind of tyrannical crusade. The men I spoke with told me Laminus was one of the places they thought about living for the rest of their lives."

"Laminus," Derik replied, "I saw that word on a sign in the scroll room under Pradicus's house. What is it?"

"A sign?" Jake asked. Immediately, the recollection dawned. *Yes, of course the sign—not the Laminus sign, but the other sign*, he thought to himself. He felt his face quickly prickle into a burning pink blush. His eyes ran toward Andi, quite certain that if Derik had seen the Laminus sign, he probably saw the other also, and he had to ask himself if Andi then saw it as well. The married life Jake once imagined for himself and Andi, unbeknownst to her, had finally been laid to rest. But here and now, months after daring to call her name out down the empty corridors of hope, he wondered if these returning thoughts were merely an echo of his own voice or if Andi may have finally answered. "Oh … um," he managed, obviously preoccupied, "that's, uh, the true name of this island," Jake said, questioning whether or not his thoughts actually were emerging over the entirety of his face, as he felt they were. *Could she be calling back? The answer to that question could change everything*, he thought. *It could be the reason she just tried to stop me from throwing my life away, why she approached me first in the cavern when Derik and I both sat on the horse, and why she called my name out for help when leaping away from Lig Nædre.* He then continued. "The government was a God-fearing people and named the island in honor of Jesus, the Lamb of God within us. They were a blessed people. But Valicious, in his rage, abolished the government and proclaimed himself ruler. He decreed that God didn't and couldn't exist and renamed the island for the absence of God, which he was sure was more accurate. He then warned that anyone referring to the island as Laminus again would be executed immediately."

"Hell-in-us, how do you like that?" Derik said.

"Well, we need to stop Valicious, then find the emerald to get us back to our time," Derik said.

Realizing his secret was probably safe, and the timing of pursuing Andi due to the lack of, he decided to let it go —for now. "There's not a good chance of that. Another time gate won't open for quite some time now that Lig Nædre's gone," Jake said.

"What about the Atlas? I thought he could go anywhere without the dragon's fire to assist him if he completed the Atlas, which he did," Derik said.

"Yes, but he jumped through the gate in a panic," Jake answered.

"And without the Atlas," Andi interjected. "Wait…hey…" she added before Derik cut in with a triumphant laugh.

"Well, then he can't do anything else. He has no power. So let's find the emerald and get back," Derik explained. Suddenly, Andi's comment caught up to them. He and Jake together turned to Andi.

"Wait a second," Derik said. "How do you know whether or not he has the Atlas?"

She answered him with an insightful grin.

"Then all he has to do is get back to the Atlas?" Derik responded.

Jake nodded. "Yes, but for some reason, I feel it's been dismantled."

A loss of comprehension enveloped Derik. "So who dismantled the Atlas?"

Andi interrupted. "Um, guys, we don't need to look very far." She pulled the glowing emerald from a second pocket on the underside of her skirt. "The pocket's for carrying important things," she said with a smirk. She held it up to Jake with a questioning expression as she stared at its glow.

"*You* dismantled the Atlas?" Derik asked in utter astonishment.

"Well…I thought we might need the emerald."

"When? I mean, when did you have the chance to—"

Wishing he didn't have to go through with it, Jake shook his head, stepping in. "That's not important. What is important is that you have the stone and are just beneath a gate. This gate will take you home."

Andi smiled, staring at the emerald. "It's not hot, even though it's glowing. Isn't that sort of strange?" she asked, pocketing the emerald again.

"It'll always glow around the dark magic," Jake explained. "And the dragon was just here. Its luster will diminish shortly."

"Well, it seems it dimmed a little," she said.

Jake raised his arms out. "Yes, let's not forget about me. I'm wrapped up in it completely. The stone should remain cool while illuminating until the dark magic is away from it. Thanks to you two, I broke free from the darkness. Perhaps I too will cease to exist in this state." He dropped his furs to the ground, revealing two well-developed arms extending out from a sleeveless tunic. It was the first time he'd given any notice to his body in months. Derik's eyebrows peaked as he studied the muscle-on-top-of-muscle definition within each arm. Andi glanced at first and then turned completely around, unaware of her plummeting chin.

"Well, this state isn't all bad, I suppose," Jake added, oblivious to the others' gawking. "But it would be great if I could get back to being the old me. Again, thank you both." Unsure about how Jake would interpret their attention, she resumed her former position and then cleared her throat to gather Derik's attention.

Derik looked down and smiled at Andi. "It wasn't the two of us. It was all her. She's the only one you need to thank. Well, and Pradicus, I guess."

Andi smiled back and then turned away in a frown as her thoughts drifted to Pradicus. "I was sure he was going to meet us in the cavern," she said, barely squeaking the words out. Eighteen months of happy and sad times swarmed within the banks of her memory. "How could it happen?" she asked. "Is it really possible that you could go back to being Jake—the Jake from a few months ago?"

"Anything's possible now that Lig Nædre is dead. The curse shouldn't keep much longer." He picked up the furs and refastened them, then gripped the horse's mane, and in a single hop, he was securely seated. "Climb up on Heracles, here, and we'll make sure you get through the gate."

Derik helped Andi to her feet and then, with a running start, managed to leap up onto the tall steed. Jake reached down and took Andi by the hand, then effortlessly hoisted her up so that she sat directly behind him. She held on to Jake's coat of furs, and Derik held her around the waist. The great horse started in on a trot and then blasted into a mad dash.

Andi laughed, as it was Derik's hind end in jeopardy this time. Heracles built up enough speed to vault off a quickly approaching peak.

Andi adjusted her grip on Jake. "What about you?" she cried.

"I'm going back for Valicious to finish what I started before he did this to me," he answered.

Just then, the emerald radiated fiercely. "Jiminy Christmas, what the…" she shouted just before the burning reached her leg. "Ouch, ouch! Get it off!" she cried, staring down at its penetrating glow from within the pocket against her thigh. "Help me! It's burning me!"

She let go of Jake and started slapping at it in an attempt to quickly alleviate the scorching. It seared a hole through her pocket and began to slide out, along with three shimmering gold pieces. "The emerald! I'm losing it!" she screamed. She grasped it but lost control of it when its heat punished her palm and fingers. It fell free from her open hand but sat hanging in midair, its brilliant glow remaining.

Jake leaned back. "Jump on three, two, one, go!" he yelled.

His leaning back caused her to shift her balance. She began slipping off the horse but was caught by Derik.

"Gotcha," Derik said, gripping her arm. The horse sprung off the peak into the sky, and all together, they ascended toward the gate. As the horse went airborne, Derik's legs and rear lifted high off the horse's back. His hold of her arm was all that kept him from breaking free. In a reflex, she seized Jake's coat of furs to anchor herself.

"Derik," Andi cried, "hold on!" He lost his hold of her as her arm slid through his grasp like a wet bass. He clutched her hand in one last-ditch effort. The grips each of them held for the other's hand began slipping away until they were connected by the tips of their fingers. The gate threshold's suction swirled, pulling and twirling Andi's hair as she held her eyes on Derik intently.

She looked past Derik. "No!" she yelled. Suddenly, a horseman's whip wrapped itself around Derik's ankle, retaining him at the entrance of the gate.

"Derik, find me!" she shouted, trying to speak over the rushing wind. "I love you." The feeble connection their hands shared gave way as Derik watched Andi, Jake, and Heracles pass through.

"Andi!" he screamed fiercely, reaching his hand out toward her fading image. Suspended like a kite, he turned to see what had a hold of him. A brutal-looking horseman unlike the others had his lengthy whip extended and was reaching for his crossbow while sitting upon his own great steed. A vague familiarity churned Derik's discernment. The word shook him, even as it slipped from his mouth: "P-Pradicus?"

He, at first, dismissed the thought but then remembered what Andi had said about dragon saliva when she was telling him about Garren and Jake. It seemed impossible that Pradicus could be subjected to the dragon's will, but the proof sat in Pradicus's robes on a horse in front of him. The horseman took the weapon in a single hand, aimed, and fired. The arrow pierced the air with terrible speed.

"Oh God in heaven, help me now I pray," he whispered, bearing clutched fists.

As Derik helplessly awaited the arrow's strike, he simply closed his eyes and surrendered to fate. Thoughts ran threw his mind of how it should have been him there all along and never should've included Andi. He drew upon the memory of her expression as he told her of his love in the field a short while ago and decided it, if any, should be the expiring image he would depart with. As he became comfortable with his final moments, it became clear that too much time had passed. Perhaps the arrow had missed him. Was he actually afforded the opportunity for escape?

He opened his eyes to an incredible sight. Time had, in fact, slowed to a near stillness, and the arrow had yet to land its deadly blow. As if someone had thrust it straight to the forefront of his thoughts, the recollection of Jake's knife sprung into his memory. *Yes, that's it.* He reached around, yanked it out from behind him, and, in a single swipe of its razored edge, cut himself free. The wormhole swallowed him instantly. A powerful light flashed, followed by a fall through darkness.

16

He awoke in the late evening under a starlit Nebraska sky. The heaviness of his eyelids kept him comfortably at rest while some semblance of alertness leaked into his sleep, more and more every few seconds. He finally made several attempts to open his eyes despite the burning. He found some partial relief after a series of blinks. Waking without memory of Pradicus or Jake, he took a quick glance around.

"My goodness, how long have I been asleep?" he muttered. He sat up, finding himself in the middle of his uncle's wheat field. "Whoa," he said, rubbing his forehead. "This is crazy."

His hands moved toward the top of his head, where he ran fingers through his hair, and sighed. Through a large, drawn-out yawn, he tried his best to recall the earlier events of his day. Images of lunch with a friend slowly materialized. "Everyone's probably wondering where I'm at," he said with a chuckle. "I slept straight through dinner. Wow."

He struggled to stand to his feet, losing his balance a bit along the way, but managed well, considering how sore and tight his muscles felt. He stretched mightily, bellowing out a fantastic roaring exhale that seemed long overdue. A gentle gust caught him just right. He closed his eyes as the wind caressed his face. He then turned to watch the tips of prairie wheat sway back and forth in response to the breeze's light, flirting touches. The night's brilliant moonlight allowed him to see for miles in every direction.

"What in the world are you doing out here again?" a tender elderly woman's voice asked. "You missed dinner again. I had the table set nice tonight just for you."

"I'm so sorry. I didn't mean to miss ..." he said, pausing, as memories of his journey trickled back in. "Wait a second. Where's Andi?" he asked. "Is she okay?"

"Land sakes, Derik. I swear, that girl's got a hold on you something awful. Well, I guess I figured she'd be the reason you'd be out here so late. You just saw her this afternoon."

"What time is it?" he asked, somewhat confused. "I had a date with her tonight. Man, I've let her down, haven't I? She's gonna think I blew her off. Is it too late to see her?"

"It is kind of late. Why don't you just see her tomorrow?"

"Can I at least give her a call?"

"Good heavens, Derik," she said, relenting. "You know what? It's not all that late. I'm sure she'd appreciate another visit." She attended his side and escorted him by the arm. "Your legs give out on you again or what? Come on. I'll walk with you."

He smiled at her. "Maybe we can keep our date after all. Again, do you have the time?"

"Hang on. I'll check in a minute," she said. She reached into a pocket in her gown and pulled out a small, smooth, chrome disc about the size of a half dollar. "Don't wanna drop one of these in the field again. That was quite the headache," she said with a chuckle.

As the two reached the edge of the wheat field and turned toward the barn, Derik realized it looked different, possibly restored. "Wow, when did *that* happen?" As the words barely left his mouth, a holographic image began to take shape above the held-out disc.

"Aunt Frieda, what the—" Derik said, taken aback by the sight.

A high resolution, three-dimensional, football-sized weatherman announced himself. "Good evening, Miss Katie. Dale E. Forecast at your service. How can I assist you this beautiful evening? And I see Sir Derik is joining you. Shall I prepare his evening cocktail?"

Derik stopped cold. "What did he just call you? And how does that thing know me? Aunt Frieda, what's going on here?"

"Derik, it's okay. We need to jog your memory a smidge. Let you catch up after that big nap."

"Wait a minute. Nap? I should have ended up back in the barn. This is all wrong. I mean, just moments ago I cut myself free with Jake's—"

"Yes, I know, Derik," she interrupted. "Everything will make sense in another second."

"But he called you Katie, Aunt Frieda," he said, staring into her wrinkled but beautiful eyes.

"That's because my name isn't Frieda, Derik. It's Katie."

The world he knew slowly came to a grinding halt as he lifted his eyes. "It's currently eight forty-seven p.m. on a beautiful November twenty-eighth evening," the holographic image stated in the background.

A vague awareness fell over him upon his glimpsing a familiar image. Katie's words began to process. *My name isn't Frieda, Derik. It's Katie.*

He freed himself of her escorting arm and approached a wonderfully filigreed tombstone displaying the name "Andrea Halle Schaeffer" in a fancy script. He shuffle-stepped his way closer toward the beautiful stone slab. It read: "Resting peacefully here and in our hearts," then had the date November 28 beneath it.

"Well, that's today." He turned to Katie with a lost expression and flooding eyes. "She's ... gone?"

Katie took him by the hand. "November twenty-eighth is the day you came back fifty-four years ago. Sweetie, we've been over this many times."

"Fifty ... fifty-four years," he whispered. He looked down at his hands and found them wrinkled and slender and scattered with age spots. Fighting back the pressing lump in his throat was like holding a dam together with good intensions. Glimpses of his surprise were revealed upon his curling frown. He gently brushed his fingers over her name on the tombstone. He heaved the words "I'm so sorry" as the lump in his throat gave way. He nearly collapsed from his wailing.

"She never made it back. Sweetie, we've gone over this many, many times for the last six or seven years. Don't you remember?"

"Andi, I'm so sorry," he cried. "It wasn't supposed to be like this." He looked back at the elderly woman. "Is it really you, Katie? Little Katie?"

She smiled sympathetically. "Yes, Derik, little Katie, although I'm not so little anymore," she said, shaking her head and chuckling.

He had the presence of mind to look down at her ring finger. It bore a plain gold band. He gazed down at his own finger.

She addressed him with a snigger. "No, Derik. You and I never … um … "

"Katie," he called through a sobbing voice, "what happened? Dear God, what went wrong?"

She stepped up next to him and held him closely.

"What did I do, Katie? She's gone."

"I know. I don't even really remember her, except that she used to tickle us. I do know that."

A sudden clarity for the life he'd lived away from Andi began to dawn. "When did I stop waiting for her?"

"Well, you let go a few years after I came to live with you."

"How long ago was that?"

"Twenty-two years ago."

He turned to her quickly. "What? Twenty-two years? You're joking."

She shook her head.

"Who were you married to? I mean ... " he said, pointing down at her finger.

"I was engaged five times, but, well, never married."

His face immediately expressed heartbreak. "I'm sorry, Katie. So whose ring?"

She blushed just a tad. "You don't remember?"

"Well, I was just asking. I didn't mean to pry."

"No, no. It's your ring. You gave it to me while on a—"

"Cruise," he interjected. "That's right," he added, squeezing her hand. "Several of us went together, and I told you on the deck one evening that if neither of us were married by the time you turned forty-nine that I'd marry you."

She grinned and glanced away.

"How did I ever forget about that? Don't tell me that's coming up soon."

"It's about time to get you in," she said. I'll wait over here while you visit with sister. Then we'll go in and have some ice cream."

"Now wait just one second. If I'm thirteen years older than you and I'm currently ... " he said, reflecting for a moment, then continued, "seventy-one, then you, of course, would be ... " He counted on his fingers. "Oh my. I'm just letting everyone down, aren't I?"

"Sweetie, let's get you in."

"Katie, what happened to me? Why do I keep forgetting?"

"We should be thankful for the warm weather this week. We need to get you inside."

"Katie, please. I need to know."

She touched his arm and then sighed, pressing her lips. "Let's talk inside, Derik."

"Katie, no. Whatever this is I'm hanging on to needs to be dealt with."

She debated for a moment and then conceded. "All right, honey. About twenty-five years ago, you fell into a depression. Apparently during that time, you had an accident here on the farm and since then have been struggling with this. The last six or seven years have been the worst. You've seen the best doctors, but no one's been able to help you kick this without medication."

"Yes, I'm starting to recall the hospital visits. How did I pay for all that?"

"Are you kidding me? Derik, with the coins. You don't remember?"

He squinted his eyes as if searching his memory.

"You came back with three coins from the twelfth century. You made a killing on them. You bought everything around here. This is all your property for as far as you can see. Derik, you're rich."

"Of course, the coins," he said quietly. "How is it that *I* ended up with those? Is that why I can't get rid of you?" he asked with a chuckle.

"Hey, you didn't let anyone know you had them until fifteen years ago or so. I was already here with you, so don't start. Besides, you offered to send me off with a small fortune years ago, and I told you where you could put it. Being here with you is my place. I don't give two hoots about the money, Derik, and you know that. Now I'll be waiting over by the fountain. Take your time with Andi," she said, giving him a short distance of privacy.

He grinned mildly and then turned to Andi's tombstone, realizing once again that she was merely part of a distant, nearly forgotten part of his life. He had previously etched the words *Find me* into the top of the cement. He suddenly remembered the very day he scripted those words so long ago. Recall instantly returned.

"I can't keep doing this. My goodness, it's like I just saw you yesterday, or today, for that matter. But I've got to lay you to rest once and for all, my love. I've allowed my feelings, my yearnings for you to consume me, and I've missed out on life. You wouldn't have wanted that for me…" He glanced over his shoulder back at Katie. "Or for her," he added. "It's past the time for me to move on. I'm not going to visit you again for a long time," he said, drawing a tear. "I've got to close this chapter of my life. But know it'll always be the one I call my most cherished, the one worth living a lifetime for. You're the most incredible woman I've ever met, Andi Schaeffer. You're the one no one else ever matched up to."

He picked up a small stone and leaned over the tombstone. He etched the word *Don't* in front of his prior scripting and kissed the top of the headstone. "Even that one," he said in a regretful tone, recalling his kiss on her forehead so long ago. Then he stood up and walked away.

17

Derik took Katie by the hand. "I once promised you that you would always be my number one. It seems funny, looking back, to make a promise like that and expect to keep it." He stopped and turned to her. "I'm sorry I didn't keep that promise."

"Well, you didn't actually make that promise. Andi did for you. I hung on to that memory for years, that night in the basement. I must have asked her about it every day after that until the day she disappeared."

She paused for a moment, tears welling within her eyes. Words tried to find their way out of her mouth but became lost in her emotion. "I don't know how to love anyone else," she finally whispered. "You've been my entire life's love." She released his hand, then cupped both of hers over her face and wept. She stepped back and muttered something through a series of broken syllables.

Derik's heart poured out to her. He stepped toward her and embraced her. "Don't talk now. I've got you. It's all going to be fine."

She gathered herself and stepped away again. "What's wrong with me that you prefer the shadow of my sister over me?" His soft expression had her recoiling. "Oh, I'm so sorry. I didn't mean that. I really didn't mean that to sound bad. I know you loved her—or love her, I mean. But you are *everything* to me, Derik. I don't know anything else. Nothing else matters in my life. I just wish..." she said, beginning to weep again. Through a series of sniffles, she managed to put together a few words. "I wish your soul's eyes... could see me."

Derik's body went limp. He sat down on the side of the fountain. *Is it possible I've thrown my entire life away for a lost hope on the wind?* he asked himself.

Regaining some composure, she glanced over at him through red, teary eyes. "I'm sorry I said anything. Please forget everything I said."

"I've been so unfair to you, Katie. How does someone make up for something like that? My goodness, I'm a wreck. Any man worth his weight would give everything he owns to have your heart."

"It's only worth it if I have his as well," she replied, considering heavily the words she just spoke. "And I don't think I do." She stirred her foot over some loose gravel on the ground. She looked back up at him. "I'm the one who's been unfair. You've been committed to the one you love, and that's the highest honor a man could ever bestow upon a woman. I will not be the one to step in between that kind of commitment. I don't know why it's taken me this long to see it, but the love you have for my sister is what fables are made of. And it's not mine for the taking." As she approached him, he stood. "You're truly a gentleman among men. And my sister, whoever she is in God's eyes, somehow deserves such a magnificent man. She must really be something else. Lord, I wish I could've known her." She placed an open hand over his heart. "This is reserved. Always, always protect it."

"Katie, no, I told you years ago that I would marry you. I mean to keep that promise."

"Funny thing about promises; their usefulness to one person is directly related to the ability of another to walk them out. No matter what life we take up for ourselves, I'd never be your number one. I think I've finally realized that won't ever happen." She leaned into him and kissed him on the lips with a passion that validated every emotion she'd ever felt for him. "If I live a thousand years, I'll live every second loving you," she said, holding his face. "Don't let her go. Whatever you do, love her until your last breath." She reached both arms around him and squeezed with everything she had, and then she rested her cheek against his chest. "You won't find me here in the morning. I've got the rest of my life to live. But I'll check in on you from time to time." She released him and kissed him once more, then turned and headed toward the house.

Derik drew his hair back using both hands and then sat once more on the edge of the fountain.

18

Five months had come and gone since Derik last saw Katie. He decided to take one last nap against a stack of hay in the loft of the barn. The entire property was set to close escrow the next morning. He bought a cabin in the woods near a river and decided to live out the rest of his days like Andi lived with Pradicus. He rested his head back against the hay and imagined Andi on the opposite side, taking in the breeze. "I really miss you," he said softly while sliding off into a peaceful sleep.

A familiar voice answered back. "Did you mean it?"

The voice startled him for half a second, then he began drifting off to sleep again. "Did...I mean...what?" he asked in a slurred, mumbled voice.

"What you said," the voice replied in a soft, whispery tone.

A snore escaped his open mouth and slightly off-set jaw, followed by a smacking of his lips. "Um, what...did I say?"

"That you didn't want me to find you."

He ever so slightly shook his head, almost to the point of not moving it at all. "I ... didn't," he said, his speech slurring again, "didn't ... mean it."

The voice answered back. "I brought you some peaches from Old Man Cutter's peach trees." She set them down in a tidy bandana.

"Andi," he answered, his face taking on a luminescent glow. "My Andi, I knew ... you'd come."

She leaned in and kissed him on the cheek. "Yes, your Andi." She frowned. "I'm so sorry, Derik." She took him by the hand. "How in the world could I have let you live an entire lifetime without me, without us?" She began to tear up. "I just can't imagine what it was like for you."

Just then, Garren stepped off the loft's ladder. "Did you find him?"

She nodded as a great swelling tear dropped from her eyelash. She glanced back at Garren, trying hard to fight off the guilt. "I'm too late ..." she cried. She leaned in again and kissed the top of his head, holding him. "Way too late. I don't want him to know I was here," she said, wiping her eyes. Her cheerless straight lips bent into a frown, and she broke. "How did this happen, Garren? It's only been a few months. You said this wouldn't be the case."

Garren quietly moved toward her. "Actually, I said this probably wouldn't be the case. But without the emerald, it was impossible to know for sure when we would arrive in his timeline. Andi, I'm sorry."

"Oh God, this means my parents and my sisters and brother never knew either. Lord Jesus, help me."

"It's not all bad. If we had the emerald, things could possibly be different. Does he know where it is?"

A glimmer of hope struck Andi's disheartened countenance.

"Well, ask him," Garren said.

She spoke softly, studying his face, taking in his every wrinkle. "Derik, where is the … " Then she stopped.

"What is it, Andi?" Garren asked.

"What if he led a good life? What if he doesn't want this? There are other things to consider here."

"Well, we're running out of time. The window won't last long. Either we get it or we don't."

She wrestled with her selfishness and weighed it against what would be in Derik's best interest.

"Come on. Make a decision."

"I'm trying," she snapped. "Didn't you see the message he left on the tombstone? It said for me not to find him. He probably put that message there decades ago. What if he has kids, a wife, grandkids? Everything will change. I can't make that call."

She stood up and then kissed his hand. She rested it comfortably on the bandana-wrapped peaches. "Derik, I'm so sorry." She then turned. "And I'm even more sorry … you've forgotten me," she said under her breath in a crackling whisper. The two exited the barn and started their run back across the field. While balancing her emotions on the bitter edge of tears, it was the managing of her amassing feeling of loss that overtook her. She slowed to a walk and then collapsed to her knees under the weight of pure, undiluted anguish.

"Andi, what are you doing? You're going to be stuck here. The window won't wait."

"My God, Garren," she answered, sobbing. "He didn't want me. I'm all alone. I've lost everything … again."

"Andi, please, I don't mean to sound insensitive, but I can't wait. I have no way to get back. I have to go. Are you listening? Andi." He called again, but it wasn't the sound of Garren's voice she caught carrying on the wind. It was the tone of an elderly woman calling her name.

Andi turned one direction, then, sitting up, flipped around to another, trying to hone in on the faint calling. She heard it again and then spotted the waving of the woman's arms. It wasn't so much a call after all but a shouting of her name. She leapt to her feet and then took a few small steps toward the elder woman.

"I'm going to have to leave you here, Andi. I have to go right now," Garren said firmly. "Come now, if you're going with me."

She swiveled her head toward Garren. "Shush, I can't hear her. She knows who I am." She turned her attention back to the woman and squinted hard. She couldn't make out the sentence, but a few words landed on her ears. "Garren, can you understand her? I think she said 'mister' and 'late.' That doesn't make sense."

"No, not 'late'—more like 'lately,'" Garren answered. "There's an 'E' sound at the end. That's all I can help you with, Andi. If we don't get back to the wormhole, we're really going to be stuck here."

"She's addressing us, Garren. It sounds like 'mister' and 'lady' to me. Now she's pointing at the barn and saying Derik's name too. Maybe that's it. She's calling out names. What name sounds like 'mister'?"

"I don't know, Andi. Blister."

"Blister?"

"I'll try to come right back soon, okay? That's if I can't keep the window open. I will find you, okay?" He turned and started jogging the other direction. "Try fister, twister, shister..." he hollered out.

Andi gasped. "Oh my goodness. That's it. Sister. Mister is sister and lady is..." She stopped. "Katie?" she whispered to herself. She turned back to Garren. "It's my sister Katie, Garren!" she screamed. It's my sister!" She sprinted off toward the woman. "Katie, it's me, Andi."

Katie started walking as quickly as she could to meet Andi in the field but lost herself in the hysterics of joyful weeping. She slowed to a complete stop, bent over at the waist, catching her breath, and then buried her face in her hands. However, the unexpected sight of her long-lost older sibling churned up painful memories laid to rest long ago, exposing unattended wounds of a family's arduous past. By the time Andi made her way nearer, Katie's joy had been snuffed by the reminiscent storms of sorrow and grief from Andi's disappearance.

Andi stopped just short of reaching her. "Is it really you, Katie?"

Katie looked up and wiped her eyes. "My, my, you look just like your high school picture," she said. "Derik always said you would." A long-repressed tear welled within her eye, finally announcing its validation. Surrendering to the tears that followed, she whimpered through an emerging frown. "I'm so angry, Andrea. I'm angry that you were taken from us, from me. You're my sister, and I never even knew you."

Sorting through a myriad of unsettled feelings herself, Andi wondered if a hug would be presumptuous and instead placed a consoling hand on her arm. "Katie, I'm sorry. You have no idea how happy I am to see you. But look at you. It seems like only yesterday you were little Katie, full of life and attitude." She steadily reached an arm around her baby sister and squeezed. "There's so much I want to say."

Katie took Andi by the hand. "Derik used to speak so highly of you. It made me so envious of the time he was able to spend with you. All my life I've felt as if I were robbed. We all did."

Andi's smile, laced with heartache, simply flattened. "What became of everyone?" she asked somberly. "Katie, please … tell me. What happened to Mom and Dad?"

Katie held Andi's hand tighter. "They all, well, we all held on to the hope that we would see your safe return. Derik never told them what really happened. As far as anyone knew, you simply vanished one day. I didn't learn from Derik his account of things until everyone else was …" She paused. "Until they all passed on—Mom much earlier than the rest of them." She shook her head, giving in to another elongating frown. "Dad was so unhappy, downright miserable without Mom for the next four years until he just … one day stopped. He stopped eating, caring, living."

Andi clutched her sister's hand, then drew it to her lips and kissed it several times. "Katie, I'm so, so sorry," she said. She then closed her eyes and enveloped her in a complete embrace.

"I just wish we could go back to that day you disappeared. Nothing's been okay without you. Even Derik's had such a lonely life."

"He could've tried to find me, Katie. I don't understand why he didn't try. He had the emerald. All he had to do was add it with the other stones that make up—"

"The Atlas?" Katie interrupted.

The answer caught Andi off guard. "Well, yes, actually. He must have discussed this with you." Silence split the moment as Andi put pieces together. "Oh," she said. "Derik never had the Atlas. Wait a minute. Garren has it. But we weren't able to use it because it was missing the emerald." She looked back over her shoulder toward the wormhole. "Oh no. Garren's taking it with him. We need to get a hold of the emerald. Do you know where it is, Katie?"

Katie grasped a delicate gold chain fastened around her neck and then drew the attached emerald out from beneath her blouse. "This?" she asked skeptically. Andi nodded and then reached for it. Katie's tone deepened while her eyes grew wide and irate. "This small green stone is the reason for … everything?"

"Well, there's more to it than that. But please hand it to me, Katie. I realize some things seem to be finally making sense, but believe me. It's not at all even close to the truth of the matter. I need to catch Garren. I need to

275

catch him now. He's the one you saw me with way over in the field. Please, we actually have a chance to set things straight. Please hand it to me."

"Derik never made a big deal out of this emerald. Out of the blue one day, he asked me if I wanted it. It seemed to me that he was about to pawn it or just throw it out, so I said I'd take it," she said, unclasping it in the back.

"I'm so glad he didn't throw it out," Andi said. "Thank you for keeping it for him." She gathered it in her hand. "I promise I *will* be right back." She turned and then sprinted off toward the window, praying there was still enough time to reach Garren.

19

Back in the loft, Derik lay fast asleep. The air in the center of the loft took on an orange hue, then all at once ripped open. A window appeared, and a slightly hunched-over man in a charcoal cloak stepped out. His face, the one Andi had seen in the cavern, which certainly must have looked human at some point, had indeed taken on reptilian characteristics with the exception of the horrid wrinkles. He had two slits for a nose, thin black slices for pupils, and the absence of exterior ears. He walked with a small limp under the assistance of a tall walking staff, much like Pradicus's. His head, torso, and arm movements were smooth and seemed synchronized with one another. An arm didn't move without also his head or torso somewhat slithering along with it. He approached Derik. "So this is the vein in which you landed," he said in a smooth yet gravelly, snakelike tone. "I've been looking a long time for you, boy. Let's have it. The emerald."

Derik didn't answer or flinch.

"Wake up, boy, or I'll gut your entrails." He swatted Derik's leg with his staff. Again, Derik failed to respond. He brushed Derik's cheek with a claw-like nail protruding out from a long, bony finger. He ran it downward toward his mouth, then hooked it under his chin and pressed in.

Derik sprung to life in agony. "Who are you?" he garbled under vocal strain. "What on earth do you want?"

"My name is Valicious. I'll have that emerald now."

"I swear to God"—he coughed—"I don't have it."

"Come now." Valicious chuckled confidently. "Do you really believe faith has any bearing here, you diseased, worthless carcass?" He applied more pressure to the soft tissue under Derik's chin. "I press any harder, boy, and you'll open. Where is it?"

Derik floundered around, struggling for a breath, landing his hands around the wrist of his tormentor. He pulled down hard.

Valicious released the pressure. "So someone values the pitiful life he lives. I feel the stone's presence. There's no denying that it is nearby." He leaned in close to Derik. "You cost me my serpent. For that, I'll have your cold, dead body on a wall until you rot."

"No," Derik said under his breath. He then leaned in closer yet, touching his cheek against Valicious's. "You filthy salamander, you won't ever see that stone again," he whispered. "And I only wish I was the one responsible for your oversized iguana's death. Then my cold, dead body could wear a satisfied grin while I rot on your wall. What the heck? Why don't I just take credit for it right now?

It died like a pansy, begging for its life. I watched it and laughed while it squirmed for its last breath."

Valicious took a step back, screamed in a fit of rage, and then wrapped his long fingers around Derik's throat. "You dare to toy with me, boy? I'll tear you limb from limb."

"Then do it, you ugly cuss. You threaten because you can't follow through. Do it."

Valicious squeezed hard, watching the life begin to empty itself of Derik's limp, compliant body. Suddenly, he stopped. "Hanging Judas," he said, releasing his hold. "Of course, you wily fox. You're protecting her."

Derik fell forward, coughing and straining for breath. "I'm not protecting anyone. Finish it, you powerless, overgrown hobgoblin."

"Yes, I see it now. How noble. Your sacrifice is commendable, but after I have the emerald, your last breath won't be a sacrifice any longer. It'll be inconsequential."

Derik looked up at his pacing adversary. "You devil. You think you're going to get away with this? You don't know what stands against you, do you? I've seen them. There are beings out there that will stop you."

"Yes, the legendary, illuminant beings," he answered. "They're someone's song of hope, someone much less heroic than you, I assure you. I have an idea. Why don't you call to them while I watch you suffer?"

"You're an idiot. You don't even know who your real enemy is."

Valicious slowly turned. "Enough talk. If you're not assisting me, you're hindering me. Where's the emerald?"

"You know where you can stick it."

"Such attitude from an elderly man," he said. "From whence does it come, I wonder?"

"What does that mean?" Derik asked.

Valicious leaned in close again. "I put you here, boy," he whispered in a slithery voice, then stood as tall as possible, intentionally lording it over Derik.

The statement threw Derik for a moment. "I've been here my entire life," he said. "Seventy-one years."

"Is that so? Then what, specifically, can you tell me about your life one year ago?"

Derik's eyes ran around the loft as he tried hard to pull a memory. Clouded thoughts of Katie emerged.

"It's not there, boy. What you have is general memories from the vein that might have been."

Derik didn't answer.

"No comeback? No foul name for me? I'm disappointed."

Derik looked away. "The cruise, the inscription on the tombstone..." he said under his breath.

"Are you that dense? I just said they were memories that might have been."

Derik was quiet again.

"I believe I'm beginning to understand. You can't comprehend it. Oh, this is laughable. Our hero *is* more dense than presumed."

Derik glared furiously into the dull, black, slivered pupils staring back at him.

"You were held at the window's threshold, suspended in midair by my servant. An instant later, you were here.

What you fail to understand, my dense boy, is that there are billions of possible veins branching out from the smallest of decisions. History reveals plainly the ones you chose, but the future is unwritten. You could end up in any one of those billions of veins from here simply because you chose left instead of right. What you see around you is a possible future for you. You're still the young, impetuous teenager you were a few months ago. You've been dropped into one of those veins for one purpose: to deliver me the Atlas sooner than later."

"If what you say is true, why didn't you show up before now? I remember waking up in the field. It was months ago."

"I placed you at the seventieth-year parallel. It took me five months to track down which vein."

"That's hogwash. You're telling me I'm still seventeen years old?"

"I don't expect a failing high school student to grasp the complexities of time bending."

"So you're saying that if I go back in time from here, everything immediately around me this instant ceases to exist."

"Bravo. He can be taught."

"That's impossible."

"It's possible because it hasn't happened yet," he snapped. "I'm through explaining this."

"No, please, sir. I'll give you the emerald if you help me understand."

He snarled at Derik. "I said I'm finished talking," he muttered. "You pathetic, patronizing mule, I had more respect for you when you were ready to die. And die, you shall."

"Who cares if I die then? I'll just show up in another vein."

"So that I can enjoy the anguish of you actually understanding your predicament, this is the last thing I'm going to say before I begin watching you die." He knelt down in front of Derik, placing a hand on either of Derik's thighs. "In your ever-present walk of life, the future is unwritten. When *you* die in one of *your* unwritten veins, you don't come back. So understand this, boy, what you see around you is a possible unwritten future. When I take your life in a moment, *you* will die in an unwritten vein. Only returning to where you once were can save you. Now let's see that heroism once more," he said, slicing his nail into his inner thigh, nicking the artery. "You have merely minutes to tell me where the emerald is. But know this: I found it once before and shall find it again without your help. Tell me now, you cursed little ant, where the emerald is. Tell me, and I'll make it painless and quick. Otherwise, you can watch yourself bleed out."

Derik's eyes lowered to half mast as he leaned back as far into the haystack as his weight would allow. The window's threshold had a constant flow of air circulating amidst the loft. He thought of the last time a window appeared in the loft. Memories began to pour in from his journey to the twelfth century. Sitting in the breeze on the porch with Andi that one evening was the highlight of his life. He pondered her words once again and how they reflected such faith. He was amazed at how clearly he remembered them. Realizing it was the end for him, he took solace in the fact that he'd at least protected Katie and hoped wherever Andi was in her maze of veins that his sacrifice would extend to her as well. Sitting comfortably still, he whispered a sentence.

"What's that, boy? You have something to say?"

He whispered again, but his words slurred as he lost consciousness.

"I believe he said look behind you," a voice called.

Valicious spun around just in time to be struck in the temple by Garren's fist.

"You son of a ..." Garren said, biting his tongue. "I'm not finished with you."

He leapt to Derik's side, examining his wound. "Come on, old guy, don't give up just yet. Andi's here. She's waiting for you."

Derik twitched and briefly opened his eyes. "My Andi?" he asked.

He heard Andi's voice reply. "Yes, your Andi."

Andi covered her mouth in horror, seeing the massive blood spilled out around him.

"We've got to move fast," Garren said. He picked him up, tossing Derik onto his back, and turned to Andi. "Try to keep up." He reached into his bag and pulled out two small vials of a powdered mixture. "I haven't perfected it, but these create sort of a hyper-tunnel so we can shoot across the field. Ready?"

He shook both vials and then tossed one out the loft doors. A small puff of smoke exploded into a six-foot window. He ran, holding Derik with both hands, and then jumped into it. He exited another one several hundred yards ahead and fell out of the air to the ground, landing on both feet. He threw another vial and sprinted into it, propelling him again several hundred feet forward, exiting the tunnel yet still several hundred yards short of the fading wormhole. Andi followed behind, then caught up and ran alongside Garren.

"Are we going to make it?" she asked frantically.

"I don't think we're going to make it," Garren said. "Reach into my bag and pull out one more purple vial."

She fumbled through a few items until her fingers lay upon the vials attached to the inside wall of his bag. She pulled one out.

"Shake it, and then throw it far enough ahead so it has time to open or we'll run right past it before it opens," Garren said. "The window will only remain open for five seconds, so don't throw it too far or it'll close before we get there. It's a built-in safety from animals, pursuers, and such, so whatever you do, don't stop running."

She held up for a brief second, quickly shook the vial, drew her arm back, threw it hard, and then started after them. It flashed open just as Garren reached it. He immediately exited another window farther ahead, ran about fifteen more yards, and then stopped, looking back at Andi with a quarter of his body swallowed by the wormhole's threshold.

"Run!" he yelled.

"Yes," she said, patting herself on the back after regaining some ground but slipped and fell to one knee. Regaining her footing, she lunged forward and quickly accelerated again into a mad dash. "Oh please, Jesus, give me speed," she prayed, keeping her eyes fixed squarely on the small window. Pushing herself harder and harder in order to catch Garren's hyper-tunnel before the five seconds were up made it seem as if she were trudging slowly along in thick, sticky tar. She managed to just reach the tips of her fingers into the window before the time had expired. In the blink of an eye, it was closed and gone before she could get the rest of her body through it.

"Jiminy Christmas," Garren panted. He watched her for another second, then realized amidst the stirring and swirling wind the threshold in which he stood was dissipating. "Andi, run!" he yelled as loudly as possible.

"I'm not going to make it," she whimpered, calculating the remaining distance with her slowing speed.

"She isn't going to make it," Garren said, watching her laborious strides.

"I'm coming," she wheezed and cried out through battered breaths. "Derik … I'm coming … Please … don't leave me."

He reached into his bag and found one last vial and started shaking it. He pulled a rubber sling out of his satchel, then sent the vial hurling out a ways in front of her. "I hope this works. Run into the window," he said.

A tunnel burst open around him, making him immediately part of her hyper-leap. It completely surrounded him and Derik and looked to him as if they were submerged under water. He'd never actually been able to see what it looked like since it ordinarily moved him instantly from one end to the other. The way the air had been molecularly separated to make room for the instant transporting of a person simply mesmerized him. As Andi closed the gap between herself and the new window, Garren had a sudden sickening thought.

"Andi!" he screamed down the tunnel. "The emerald! We can't guarantee Derik's safety or anything else without it!" With only a few steps remaining, Andi pulled it from her shirt pocket just as it brightly burst into illumination. In a final lunge, she dove into the hyper window and was transported immediately and directly into Garren's torso. She, Garren, and Derik all collapsed onto each other and disappeared into the wormhole as it faded into a puff of smoke. All three of them emptied out of another wormhole, landing in unison onto the haystack in Derik's loft. Garren rolled Derik off of his chest and took a look at his paling face. He was seventeen again.

"Let's take a look at that wound," he said, quickly eyeballing Derik's inner thigh. The seeping from the wound, in just the small amount of time he'd been carrying Derik, was concerning. When his fingers settled lightly against Derik's pant leg, they left a saturation impression. Large intermingled splotches, scattered smears, and countless peppered droplets of Derik's bloodletting extended to most of Garren's clothing and upper body.

"Andi, I need your help. Now, Andi. We're losing him." He glanced over at her and then gasped at her limp, lifeless body. Protruding out from her chest was the unmistakable arrowhead of a horseman's arrow, which he immediately noticed was also gouged into her back.

"What in flaming Hades … Andi, no, no. Oh my God in heaven, how could you have let this happen?"

He leapt to her side and checked her pulse. There was nothing. He grasped her wrist and tapped it determinedly. "Andi. Come on, Andi. This just can't be. Come on, girl. We've got Derik back. Please, please … "

He paused as the realization began to settle in. She was gone. He snapped the arrowhead off with a single angry twist of his wrist. "God, no, not her. Why her?" he wailed through clenched teeth. He gazed across at her body toward her other wrist and found, still wrapped within her fisted fingers, the emerald. He peeled her fingers back. A weltering blister in the center of her palm, as well as along the inner recesses of her fingers, remained from its scorching.

He removed the stone, pocketing it. He brushed the hair from her face, studying it, and then pressed his lips together in a somber expression as his favorite memory of her swept into the forefront of his thoughts.

Then, as if a voice had whispered into his ear, he quickly picked her body up into his arms and rushed back to the wormhole, taking one step into it. The circulating wind had her gown flapping and fluttering about her listless, draped legs. He took a long last look upon the unemotional expression she wore, watching her hair dance in the spiraling airstream, and then released her. The thought of a rag doll came to mind at the sight of her limp arms and legs swaying about by the air's stirring.

Then, in another second's passing, she simply vanished before his eyes. He stepped back out of the wormhole and watched as it too evaporated into a tuft of smoke. He immediately returned his attention again to Derik. He reached into his satchel and drew out a leather sack. Emptying its contents into midair, the stones instantly aligned themselves, and the Atlas was formed, short of one stone. He pulled the emerald out of his pocket and placed it in its precise location in the Atlas. He spoke to the Atlas. "Okay, do your thing. We have a remnant of evil lingering, about to take Derik's life. He hasn't much time."

The Atlas hovered over Derik's body and drew out a small wispy stream of Valicious's darkness, and then it descended upon him. A moment later, color began to return to Derik's face. He started mumbling.

"Don't talk," Garren said. "Just let it do its work." He knelt down and gathered Derik into his arms. "I know you're finally home now, but you have no way to answer me, so I'm making a judgment call. I believe it's what you'd truly want. It took Andi a while to find you, and now it's gonna be your turn to find her."

Vague pieces of Valicious's visit with Derik began filing into his memory. "Where's Andi?" he asked.

"That's not important right now. What is important is that we get you back to the twelfth century before this mess gets too far out of hand. She was killed in one of *your* future veins, not one of hers, meaning there might still be a chance to save her. I'm afraid we're not going to be able to track her without some help."

"Help? From whom?"

"Hush. Just relax."

"There's nobody left," Derik slurred. "Where are we going to find help?"

Garren raised his eyebrows. "Lig Nædre," he said in an ominous tone.

Derik's body jolted and his eyes, heavy as they were, peered back at Garren boldly.

"You ready to do this, bud?" Garren asked.

Derik closed his eyes and sighed. He then looked up at Garren again. "I'd move heaven and earth for that girl," he said with solemn determination.

"I'm really glad to hear you say that," Garren answered. "Because I don't know if even that would be enough," he added under his breath. He addressed the Atlas. "Well, don't make me scrunch down. Come on. Give me a hand."

The Atlas immediately expanded large enough for him to step through with Derik in his arms. After doing so, the Atlas collapsed behind them and vanished.

20

Andi's body was returned to the exact location of her passing. It lay in the open field of one of Derik's possible futures. Thick horse's hooves approached her body and then stopped a few yards short. From behind the horse and rider, a man in a dark cloak, its hem dragging along the ground, approached her a moment later.

"Blasted apprentice," Valicious said through gritted teeth. He turned toward the horseman and then sneered. "You taught him well, my brother. His quick thinking just might have saved her life. Well, perhaps that means they'll be looking for her, doesn't it? In which case, I'll have my revenge after all."

The horseman began to step down off his steed but was halted with a derogatory statement from Valicious. "Leave her to rot, you half-wit. It's entirely possible she won't recover." Valicious turned and began walking. The horseman circled around with him. "We have a lot of work to do because of the Everal—her companion, the newcomer," Valicious said. "He cost me my dragon. I'll mount his head on a platter. I swear it."

A sudden shift in the wind caught his interest. He stopped and turned his attention to the elements. His shrouded face slowly turned back toward Andi just in time to see a thin, glowing, vertical strip of light rip through the air from approximately sixty feet away. Three well-developed men leapt out of the prism-esque crease, each wielding a bow, a blade, and a quiver of arrows and landing, with Andi at their feet. The first two wore animal skin vests and loin cloths, while the more muscular third opted for the loin cloth alone, sporting also a bear-tooth necklace and a whip at his side.

Jake, the brawnier and third one out, landed and caught a glimpse of Andi's life-lacking body. He immediately drew his thoughts upon her in the ravine, where he found her nearly three years prior. The vow he made in that moment when he said his farewell to her sprung into resurging life within him, churning, tearing at the core of his heart. A reason to live, to press on for a better life, suddenly dawned over the darkness of years past. "I'll *never* leave you again," he murmured.

The color-laden rays bursting out from the crease had Valicious gazing in a thrilled yearning. "The Atlas, finally."

Realizing Valicious had assembled the Atlas, Garren, the second one out, knew it would respond to Valicious as a higher authority.

Valicious drew a fist, and the Atlas took action. It closed the crease and hovered as a small sphere just long enough for Garren to dive for it. The Atlas zipped to Valicious directly.

"At long last, the Atlas." Upon examining it, he realized it was short a ruby. "Blast you!" he roared. "Unhand the ruby and I'll spare you a tortuous death."

Just then, Jake, who had maintained several characteristics concerning his previous identity as a horseman, quickly drew his bow on Valicious. "Hey, remember me? I heard you might be here. I was hoping I didn't miss you. I never did get completely back to myself, but thanks to you and that stinking dragon and his fire, I'm still dead-on with a bow."

Derik, the first one out, quickly knelt down next to Andi and touched her face. "How could I possibly have forgotten how beautiful you are?" Derik said. Garren joined Derik in tending to Andi. Derik broke his gaze away from Andi for just a second to address Garren.

"I owe you my life a thousand times over, my friend. Thank you." He glanced up at Valicious and scowled. "I mean to finish you this day."

"Oh, a hero after all," Valicious said. "This is interesting. The hero has no idea what he has jeopardized for the soul of a wench. Now hand me the ruby."

"Mind your tongue, you bastard," Jake said.

Derik threw an overly unkind glare at Valicious. "Did he tell you he's a spot-on shot? Take him, Jake."

Jake released the arrow. It traveled the air with urgency, narrowing the distance between them instantly, and just as it readied its landing toward Valicious, it burst into splinters under a resounding snap. The horseman,

Pradicus, had clutched his whip and cracked it against the arrow upon its arriving.

"Oh, you want to play," Jake said. He unraveled his whip and wound it out off to the side. He then went through a demonstration of whip-handling brilliance, snapping and cracking it in various places overhead, behind, and before him. "Let's see what you got," he said, approaching Pradicus.

Without hesitation, the horse progressed forward upon Pradicus's prompting. Pradicus then dismounted. He advanced toward Jake with purpose, like a determined lioness upon a fawn. He cast his whip forward and back, performing a series of exhibitionary snaking maneuvers, then threw in a crack at the end. He stopped and waited for Jake to engage.

Jake stepped toward him and then started a dead sprint, which quickly transformed into a smooth display of zigs, zags, and rotations, all the while controlling the whip effortlessly. A symphony of sounds split the air in streaking *howls* and *swooshes*. In the middle of his performance, he rotated a quarter turn toward Pradicus and unleashed a wailed lashing upon his face. His cheek split instantly, and a splash of blood sprayed out. Pradicus responded with a lightning-quick snapping back that Jake evaded with a half tuck and spin, which culminated with another crack across Pradicus's face, presenting another laceration, this time above the forehead.

Pradicus continued as if unaware of his thrashing. He started in on a series of fantastic *thwacks*, one after the other, all landing absently where Jake had just been a split second before, until *smack*, Jake took one on the back between the shoulder blades, and he unleashed a scream of pain. Jake stopped and threw Pradicus a look of determination. "Okay, no more toying." He winced, gritting his teeth, and then tossed Valicious an evil squint. "After I'm done with him, I'm coming for you."

Valicious returned the threat with a barely discernable grin.

Jake began his attack, winding his whip in several serpentine weaves while circling Pradicus. Halfway around, he cut in, evaded a lashing, and then turned and delivered four more strikes in succession, each in a fleshy part of the face. He then rolled and stepped within an arm's reach of Pradicus, pulled a blade from Pradicus's sheath, ducked, and spun around behind him, landing the blade in the upper right quadrant of Pradicus's back, which had little effect on the horseman being a solitary incision. Jake tumbled to the ground, cast his whip around the one Pradicus held, and yanked it out of his grasp. Jake then wielded both whips in an impossible display of half turns and revolutions back and forth, cracking them in an amazing, concerted effort.

He turned his attention to Pradicus, who stepped to his horse and withdrew the metallic-looking whip. He unraveled it and then cast it toward Jake, who either stepped out of its way or blocked his opponent's efforts with one whip and landed another lacerating *whack* with the other.

Finally, Jake started closing his distance from Pradicus, bearing both whips, neither out of sync with the other and then, with one valiant effort, cast one lashing around Pradicus's neck. It wrapped around like a python. In a one-handed cartwheel, landing him once more within arm's reach in front of Pradicus, Jake spun around behind him again and pulled the slack. His strength, still considerable, had the horseman on his toes, reaching and clawing with his hands.

"Yield!" Jake yelled. "Yield!" While pressing his chest against Pradicus's backside, Jake's shoulder took on a vague illumination where the blue arrow had struck him.

The light spread to Pradicus, who, suddenly and for only a second or two at a time thereafter, had strangely experienced freedom from the snare of the horseman's curse. Lucid moments of clarity returned to Pradicus, the man, only to be overpowered by the inner wrestling. A great battle for the control for his mind was underway, like two mythical titans vying for a peak's highest ground. As the horseman resurfaced within his eyes, he drew the longest blade he had access to, positioning it merely inches from Jake's ribcage, preparing a hearty thrust.

Just then, the man, Pradicus, emerged again, having a mere solitary moment to survey and act. While realizing he was moments from his own suffocating death if he did nothing, his eyes inadvertently fell on Andi. A horrified expression swept his face, and he gasped. "Andi, no." Awareness suddenly set in, and he was able to see what a gift she was to him.

In the darkness which was his world, a light had been sent to show him the way. And it was anger—perhaps his own anger—which ultimately eclipsed her brightness leading her to this end. Every good, noble and caring deed she had offered him abruptly rushed to the forefront of his mind. Memories of her character—her quickness to forgive; the kindness she showed despite her circumstance; patience in the midst of difficulty; a fresh, "I'll be praying for you," and the way she ended almost every prayer with, "And kind Father, it's Your kindness which leads me to repentance," nearly every day—flooded his mind's eye. Her prayers finally had taken root and begun springing up everywhere within the arid land which knew no Savior: his innermost being. In an instant, it was made known to him, the love of a loving God.

He smiled just slightly and spoke his first words to a God he only knew through the eyes of one incredible girl. The words simply leapt out from within him. "Kind Father, Your kindness leads me to repentance." He raised his eyes to the sky and found himself remorseful for a life full of anger. Lacking the ability to understand his heartfelt change, he uttered the words, "Jesus, God of gods, Savior of souls, I choose your love in place of my anger. Save me."

Without a moment's hesitation, he experienced a freedom he'd never known or could have imagined after a life of shackles. He gathered a breath—his first truly fresh breath of freedom.

But just as quickly as he gained comprehension of his newfound liberty, the monster within him began taking over again. He fought a desperate internal battle to keep hold of his mind and take back his life, all the while ensuring no harm came to Jake. A depth awoke within him he hadn't before been aware of, a reach which extended to his eternal core. An epiphany jolted him, one which acknowledged that the struggle had not only taken place for dominion of his mind but, much more importantly, ownership of his everlasting soul.

"A battle...why is it I never saw this before?" As understanding began to flow, he found himself drawing upon the threshold of a whole new concept: significance. His eyes shot back and forth across the ground, attempting to rationalize the wondrous rush he was experiencing, while purpose started its unfolding like a blossoming rose. "I was meant for something," he whispered.

Marveling at the recent discovery, yet powerless to truly grasp the revelations rolling in wave after wave, he abandoned carnal reason and simply embraced the new, fresh way of thinking, of living. He felt liberated, new somehow, as if nothing he did previous to that very moment bore any weight in his value. What lay ahead was all that mattered. How he viewed his life had completely changed, and all in the blink of an eye. So who was he now?

A discernment arose within him, one in which he felt the essence of his entire person, newfound identity and eternal worth highly sought after by two clashing kingdoms. In his estimation, this discernment revealed that the battle had been lifelong, going on without his knowledge from his first breath, and had ensued for the claiming of his very soul.

He mouthed a few silent words, holding his gaze on Andi. With what dwindling sliver of his mind he'd clung to, he found the alertness to surrender the blade, dropping it to the ground, just as all that remained of the man, Pradicus, was seized by the more physically dominant monster. Pradicus, the horseman, once again fully in command, immediately began implementing a plan on the fly to rid himself of Jake and following close behind, the annoying presence which, for several seconds, had unseated him.

Within seconds however, and without warning or explanation, the more-than-capable horseman within Pradicus found himself suddenly fighting for control of Pradicus once again. The mind of the horseman attempted to draw power from the curse, demanding it be recognized. A desperate, violent flailing followed as the life which the horseman claimed rights to was systematically removed from his control as something holy and far greater asserted its will. The battle was over swiftly like a row boat waging war with a battleship. In the time it took Pradicus to merely open his eyes, it was finished, the curse was defeated, and Pradicus stood silently, completely free.

Garren looked up. A feeble breath fell on his lips as surprise swept his face. "Pradicus."

Jake understood the flailing as opposition. "I said yield." He gave Valicious another squint and then yanked violently, breaking Pradicus' neck.

"Jake, no!" Garren screamed. Pradicus's body fell limply to the ground.

Garren's eyes darted toward Derik, who stared on, traumatized. "This wasn't the way I saw it," Garren murmured. His eyes rose slowly, filling with tears, until he was gazing just above the horizon, trying to decide between gladness and regret. He then said something Derik didn't understand at all. It was just the four simple words, "Yes … I heard him."

Derik spoke out loudly to Garren. "H-he, Pradicus, was already gone, right? There was no chance for him to come back like Jake did … right?" He laid his face into his hands and sighed. "Garren, this is all wrong. We were just supposed to grab her and go. What happened?" He peered out of the slits between his fingers and stole a look at Andi. "What are we going to tell her?"

Garren despondently lowered his eyes. The concerned frown he wore for Pradicus quickly evolved into a deeper concern for Andi. "We've got to do something for her. She has a light pulse, but she won't make it long. And the gate is closed."

Derik lifted his face, shaking his head. "If Andi were able, she'd summon those glimmery guys. Where are they now?"

"Derik, she didn't summon anyone. She connected with God while she was here waiting for you. She lost her way and reached out. Jesus was waiting and reached back. He's the one who sent the '*glimmery guys*'—to fulfill His purpose. God will stand by and let you walk out your plans your way, but He'd rather help you. The guys you're talking about serve a function. Their assignments are part of a higher mission. They aren't permitted to help as they see fit. It would interfere with His mission. God's help is available, but, in a sense, His hands are tied until you ask for it. She knew how to ask for it. God's paths are already formed. It may be a difficult trail, but be assured, He provides where He guides. And with God, there is the assurance of hope. Let these words churn within you, Derik. With hope on God, on Jesus, there's always a promise just around the corner."

Garren's last few words resonated within Derik. He thought back to what Andi said about hope. His eyes drifted away from Garren, then back toward him, and then away again. It began to make sense, but the second he entered into a critical assessment, the idea evaporated, like an illusion. He snapped back into his rigid thinking. "God can keep His hope. I'm not asking Him for any help. He screwed up my life by letting all this happen. Where was He for the last two and a half years? I could've used His help to get here sooner, Garren. He has nothing to offer me."

"It's about surrender, Derik. It sounds like you're not ready. You, my stubborn friend, won't see His help as valuable until you come to the end of yourself."

"You don't think this is me being at the end of myself?"

"No. You're still trying to do it your way."

"You think this is my way? Fine, I'm at the end of my road. My toes are hanging off the ledge here, Garren."

"It's your way until you're willing to step off the ledge."

"Well, why don't you call those guys down? Don't you have some kind of relationship with them? I mean, you're an Everal, right? You must have been able to connect with God after all these years."

"First of all, Everal's aren't special. They don't illuminate or fly or appear out of nowhere, and secondly, they're just humans like you, and they don't have any different connection to God than you or anyone else."

Suddenly, Andi flinched. Both their eyes rushed to her.

"Call on them, Garren," Derik said. "We need their help."

"I, I can't."

"Do it."

"There's more you don't know, Derik. It's...impossible. But you can. Derik, step off the ledge. The time is now."

"No. We're doing this my way. I've always managed on my own." He pursed his lips, thinking. He spun back around to Jake and Valicious.

Garren held his gaze on Derik for a lengthy moment. "Very well," he said under his breath. He then returned his eyes to Andi.

Looking down at his lifeless brother, void of concern, Valicious chuckled wickedly and then refocused his attention on Jake. He reached into his garments and palmed *vis aduro*, a ball of dragon fire, from a pocket, then surreptitiously dropped it to the ground behind him. He placed a heel over the radiant orb and then quietly crushed it.

The fire penetrated the soil of the earth, combusting beneath the surface. It produced a nearly unnoticeable detonation radius, which reached Jake almost instantly. Jake responded with a sudden loss of equilibrium, which he promptly recovered from, but the *vis aduro* had already begun its act of reclamation. The poison of revenge, venom of fury, and a myriad of other toxins made their reintroductions from whence they were cast two and a half years ago in the cavern. Like blood to a vampire, Jake nearly fell drunk drinking them in.

"Very nice, young one. Such talent. You served me well. I am not slow when it comes to selecting my guardians. But the day is far from over. Did you think for one second that I would not have come prepared for such an end as this? Indeed, you served me well and shall again before the day is over."

"You vile slug, I'll die before I serve you again," Jake said, jumping toward Valicious in radiating confidence.

A small snicker crept out Valicious's reptilian mouth. "I'm sorry. That option is not available. I'm afraid you have no choice in the matter," he said bluntly.

"We'll just see about that, won't we?" Jake started marching toward Valicious, who drew out a whip from his garments. He unhurriedly let it unfold to the ground, and when it did, it took on an electrical charge. "Your rage, its fragrance is … enchanting. Use it. It shall bring you strength."

Feeling more empowered by the minute, Jake swooped an arm down and snatched up Pradicus's metallic whip. "Count on it."

"Jake," Garren called frantically. "Don't listen to him. The rage is a trap. Keep your thoughts focused. Anchor them on something good."

Jake held knives in his eyes for Valicious. He made a fist and threw it violently. "He's nearly killed the only girl I've ever loved. I mean her to be mine once again."

Derik attentively looked up with a glower. A moment later, he peeked at Garren and then lowered his eyes back down upon Andi's pale face. He brushed his fingers across her lips and then swept her hand up into his palm. "Come on, Andi. We've only been gone a moment. Stay with me. It's you and me forever," he said, trying to gauge Jake's last comment.

Garren met Derik's momentary glance, then shot his eyes back to Jake. "You must not let your focus come from anger, Jake."

Derik contemplated the remark. "Maybe that wouldn't be so bad for a few minutes. We need a diversion."

"No, Derik, for him it very well could entail death. He must not give in."

"What do you mean? We need Jake to distract Valicious … and, of course, I'll be needing the ruby." Garren reached into a pocket and then held it out. Derik swiped it off his palm, then leaned down and kissed Andi ever so softly on the cheek. "Just another few minutes, I promise." He stepped away, recoiled, and then bent back down. He cupped her chin and kissed her square on the mouth. "Sorry. I've waited a long time for that." He stroked her cheek and then slinked away.

Jake rotated just enough to catch a glimpse of Derik pulling away from Andi's face the first time. Conflict arose within him as he witnessed the kiss. *That should be me tending to her, not him. Who does he think he is? She's not up for the taking. She loves me. I saw it in her eyes several times. He thinks he's going to steal her from me. How did I not see it? It's all been a ploy to take her from right under my nose.* A spark of scorn ignited an inferno of rage. Jake turned away and sized up Valicious, who now stood solely as an obstacle easily eradicated after the elimination of Pradicus.

Valicious witnessed the transition within Jake's eyes. He caught scent of the fumes of Jake's fury and then beamed. "Yes, take it," he said in his most persuasive tone. "It's time to take what is yours. You deserve it. I'm part of your pain. I nearly killed the girl. I'd do it again and succeed and then leave her to rot, feed her flesh to the birds."

Circling Valicious methodically, Jake heaved heavy breaths, imagining Valicious's death and planning how he was going to do it.

"They," Valicious said, pointing toward Garren and where he thought Derik was, "are your misery. I am your affliction. Come, valiant warrior, and kill me, then seize what belongs to you." He leaned toward Jake and raised a fist. "To the victor go the spoils. This is your moment. It *is* your reckoning."

Scarcely able to control his seething, Jake grinded out a sentence through his gnashed teeth. "I'll never forgive you for her suffering, and if you run from me today, I'll hunt you till you meet the brunt of my blade."

Valicious replied with a quiet laugh.

Jake, having amassed a plan, suddenly ran forward and then stepped into a winding, twisting advancement.

Through acts of calculated finesse, he wielded both whips again in a ballet of air-piercing *whooshes*. At just the right moment, he brought the metallic whip down with urgency, which Valicious blocked with his own. Sparks accompanied by a flash of light exploded, igniting a charge to Jake's metallic whip. Valicious returned with a brilliant maneuver of his own, and the two danced in fatal eloquence, intercepting one another's *snaps* and *cracks*, all the while stepping aside from ones they didn't.

The clash elicited a stunning display of flashing and bursting light, likened to a fireworks presentation. Jake then began another circling forward progression. After his third rotation, he sent a lashing down that broke the air with a fantastic *whoosh*. Valicious readily intercepted it in a defensive execution. With a powerful jerk, he snatched Jake's whip from him. He then cracked his whip like lightning across Jake's back, then, with a sidearm casting, robbed him of his other whip. He struck it again against Jake's chest and then sent a sweltering lashing upon his abdomen.

Jake dropped to the ground, reeling in a searing blaze of pain. Refusing to surrender, he stood to his feet, doing his best to separate his determination from the torment. He reached down and unraveled the whip from Pradicus's neck. Stammering toward Valicious, he laid out its length in full, weaving it back and forth. His shoulder began to radiate once again, then suddenly flashed out from the piercing. In that moment, Jake had sudden clarity. Comprehension of what he'd allowed to happen to himself seized him. His face, emanating remorse, fell into despondency.

Out of the corner of his eye, he caught Derik placing the ruby back into the Atlas. It instantly expanded into a whirlwind time gate. Valicious twirled around in outrage. Realizing he only had seconds to act, he turned and threw a whip around Jake's leg and jerked him off his feet. He then headed straightway for the Atlas. Derik sprinted back to Andi and positioned himself in order to hoist her onto a shoulder when Jake cried out a heart-wrenching plea. Derik paused and then looked up. Valicious was about to enter the Atlas, dragging behind him a pleading, defeated Jake.

"Derik, please help me. I can't go back. It's taking control of me, Derik. Please, do something. If he takes me, I'll never see her again. You and I, we'll never talk again. We've become friends, Derik. You're the brother I never had. Please help me. It's so lonely, so empty; I can't go back with him."

Derik stood then drew his bow.

Valicious stopped and glanced at Derik. "How interesting. Our hero thinks himself an actual hero at heart. Go ahead and shoot, boy. I fall into the Atlas, it collapses behind me, and your rag doll, Andi, dies. You save the rag doll, then the warrior here is my trophy. It seems our hero finds himself on the brink of a tragic moral choice. This *is* laughable."

"Wait," Derik said. He glanced at Garren, then at Andi. "Take me. I can lead you to the dragon. We resurrected Lig Nædre. We had to in order to get back here."

Silence fell powerfully. Staring seemingly through Derik, Valicious considered the veracity of such a statement. "Don't insult me, boy." He drew out another *vis aduro* out of his cloak and tossed it at Derik. It exploded, knocking Derik off his feet. The impact of *vis aduro* had Derik fighting consciousness for several minutes.

Garren held a contemptuous glare at Valicious. "Come on, come on, already," he said beneath his breath. He closed his eyes for but a moment then opened them with a renewed fierceness. "Thank You. It shall be done according to Thy will, my Lord," he said, then stepped forward, empty-handed.

"You dare challenge me, Everal?"

"Dare? Oh yes, I dare, and this victory belongs to the Lord." He immediately burst into illumination and approached Valicious.

"What trickery is this? You're no Everal. Curse you!" Valicious shrieked, cracking his whip onto Garren.

Garren waved off the strike and then gestured for the whip to be thrown aside, and it was instantly. "I'm not permitted to destroy you until the appointed time. But you are defeated."

"You forget your place, illuminated one. I *can* destroy as I see fit and without permission. And let us not forget, the Atlas affords me such a luxury." He raised his arms and then, in a clenched fist, heaved a deep bellowing voice into the Atlas. "Arise, Lig Nædre!"

Instantly, the gate expanded, and the great Lig Nædre exploded out from it. Valicious reached for his whip and then closed his fist as if stealing it out of midair. The whip leapt into life from its place and cast itself to its summoner. Valicious then cast it toward Lig Nædre, wrapping it around its neck. He was snatched away immediately, positioning himself upon its shoulders at the base of its neck. A much younger Lig Nædre than was previously killed by the kraken sprung high, then circled back around and blasted a blanket of fire upon the lot of those on the ground.

Garren extended his arms and then raised them to heaven. "Holy Lord of all, Jesus, grant me protection for them." A splendid crystal dome or hemisphere appeared over all of them.

When the fire ceased, Valicious surveyed the toll from the air. To his alarm, he found no illuminated being; no Andi, Derik, Jake, or Pradicus; and, to his outrage, no Atlas. "Curse you!" he yelled. He took the dragon up high into the sky, then, using its fire, created a wormhole and vanished into it.